Hand Me Downs

A Compilation of Short Stories

United States of America

Publisher, OSAAT Entertainment

First Edition. Fiction

Contact the Author Visit: oebooks.blogspot.com
Email: rycjoebooks@gmail.com

Library of Congress Control Number: 2023916236

ISBN: 978-1-940994-2-39

Printed in the United States of America

Hand Me Downs

*for the little people
and the big people
for the tall people
and the short people
for the mean people
and nice people
for the white people
and the black, brown, red
yellow and green people
for all the people.*

*i love customer service
i love people
even one reader
means the world to me.*

A Word from the Storytella

'it's amazing what can be found when least expecting...
or looking for it.'

Yes sirree...and ma'am... this is some renewable kind of
energy enclosed in this book. After going through old
books I previously published, and pulling out favorites,
dusting them off, and ironing out the wrinkles, I gently
placed this now spiffed up, polished collection under
this cover...i.e., and thus Hand Me Downs.

Old Stories: The one commodity more valuable when
used. Don't sleep on the wisdom.

Expect to learn, laugh...and be touched a whole lot.
—Enjoy!

Content

MORNING

Yellow Ribbon

~~

"An elementary school teacher shared this tale, or some semblance of it. That day I ran all the way home and tried to repeat what I heard."

~~

When this young girl laid eyes on her mother splayed out, on her back, on a daybed, with a yellow ribbon tied around her neck, she wanted to know why. Why was her mother, a beautiful woman, with long precious hair and milky silky skin, so fair and wrinkle free, laying on a daybed wearing a yellow ribbon tied around her neck.

So, stroking her mother's hair the little girl asked why. "Mother, what's wrong? Why do you wear that yellow ribbon around your neck?"

Her mother smiled and beckoned for a pen and a piece of paper. The yellow ribbon seemed to prevent her from speaking. 'Darling,' wrote the mother. 'Go ask your Father.'

So, the little girl did as told. The very next day she asked her Father, to which came his reply. "My love, your mother must be thirsty. Go fetch her a cold drink of water."

The following day the little girl did as told once more. She fetched the cold water and returned to her mother's bedside with the same question.

"Mother," she exclaimed. "Here's the drink of water Father asked that I fetch for you, but he did not tell me why you must wear that yellow ribbon around your neck. Won't you please tell me why?"

The child's mother held up a finger to her lips,

silencing the curious child, and motioned for yet another pen and piece of paper. 'My darling daughter,' wrote the mother. 'I cannot speak about my illness. Only your father can explain. Go and ask him to show you his sword, and then maybe you will know.'

And off again the little girl went, more puzzled than the day before. She asked her father to show her his sword, to which he replied. "Hush, hush my curious child. Take your mother these lovely flowers, and send her my love."

And so off again the little girl sauntered. She took the flowers to her mother with that nagging question still unanswered. "Father asked that I bring you these flowers. With them he sends his love," she softly replied, though unable to hide her growing exasperation. "Now, will you please tell me why on God's Green Earth you wear that yellow ribbon?"

Again her mother motioned for a pen and a piece of paper. 'My darling daughter,' wrote the mother. 'You may untie the yellow ribbon, if you must really know.'

And so the curious child, who really wanted to know, did just that. She untied the yellow ribbon and off came her mother's head, rolling to the floor.

Moral of the Story. Don't ask so many damn questions you do not really want answered. My mother laughed. I did not. I didn't get the moral then, though I do today. Frightening.

cody & crei

~~
"…And so here comes Crei."
~~

Some say Cody and I were evil. Don't know why they said this about us. I guess it was the way we made those mean cherry pies. And they were some mean cherry pies too. They had this extra special bite to them. We picked the berries…I mean the cherries right out of the garden. The garden Mother and Mrs. Kelly, that's Cody's mom, told us to stay away from. They said those berries were poisonous.

But Cody and I were curious. We wanted to see if those berries…I mean cherries, really were poisonous. At least we weren't evil enough to try eating them first. We tried to entice the other kids in the neighborhood to have a bite. If they took our bait, and so very few did, no one ever trusted us, but if one did, we would then stand back and wait to see if they fell over… the way it was done on television. Not one child fell over. They each lived to tell on us, and get us in a heap of trouble.

Cody's imagination though was much wilder than mine. That's because Cody's parents had more loot. She could jazz up any story and her family would play along… going so far as to set a place at the table for her imaginary friends. They'd even put food on her imaginary friend's plate too, if Cody said her friend was hungry.

My family wouldn't buy it. We were too damn poor. Just getting bare necessities on our table, like bread and butter, was such a chore that I was liable to get more than my feelings hurt making up friends and talking about things like money growing on trees when wasn't nothing growing on trees but leaves.

But Cody and her wild imagination helped me think. She really helped me think when we would do things like make prank phone calls. Cody could make up the wildest stories. If a woman answered she would lead them on with something about a suspicious man creeping around their house about to break in, trying to see if she could persuade the woman to call the police. But if a man answered the phone she would tell him how much she had been watching him and loved him. Those were the best prank calls because they sometimes lasted hours. Sometimes we would even save the number to use later, often vouching our undying love to old men who sounded like they could be our grandfathers.

So Cody started it. She started it by her wild imagination, telling me things like how mean Mrs. Kelly, her mother was. She said her mother was a real live one, even lifting her arms to make like a bat, hissing through her little termite teeth.

I didn't really believe Mrs. Kelly was a witch, but Cody did convince me it was a good idea to run away. It sounded a lot like taking flight. I'd always imagined being a bird… ever since my first scuffle at school. If only I could fly I would escape all of my troubles. There's even this bird that sits in the tree outside my bedroom window. It just stares at me though, real sad like, I guess telling me that even birds have its host of problems up there too.

Still, Cody's plan sounded way too cool. She already told me how easy it was to hitchhike. Truckers regularly picked up hitchhikers she told me. We just had to make sure we didn't look too young. That's why she gave me a pair of her go-go boots. Since my parents couldn't buy me cool clothes, she was going to let me borrow some of hers.

The evening Cody and I were to leave I was so excited I didn't eat. I pictured Cody and me bouncing up and down, two small faces looking out of one large window riding across the country waiting on California to show up. That's where we were headed. To sunny California, full of palm trees, beaches, and where people always smiled and it never rained. Our parents were going to be so surprised when they turned on the TV and saw me and Cody grinning ear to ear from Hollywood.

We packed, both of us realizing about the same time we had too much stuff. So we kissed or favorite dolls good-bye and just packed the things that could fit in a suitcase. Well Cody planned to carry her lavender Barbie suitcase. I had to carry a pillowcase. Cody was going to let me borrow her other Barbie suitcase but I thought her mother might get suspicious if she saw it missing, and Cody agreed.

Besides, we were going to be able to buy lots of nice things once we got to California. Cody said California had all sorts of cool things, and I agreed. The prettiest people lived there. Marilyn Monroe, Marlo Thomas, Judy Garland, and Elizabeth Taylor.

Cody always thought she resembled Marilyn Monroe, even showing me a mole above her lip. I only saw a faint brown spot so she colored it in with a marker and told me to move closer. Still didn't see Marilyn Monroe in her. I didn't see any of them in her. I wanted to tell her I thought she might pass for Pam Grier but didn't want to make her angry. She always went for the stars with long straight hair, and not so black.

Cody, though, told me I could pass for Diana Ross. I thought she was wrong about that one too. I liked Cleopatra best. Cleopatra was all the way to the sky gorgeous... sexy, brown like me, and she had a real mole on her cheek!

As soon as we got to California the first thing we planned to do was get all new clothes. Then we were going to the beauty salon and having our hair done and faces made up. After that we were having our pictures taken.

I couldn't wait. Cody told me to meet her after dinner by the lamppost at the end of our street. I happened to live at the end of the street (by the lamppost), so that part was easy. All I had to do was stand on the corner and watch her house, which was a few houses down from mine. She was going to flick her light three times to let me know when she was on her way.

As instructed I stood beneath the lamppost intently watching Cody's bedroom window. The light from behind her sheer pink Priscilla curtains was blazing yellow. I imagined Cody packing some last minute things… probably snacks for the trip, I hoped. My stomach had started growling as I had passed on dinner I was so excited.

Standing there, clutching my pillowcase with much anxiety, I all of a sudden see the porch light at my house turn on. It frightened me so badly that I dropped the pillowcase, and thinking quickly, kicked it down the sewer. I started to hide behind the lamppost but Mother saw me first.

"Crei!" Mother yelled. "What are you doing standing on the corner? Get your butt up here and in this house!"

My heart sank as I plodded up the cement steps. In just that instance, brooding about Cody leaving without me, I happened to see her light flickering. So badly I wanted to turn around and run to tell Cody we had to get going. Only I knew Mother would catch me before Mrs. Kelly could open the door. I had no choice but to sulk up to my bedroom.

All night I cried in my pillow thinking about how much fun Cody was having without me. She had almost reached California I imagined. The lights of Hollywood's grandeur just creeping up over the highway.

Cody's eyes, big as saucers, were probably glowing too. I pictured her smiling, just as close to becoming a movie star as we had ever dreamed. I wondered how much she thought about me… and what I was missing out on. In a short while she was going to have it all, and be on TV. It was always like that with Cody and me. Cody getting it all, and me glumly looking on.

I cried and cried…to the point of wanting to commit suicide. There was no way I wanted to live another day seeing Cody on television enjoying the Hollywood I almost, but didn't get to see. I could slit my wrist, or take a bunch of pills. Or maybe Cody might write to me, telling me how she got there, so I wouldn't get lost.

Sometime around midnight…or it could have been later I awoke to screams that sounded much like Cody's. Often when my bedroom window was open I would hear Cody screaming like this. Usually it was because Mrs. Kelly was whipping her. Cody got lots of whippings. She always got into things and then later would get in trouble for it.

I sat up wondering what had Cody done now. Maybe Mrs. Kelly saw her packed suitcase. But it was really late. Cody should have been in California by then. Maybe Cody had changed her mind when she didn't see me at the lamppost and got in trouble for something else. Or just maybe Cody had waited for me by the lamppost…oh God! I hoped it wasn't me who got Cody in this trouble.

The next day after Mother finished making breakfast I rushed over to Cody's house. Mrs. Kelly told me Cody was on punishment and couldn't come out to play. So I asked if it was okay for me to come inside.

"Please Mrs. Kelly," I begged. "I want to borrow a pair of Cody's go-go boots…" I continued to explain, swallowing hard and thinking faster. "…to wear for show-n-tell at school," I lied.

Mrs. Kelly thought for a moment and then let me

in. "Just be quick," she warned in a stern voice. "Cody might be sleep," she added as I was halfway up the stairs.

I peeked in Cody's room before easing in. "Cody," I whispered, seeing her partially hidden beneath a gathering of pink Priscilla bedding. Slowly Cody lifted up. She rubbed her eyes and then stretched them open before reaching for her eyeglasses.

"I'm sorry," Cody said. "We can't go to California now."

I was so relieved that Cody wasn't angry with me. Mrs. Kelly must have caught her before she got to the lamppost. "That's okay," I stiffly smiled. "Maybe we can try going to California another time."

"I don't think so," Cody said disappointed. "The spot where truckers pick up the hitchhikers must've moved."

Oh Wow… Cool! Cody really tried going to California without me. This was why I liked Cody. She was so brave. To not see me at the lamppost and just go on without me was the coolest. I would have never left without Cody. I would have never been that brave.

I was glad Cody never got there though. When she didn't see me at the lamppost, and saw no light on in my bedroom, she figured I had been found out and walked a few blocks and caught a city bus that she thought would take her to the spot where truckers picked up hitchhikers. She rode the bus for hours looking for that spot. Eventually, when she was the only passenger on the bus, the bus driver turned around and asked where she was headed. She told him to the spot where truckers picked up hitchhikers. Promptly the bus driver called police. And promptly police took her home where Mrs. Kelly promptly lit into her for hours.

Cody threw back the bedding. "See! See what that witch did to me!"

crei HATES bullies

~~

*"…first time I stood up for a principle
for which I believed deeply."*
~~

Forget natural selection; how animals straying outside its herd became susceptible to falling prey to wild dogs and hyenas, which in turn helped naturally control the animal population. Despite this order, God's constant reminder about this process, a law and order founded in the principles of physics, I was in the third grade when I figured out all on my own how much I despised herd mentality. I HATED bullies.

Lo and behold, late one afternoon one of my classmates, without warning, began verbally assaulting a girl who sat beside me in class. Like dominos falling, the rest of the class chimed in. As it would be, this all got started just after the girl seated beside me had poured out a story both terrifying and touching. My new friend almost died from an appendicitis attack. I had all sorts of questions, and was grilling my new friend when an eggplant head girl sitting in front of us told my new friend to shut up.

Ironically, Mrs. Cobbs—the teacher—wasn't in the classroom as all hell was about to come loose. She had stepped outside the room to have a word, apparently quite a lengthy word with another teacher…when I decided to become like Jesus in defense of my new friend and her story clinging to me like skin.

The thought of my friend being hurt all over again, was for me, like watching Jesus being nailed to a cross right before my eyes, all over again. With no mercy or reason, and very quickly, these kids immediately took the popular (eggplant head) girl's side!

I didn't hesitate. It didn't take a minute, not one iota of a second to stand up for my friend. These mean sheep taking the popular chick's side, before hearing my friend's horrifying story, was just too much sorrow for my 8-year old mind to bear. It was like seeing the faces of Jesus' persecutors, seconds from nailing my friend to a cross. I had to stand up.

Whatever possessed me, as I'd never fought anyone a single day in my life, all three pints of me rose up out of the chair. One by one, from the popular chick with the flapping gums and eggplant for a head, to the tongue-tied grizzly bear of a hippo with the dark circles around her eyes and black stripe running down the center of her tongue, I fought all these mean sheep with pretty nasty third grade language. I singled out the ringleaders, calling out their worst flaws, and launched a vicious verbal assault. From the girl with the big hairy nose, to the girl who wore the same too small dresses showing her dirty panties, I took 'em all out! I even got a few boys who tried to get in my way.

Lips littered the floor when I was done. Even I was shocked. My lips were the only lips that kept moving… along with my eyes and neck rolling in sync with my mouth. I was on a roll. A sugar roll without the fructose. I gave everyone that dared to open their mouth a taste...since...umm...I was already promised a butt whipping after class...at 3pm.

Yeah, this was in the era of '3pm fair-ones', when fights didn't break out during class, or else I very likely would've received the butt whipping promised ...unless a miracle materialized... either incentivized by my psychedelic subtleties, or God Thyself.

Sure enough, as it came to be, the talk Mrs. Cobbs excused herself to regale, was about me. A teacher stopped by to remind her about a newspaper club meeting I needed to attend. Now that was God! A godsend I never saw coming!

The next day I came to school prepared. I knew them kids were out to get me and had my mother pull my hair back in a tight ponytail. I asked my mother if I could wear my leggings and a turtleneck too. Wasn't nobody about to…easily… pull my clothes off. I made sure to wear stuff that hugged my small frame. I also carried an exacto blade, unheard of back then.

When I arrived in class I told my classmates 'the first person that came near me at recess was going to really get it, emphasizing how I might get beaten down afterwards, but before I was going down, I was taking one of them down with me. Surprisingly, none wanted to go down, thus no one wanted to be first to approach me. Just like that the incident was forgotten… yet the moral of this tale lived on… especially for me and my friend.

tellin' on it

~~

*"…and they wonder what's wrong with
younger generations…"*

~~

liar! liar! pants on fire! That's what I wanted to tell grown people who lied on children.

I was upstairs in my bedroom minding my very own business when Dad got to yelling, "Crei! Crei!" And he's yelling at the top of his lungs too. "Crei get down here now!"

Here we go, I'm thinking. By the sound of the yell I know I've done something wrong—again—as such was my life. Always doing something wrong. The way it was for most children. They were wrong, the grown-up right, no matter what—end of discussion—extent of the law. Didn't have to like it, but learned I had to take it. Too bad they couldn't take what they dished. Cried like babies all through their Civil Rights fight though didn't they!?!

"Yes," and I always answered nonchalantly. No matter what, I already knew I was guilty of something.

"Did you roll your eyes at Mrs. Baron when she asked you to help clean up," he spat no more than inches from my face.

Now this hadn't happened. What did happen was the bitch told all of us, speaking in general to everybody in the room, to "quote" put everything away. Well, I had been reading a book, which I DID put back where I got it…back in the bookcase…and went wherever I went. I'm not sure what the other kids put back, or didn't put back, but far as I was concerned, that was on them if they were so scatterbrained that they pulled the room apart trying to figure out what they wanted to occupy their time. If everyone had pulled out one book like me, and put away that one book like me, there'd been no problem, right?

At any rate, this all happened so long ago I only remembered it because it was one of the rare occasions I was in old lady Baron's wake. Actually, thinking back on the last time I'd even seen Mrs. Baron, I think I waved and smiled at the old heffa, which was highly unusual given how much I absolutely loathed the woman. And still, as much as I hated her, I would never openly disrespect her to that magnitude.

"No," I answered looking down towards Dad's knees. Looking directly at him would have made him even angrier. The contempt wrangled inside me would have shown on my face, and screamed louder than if I had yelled, 'Mrs. Baron is a bald flat-fat face liar!'

"You owe that woman an apology! Who do you

think you are!?! I'll break your damn arms off your shoulders. You go over there and apologize right now!"

I turned away and marched right on out the door in such a fury I couldn't even see straight. In the past when I was just getting to know Mrs. Baron's two-faced habits, she had said and done many things to me, but this was the straw that broke the camel's back. People always said I was an evil, spiteful child, but I doubt if the way I was feeling was anything near to what they meant.

Oh, Mrs. Baron, and I called her that with a plank tucked up my sleeve and hidden behind my back, was going to really get it now. I didn't know how or when, but sure as the sun would rise after the last species had curled up and died, she was about to meet a fury of an absolute ferocious most brutal kind. The next time she'd see the sun she was going to be looking through it and not up at it.

There was no way I was knocking on her door. No way! Had I, and I would have beat the injurious vengeance out of her right then and there. Dad hardly would have had to break my arms off. I would have beat her so long my arms would have on its own fallen off!

God, I prayed. I have done nothing to anyone, so why do You send this evil woman to me? This mean-spirited soul has risen in me a vim of ill so iniquitous that I would rejoice at seeing every part of her plucked apart, pore by pore. Is this why You sent her to me?

I hear no answer from God. I have to assume he's nodding and answering, "Umm hum." He's put this eye sore in my sight for a reason. But at least He's given me enough sense to walk around the block instead of con-fronting her head on.

Before long much of the anger had worn off. I found myself inventing the lie I was going to tell Dad for why I didn't get to apologize. I reasoned it'd have to be better than having to invent the bigger lie I'd have to tell police, detectives, the courts, and everyone in the neighborhood, to include Dad and Mother. They would be so heartbroken, as would Mrs. Baron, too.

Running away occurred to me as well. I smiled when I thought about it, thinking about Cody and all. No, running away was out of the question. I probably wouldn't get as far as Cody had. I didn't even have thirty-five cents to my name, let alone on me. I'd have to start hitchhiking from where I stood, a street where not a single solitaire bus ever rolled tires over.

I was just going to have to tell Dad the Baron's probably weren't home. In all likelihood, I would throw in, they probably looked out the window and seeing it was me, refused to open the door. Mrs. Baron had done that to me before. The more I thought about it, I believed she just hated my face. She had some kind of nerve though. I heard her mother was black as tar. Thought it was a sinning in a shame she hated her own mother because of her skin color…as if her yellow moon pie face was a treat for white…or any eyes. The woman looked like a Dalmatian, and had the unmitigated gall to introduce her own mother as the maid. What a disgrace. People had to put two-and-two together to figure out it was her own mother she was shunning.

When I got back home Mother was there, but Dad was gone. He probably felt guilty and went out for some air. Or maybe he had followed me and was working off what he planned to do to me when he returned. Whatever. I was relieved he wasn't there. If he was going to let me have it later, I'd just grit my teeth and bare it like I always did.

"Mother, you know Mrs. Baron lied," I said as soon as I entered the kitchen.

"Crei, but that's your father."

"I don't care who he is! He's wrong!"

"But he's your father. We need to respect him."

"No, Mother! You need to stand up to him. You know what he is doing isn't right and you need to say something!"

Mother sighed like she always did and looked away. It was no use dealing with her. She was just as humbled about getting at the truth as all the rest. That's how she could sit around women who had far more than we had, listening to them boast on about their kids, their spouse's jobs, and incomes, their homes, the trips they'd taken, and giving her hand-me-downs, without having one thing in her favor to add…including having nothing good to say about any of us. Mother didn't even ask if I had apologized.

It couldn't have been more than a week later when I finally ran into Mrs. Baron. Me and my sister Cricket were in the grocery store with Mother shopping. Mother, however, was an aisle over from where we were, when the crookedest couple on the block out of nowhere appeared.

As usual she was cheesing and grinning chessy-cat wide, while Mr. Baron sporting the whole white shirt and after six necktie look lagged behind. When they saw us headed towards them however, their faces dropped… especially the liar!

Mr. Baron looked as if he was trying to decide if smiling was appropriate, while the rotten onion displayed a façade that had the good instinct to see trouble coming.

I turned to Cricket and whispered, "watch this!"

…To which Cricket, so appropriately named, got to quivering over my shoulder asking, "oh my God Crei, what are you going to do? You know Mother is in the next aisle."

I ignored Cricket, and the fact that mother was an aisle over. I marched right up to Mr. and Mrs. Baron and stopped dead in front of the cow, no more than a centimeter away from her face, stomping my foot as hard as I could without breaking my ankle. I'm saying, forget smelling my breath. The woman could read my mind and she wasn't guessing.

"LIAR!" I hissed in her face. "Now go tell him what I said, and while you're at it, tell him I fucking sent you because that will be the fucking truth!"

I kept walking, Cricket on my heels the whole time trembling in my ear, "Oh God Crei, I can't believe you did that! Now we're really going to be in trouble!"

"No we won't," I answered defiantly. "She won't have the nerve to tell the truth. And even if she does, Dad will never believe it."

ms. hall's class

~~
"Every job should be handled with passion…and kid gloves."
~~

I had just been transferred to Ms. Hall's class. There was some kind of mix-up in the beginning of the year where I mistakenly was put in a class we students used to call RE. And not RE as in the proper term school officials used (Remedial Education), but RE as in retarded. But a few months later Dad stood on someone's desk and I was bumped up to a class supposedly more to my speed… the class just above RE.

But I wasn't balking about the whole thing. I had long ago given up on anyone of adult-size doing right. I was going to have to figure things out for myself, sitting on the sidelines taking it all in. After all…I always felt destined to be a writer.

That's how I came to Ms. Hall's class. Moving right to the sidelines taking note of how she, too, had given up. She said she was only teaching those who wanted to learn. Everyone else she was letting fall by the wayside. But what really was happening was no one was learning because those who didn't want to learn were being so disruptive that those who may have wanted to learn couldn't hear a word of what she was saying.

I felt that evil thing people talked about seeing in me creeping up, and crawling up my neck. So what I didn't need her lessons to learn, but there were at least two students, both females, sitting at the front of class looking frustrated trying to take notes.

One girl even said it out loud. "Ms. Hall, it's not fair. Some of us can't hear you."

"Too bad," Ms. Hall said clear as the day was long, before going back to this mumble in protest of those who refused to learn.

I sat back and watched. Ms. Hall was a math teacher, so she was writing equations on the board and mumbling stuff like, "...the mean set of integers, and common denominators, and when you divide this, you get that..." stuff most in class could care less about.

While she went on mumbling, the class went on ignoring her. From my standpoint, at least this was one class where I wouldn't have to deal with homework, or pretty much anything. This was straight-up recess, one of my favorite things about school. It wasn't so much that I hated school. I was bored! I needed to learn. See stuff I'd never seen or done before. Watching someone do a math drill (over and over and over) could kill a child like me!

And yet, this didn't mean I wasn't taking in what was happening. I was thinking about the repercussions if other professionals; doctors...pilots and such decided not to do their jobs because of inconveniences. Seemed the same as teaching to me, and I was pissed about it, the reason this Friday remains so clearly etched in my memory.

Turned out Ms. Hall wasn't the only one about to cash her final, much undeserved paycheck. With her purse dangling on one arm, mumbling and scribbling numbers on the board, the class started getting its Friday celebrate on! Little did anyone know how we were about to become the teacher, and the teacher the pupil.

Just so happen this day Floyd was joining the class. He was the brother of Lloyd. Though cuter, Lloyd was the real terror I thought. I'd seen Lloyd do some wicked things, and it didn't matter whether you were male or female. Outside of tripping girls when they passed by, or flinging paperclips and other objects at them, he beat people to bloody pulps, would cut them up if he had something on him, or set them on fire if he wasn't stopped. With his blotched complexion, jagged crooked teeth, and hornet green eyes, he was the epitome of terror.

Floyd was older than Lloyd, so he shouldn't have been in this class, but because he was left back a grade, both tyrants, him and his brother, were in the same grade… my grade. And of all aches and pains Floyd was now in my class. He had just been released from a detention center. That's the way it was for the brothers. One week Lloyd was in, and the next it'd be Floyd.

So now here's Floyd, freshly released, walking around the classroom looking for another reason to be sent back to Juvy Hall. He loved that place. All day long in fact, he'd been bragging about just getting out, and begging, so it seemed, to go back in.

I tried to keep away from him. I didn't even want his eyes to rest on me. If he sat on one side of the room, I sat on the other. I didn't make it obvious, but I obviously stayed out of his way. Ms. Hall, however, wasn't as lucky.

She was up at the blackboard with that purse swinging on that one arm, mumbling as the class started getting louder and louder…you know…getting our celebrate on, while Floyd was getting busier and busier.

There also was another vice in class. Actually there were quite a few more vices in class, just none as caustic as Floyd, and a vixen named Iza. Iza was another born hell-raiser. She was a little odd for this day and time however. Most girls didn't openly profess to being butch. Iza was butch, and would say so if questioned.

I had seen her father up at the school for other incidents; once she kicked out a window, and there were the numerous bloody fights she got into ...never herself doing any of the bleeding, unless the blood on her knuckles counted.

I'd seen the girl beat the living crap out of a classmate. She loved to box, and was really good at it, walking around with this hard stroll, wearing bandanas around her baby fine hair, and talking trash in a hardened voice all tough and mean. That girl really had me believing that there just may have been something to the contention that a mysterious plague hit the children born in 1962...something like whatever hit those kids in that 1960-something movie 'Children of the Damned'. If rumors were correct, it would explain so much.

I sat in the corner opposite Iza, Floyd, and some of the other hell-raisers, with a lesser unruly hell-raising group. Two of the girls I was with were my cousins, none of us being the wildest, though too, we also weren't exactly the ones who really cared to figure out what Ms. Hall was mumbling about. We had our own thing going on. We were beneath desks laughing about silly girl stuff, like watching one of the fresh boys make out with the hot girl Pepper. It wasn't the real make out deal. He was just pinching her butt, and French-kissing her and whatnot. Nothing too serious, but fun to giggle about.

All the while, though, I kept my eye on both Iza and Floyd. With as loud as the class was getting, and it being Friday and all, I could feel something serious was about to go down.

At one point we went beneath the desk. Can't recall if it was to shield the fresh stuff going on, or to avoid objects that started flying around the room. Every so often I lifted up to see what was going on outside of what we were doing. At one lift up I saw Floyd standing over Ms. Hall who had finally done all the scribbling she was going to do. She was sitting at her desk hunched over, her purse still dangling on the one arm, mumbling and fanning Floyd away.

"Stop it Floyd. Stop it," she mumbled.

Floyd laughed and looked over at Iza and the others taunting him to continue. He had been messing with Ms. Hall's hair.

Now, in addition to the purse, Ms. Hall also wore a wig. Everyone knew the bronze mop on her head was not real hair. It was the talk of class since I got there… "Ms. Hall, ha, ha, wears a wig."

So Floyd had been picking at the removable straw since she sat down. At one point he grabbed paper off Ms. Hall's desk and pretended to be reading. When he finished pretending, he shredded the paper and sprinkled it over her head.

The class laughed. Admittedly, I too wanted to see what her head looked like without the orange hairy hat. But Ms. Hall kept brushing the paper out of her hair. I thought Floyd was never going to get around to lifting that mop. It took Iza and them to convince him, egging him on, daring him to lift the wig. Finally he went for the hair, aggressively grabbing chunks of paper, as if he was helping the teacher. Of course he wasn't. With each pick, he intentionally tried to lift the wig. This got her to batting his hands away as someone in Iza's group decided more paper needed to go on top of her head…so the taunting and laughter could continue.

I was almost purple with amazement. Watching my classmates etch up this 'sort of' heyday, payday was new. Nothing I'd ever seen before or since.

At first Iza and a few others started throwing spitballs to keep Floyd going. But after a while, the spitballs, even saturated in a gook of spit, wasn't sturdy enough to get across the room with the force required to reach Floyd…or Ms. Hall. To accomplish this hard objects were attached to the spitballs to get them to propel the reach of Ms. Hall's desk. A few of these hardened spitballs hit Floyd, which took his attention away from Ms. Hall and onto those throwing the wadded up spit.

Within seconds a huge spitball war erupted. Pencils, pens, rulers, protractors, and any object that could be snapped were being snapped in half and hurled across the room.

Floyd also armed himself with chalk, erasers, paper clips, and anything he could get his hands on lying around Ms. Hall's desk.

Instantly, whether involved or not, everyone took cover beneath the desks. Between the desk's slats I could see objects flying around the room with such force that chip marks began showing up on the blackboard. Dozens of small holes begin pelting the shades, shredding them to strips, leaving them hanging over the window ledge. I heard one window shatter, and watched the glass split into a large cobweb. Damage to the blackboard started taking its toll, turning the math problems Ms. Hall had scribbled on the board into a white slated hierogram of scientific marvel. The simple arithmetic problems looked like a chalk hurricane had hit with a category 10 or 12 force.

Ms. Hall tried several times to leave the desk to get to the telephone. The telephone was about 20-25 feet from where she was, but she couldn't get to the phone because every time she tried crawling from beneath her desk, someone pinged her from behind.

It was a tantalizing inspection watching her trying to reach the door, and thus the telephone, with that purse still dangling on her arm, while holding her wig and trying to crawl at the same time. She would get about two or three feet before she'd have to scurry back for shelter.

Finally, when the spitball fight became so intense that it actually looked as if it was hailing nails, Ms. Hall in a last ditch effort scrambled to the door in a rolling fashion. I could not believe my eyes. She literally rolled across the floor away from her desk, holding her wig with both hands, with that purse still dangling, the way I'd seen it done in some of those old World War II pictures.

When she reached the door she scrambled to her knees, crawled up the wall and grabbed the phone. Frantically she pressed buttons and ran outside the door-phone in hand, screaming... literally freakin' screaming to the top of her lungs… "Emergency! Emergency! Help! HELP!"

Never, during the entire time I had been in this class had I heard her voice go above a low grade hum! I mean, no mumbling whatsoever. She was clear as a bell. I was simply astonished she could speak at this volume. At that point though, the war turned full force on the door. I think everything to include a few desks and floor tiles was thrown that way.

But this was our last payday. There were no more celebrations. Ms. Hall never returned. Instead, we were assigned a new teacher. This one was hardcore, and more dramatic. She bragged about a metal plate installed in her head. Seriously. The teacher claimed she was in a motorcycle accident. I honest to goodness thought I was seeing a 'Hell's Angel'. We weren't about to test her; someone wearing the equivalent of a cement helmet, and tatted up when tattoos WERE NOT popular! Some might not know this, but it ain't no kind of fun busting up concrete. Surely those that wanted to learn, got to learn for the rest of the year.

irrelevant

~~
"Right and Wrong is a figment of imagination."
~~

Get a good education. Right and wrong becomes irrelevant when pass or fail is the test. I'm sitting in class, ninth grade to be exact, looking at a big fat effluent "D" scribbled on a test I had taken. Assuredly I'm not happy about the "D" even though I hadn't studied for the test. I'm only sulking because in the face of this big fat hefty "D", I get to look over to my right to see this big fat hefty "B" scrawled on this other girl's test.

WTF!?! How did she get a "B"! She was just like me, hardly ever in class, and I knew she hadn't studied either. So I'm mad as hell wondering how she got that "B" when everything we ever handed in and got back, came back with no more than "D's". What did she have up her sleeve? One thing I knew, it wasn't an epiphany.

She caught me looking at her greasy slimy "B" too. She actually meant for me to see it. Normally she'd fold the paper in half and juggle her shoulders like she always did when she was saying so what, she didn't care.

I looked in her face, a pretty face, but wearing a smirk that made me want to roll my eyes real hard at her. Cheater! I hissed beneath my breath. The teacher must have made a mistake, or rather a whole bunch of mistakes, I grumbled out loud in my head.

I looked away, back down at my hefty "D", mad that she had seen it, when she leaned over and whispered in a tongue-tied lisp. "I know how you can get a better grade."

I'm like, "how?" And then quickly my mind leaped over to shout! I knew it! I knew damn well that wasn't a legit "B"!

I stopped sulking for a minute and was all ears. Like what did she do? Had she looked over some one's arm and got the answers? Or had she written the class notes inside the palm of her hand? It would have been miraculous be cause it was a science class and her hands weren't that large.

Or just maybe the teacher really had goofed up and made that many mistakes. It had to be something she did outside actually studying.

She told me the teacher would tutor me...after school... in his home, she threw in.

I scrunched up my face because that didn't sound right. If I wanted to pass the test that way, I would have studied. Why would I need tutoring? Maybe I heard her wrong, which when I started to ask more questions, I looked up to see the teacher looking our way. He shot us a hostile look that made her lower her voice.

"I'ma have to separate you two if you keep talk-ing," he leaned over and told us.

After he turned and walked away we looked at each other and giggled. The teacher turned around and again shot us that same mean look. And we again tucked our heads down, giggling.

I, however, was more than curious to hear how this tutoring thing worked. She was trying to fill me in but between her lisp, trying to whisper, and the teacher continuously spinning around each time he thought he heard our voices, there wasn't much to make out.

I know I heard couch. In fact, couch echoed so loud in my head I couldn't hear much else. Eventually she got tired of trying to explain things and just gave me the teacher's address and telephone number.

I sat there staring at the little ripped off square of paper, and her fat sloppy handwriting, wondering how she got his address. I imagined her going up to his desk after class and asking for a better grade, like she did in other classes we shared. This was the help he gave her.

I thought about this arrangement for a while… sifting through the should I's, or shouldn't I's and what if'isms.

Like what if I walked in his house to face another classroom setting, and he sat me down with all kinds of mad science books to read. That would really suck. I would hardly want to waste carfare on that trip.

Back and forth from the ugly dingy "D" staring up at me, poking fun at me, mocking me; to the stingy, though cheerful bright "B" snickering over my arm, made me envious it wasn't already on my test paper. Busily I sorted through the likely scenarios.

Scenario One: Getting over there to find myself-sitting in another classroom-like vibe.

Scenario Two: Getting over there and things going just as implicitly implied…but then getting my next test back and finding a crazy "C" scrawled on the paper. That would suck even more, especially if I looked over and saw another "B", or how about an "A" on her test.

All I could think about was how could I be sure I would get the "A". Other scenarios I ruled out, since distinguishing between right and wrong, at this point, was irrelevant.

fallin' angel

~~

"Least likely to make it."

~~

Contradiction. Mr. Rutherford said the problem in the world was 'people had too much'. What that had to do with teaching American History and how the "negroes" he called them, fought for human rights made zero sense to me.

Halfway through the school year I debated Mr. Rutherford on every other sentence that left his mouth. Not because I didn't like him, or thought he didn't know history. I sincerely was confused...and angry about it.

Case in point:

"So how did Columbus discover America if it was already discovered by the people here," I blurted.

"Everyone, please turn to page 243," was his response.

"I don't have a book." And I didn't say it nicely.

"Share your neighbor's," Mr. Rutherford replied.

But I looked at my neighbor; a boy with blood-shot eyes resting his chin in the palm of his hand. He had the book open, but it wasn't open to page 243.

"And look at these books!" I called out. "They are old as methuselah! When were they written? At the turn of the century?"

Mr. Rutherford interrupted his lecture to address me. According to him, I was disrupting class. If I was that concerned about the textbooks, then I needed to take the matter up with my parents and have them contact the school. Otherwise, he couldn't do a thing about it. Just like he couldn't do a thing about the fact that out of thirty-some odd students sitting in class, and there were only fifteen textbooks. He could only insist that I scoot over and share a book with a boy who was high as a kite.

"And look at this classroom. It's falling apart!"

And the room was falling apart. The bookshelf that once held the fifteen books looked like a seesaw with the books all gone. The other shelves...the three above it and the one beneath...were crammed full of other just as dusty and raggedy books. Most didn't even have spines. And the few that did, looked as if they were held together by clay...clay and cobwebs.

It smelled musty in the room too. That was due to the layers of dust blending in with the waterlogged floors soaked from all the rain that had seeped through visible cracks running like lightning down the walls.

And it was dim in the room. Only one beam hung over Mr. Rutherford's desk, but half of the beam was burnt out. It was like that all semester. Apparently Mr. Rutherford hadn't caught that one either. The only thing Mr. Rutherford caught was my attitude. Another outburst and he threatened to put me out of class. See! Another contradiction! Though that one on my part. I could care less.

So, when he asked us to write a 500-word essay on something significant we learned in his class that year, here's what I wrote:

Creschenda Sweets
History: Mr. Rutherford's Class
October 17, 1977
<u>500-word essay</u>.

Title: What Do People Want?

Take for example, my friend Phango; a decent man who happened to be 65-years old, a philosopher, world traveler, and mentioned in our old textbooks on page 243.

Every few years or so Phango took these long 'what in the world' excursions, and returned with yet another version of what he witnessed during these abnormal voyages.

Now first off, most could care less where Phango had been and what he saw. Out of sight, out of mind. People was busy hunting and gathering food and jobs. No one could care a Canadian coin where Phango had been and what he was up to.

But I, for a change, DID CARE. The first time Phango returned he said he saw sawdust...red sawdust. On the next return it was charred wood, followed by burnt ash. The next time it was charcoal. And before long, it was graphite.

Now, Phango wasn't making things up, or stretching out a sighting just to get attention. No one but me was paying him much attention anyway. People hummed and whistled right on by him, coming and going back and forth to markets and 9to5s.

And then one day came.

One day Mrs. Shirley Latherdale saw a diamond on the neck of Mrs. Ethel Swangladang that she swore she would burn down all of Rome for. All kind of marlock got going when Mrs. Latherdale saw that diamond.

She immediately hurried home and told Mr. Latherdale about the rare precious jewel. Without a gemological tool to determine the quality of the diamond, not even a second set of eyes, Mrs. Latherdale swore up and down she saw no flaws. She convinced her husband to meet with Mr. Swangladang, to purchase…or pry the diamond away from his wife.

But Mr. Swangladang was no fool. He knew, all be dang, that all the worldly goods in the world wouldn't be payment enough for the diamond. Not only was the diamond scarce, the diamond was even scarcer than scarce. Mr. Swangladang received the diamond right from the palm of Phango, when Phango gingerly tossed his last sac of graphite over to him in a 'catch it, you can have it' sort of gesture.

Phango had given up on studying the floors of other worlds. He had moved on to something else, showering the graphite he had collected into the sea… since few to none gave a sulfur dang about him and his travels.

Mr. Swangladang, as it happened to be, was there when Phango tossed the chalk in the sea. He caught the small remaining sac, and not giving it much thought, stuffed it in his pocket to later look at when he got a chance.

Months crawled by before Mr. Swangladang

came across the sac again. Mrs. Swangladang, in the interim of time, had washed and dried his cloak many times over before he really looked at the sac covered with the funny substance. All be darn the cluster remained in tack, nothing to sneer as he knew the method Mrs. Swangladang used to cure sullen wool of stubborn stains. It wasn't no compassionate process. With the stump from a tree, and an agent tougher than borax, she beat his garments into submission.

So, naturally Mr. Swangladang dutifully looked over the cluster before taking it to another guy for a closer inspection and second opinion. After the second guy shook his head Mr. Swangladang carried the cluster over to yet a third guy, who happened to be in the business of diamonds. The third guy, an honest old man, told Mr. Swangladang exactly what he held in his hand. It was the residue of Poseidon.

The honest old man and Mr. Swangladang treated and massaged the graphite into rainbow clear form, perfect for wearing and showing off. It was beautiful, and indeed flawless. So there was no way, especially knowing how the jewel was acquired, that Mr. Swangladang would take any amount of offering for the diamond. He didn't want three goats and a mule. He wouldn't take a whole farm and a barn. He didn't need a vessel and twenty-nine slaves. And he wasn't moving into the Parliament, not even for one second. Mr. Latherdale might as well quit his bother. Mr. Swangladang wasn't parting with the diamond for all the rare China in Sweden.

The diamond remained around Mrs. Swangladang's neck, and the Mrs. Latherdale remained breathing hot and heavy down Mr. Latherdale's neck. That's how…and why he turned his attention directly on Mrs. Swangladang.

First he invited Mrs. Swangladang over for tea. He was going to slip her a Micky. After she'd fallen into a deep sleep, he planned to slip the jewel from around her neck. But Mrs. Swangladang was a solid drinker. She could drink Mr. Latherdale, Mrs. Latherdale, and a whole brigade of seamen over the side of a vessel. Mr. Latherdale would need more than a Micky to get Mrs. Swangladang off her feet.

Mr. Latherdale next called Mrs. Swangladang to help him thread a needle. He figured he might be able to woo her in his arms, and after an intense kiss the night would lead to a course of mad passion where he would snatch the jewel from around her neck, and promise to return it after he fixed it himself. But Mrs. Swangladang was a real humdinger too. She flipped and tossed Mr. Latherdale around so much, he never got a chance to see the jewel, much less rip it from her neck.

At this point, Mr. Latherdale was only too sorry he had befriended Mrs. Swangladang. He wished he had taken care of Mrs. Swangladang the first afternoon she stopped by for tea. Instead of slipping her that Micky, he should've been far more aggressive. In no time flat he should've knocked her off her feet...for good! But now he was falling in love with the woman, threatening the original intent, plus his feelings for Mrs. Latherdale.

After a few wild rendezvous with Mrs. Swangladang, where he took every opportunity to leverage the diamond, he ended up bribing the old woman. He wouldn't tell Mr. Swangladang about the affair if she handed over the jewel.

Just like that, after all the bother, Mrs. Swangladang turned to her lover and said, "What? You want this old thing?" She took the precious stone from around her neck and tossed it to him. "Here!" she said just like that. "This is nothing but some old rock!"

I got a B-. Why? Because Mr. Rutherford said the essay was too damn long!

the vagabond

~~

"Great teachers teach you how to think,
not what to think."

~~

You never know. The first day of any class I always sized up for pass-ability by the teacher first. In other words, I was destined to fail the class if I had a problem with the teacher, regardless of how much I loved the subject.

But a good teacher could change all this. A good teacher had the power to teach about the discovery of chalk and make it interesting. Not tell me things like how I needed to buckle down, and in essence, do the work of teachers!

This was my problem; the radical philosopher I was. It wasn't as much about me learning, as it was about teachers teaching. This would mean, you, the teacher, anointed the special powers should take your own superficial advice to buckle down and find creative ways to teach so that students, like me, with many learning aptitudes could learn. And I always wanted to add, my favorite by-line, "dumb ass!"

No one was paying me to come to class, so why should I have to do this work? Maybe others needed to be in class to learn, but I could've stayed home and taught myself how to learn if they couldn't teach. How was that for a bit of amateurish, on her way out, mad as hell, had given up, recalcitrant, disgusted, rebellious, and milking a sour cow philosophizing?

Blind Raiser, or Raze for short, wasn't like most teachers. He was one of my English teachers. I gave him this name for raising the blinds. A sort of hard nose, hardball paradox, type of word pallbearer, I found him sitting on the edge of a desk when I walked into his English calamity. A tragic deluge it was.

Of course hard noses like Raze came with no syllabus. The only slight hope I had in this class, and it was ever so slight a hope, was that I read like I ate. Like a hog! And that was the real kicker here. I was almost renting space in the main and local libraries. Two large dictionaries and one Encyclopedia set even had a mold of my face plastered and imprinted in it. Taking a wild guess, I might be talking in the upward numbers of a hundred-thousand pages with an image of me in it.

Who me? I loved to read. Another English teacher foreswore in red ink I was a master at reading and interpreting Shakespeare's work. It was hogwash, I thought. I was no master at interpreting that man's work. I hadn't even read his work like I was supposed to. I just glanced over a few of his plays, namely Macbeth and Hamlet, and guessed the man was one terrific freak. He wrote like a madman, and I discovered this just counting the exclams he used!

If the stuff that man wrote had been spelled out in plain English, the entire school board; along with principals, administrators, teachers, and even the school crossing guard would've been carted off to jail for child abuse. That's why the book police in his day didn't want to publish him to begin with. Come a few hundred years later when no one knew what in the hell he was talking about, he becomes this celebrated contradiction. I didn't spell this out in these exact words in papers I wrote, but spelled out enough to be graded highly at interpreting his highly-lauded masturbating murderous efforts.

By the time I got to Raze's class, I was a contradiction of sorts myself. I feverously doubted at the outset I would bluff this man by my guise. Coughing up names of literature specialists like…Sterling Brown, Vonnegut, and one man's name that I never found in any of the ten libraries I visited, it became clear what I was in for.

I was going to have to lift the wool from covering my own eyes and jump in bed with all the whores Raze celebrated first.

Surely Raze would love me for doing this, especially since "a madman nobody understands his cracked ideas but me…" was one whore he'd regularly gone to bed with. He aimed to get all of his students in the same bed, the same way. A bed set up so high that you'd really have to want to learn to reach it.

So there I was, selfishly leaning back in a chair, sizing up Raze, generously following his sumptuous chapped lips and huge mannish teeth, musing over the prosperous swatch of mixed-matched plaid and checkered fabrics he chose to wear. I imagined he lived in a wifeless dingy shack just following the beard that wanted to grow but couldn't. One cardboard box and a missed bath, and he could be Crusoe's Uncle Tom.

That's what the mind does. It wanders when a teacher using their anointed powers comes in and really teaches. Most don't really want to learn though. Most preferred to work hard for what ended up amounting to nothing.

But I liked Raze's style because he worked the other way around. He'd hate me for saying this, but then why would I care since every solitaire literate one of his students were crazy about hating him. But his bed became my refuge. Knowing I'd never beat the master at his own game, he had too many years ahead of me already, yet in his sanctuary, my asylum, I acquainted myself with his stepladder, since I needed it to reach the bed to prowl One Thousand and One Nights, daring to free myself from human loneliness.

I had to unlock the Lady Dedlock's secrets too, and to humor myself levitating over vulgar faint ideas I had means to address, but no manners to court. And I certainly needed his ladder to shout down below, "Who do you think you are, if you even so do care!"

That got him, so he shouted right back at me, though it really wasn't him speaking. Someone unlucky enough to have the name Poe, first wrote it; "...and men have called me mad; but the question is not yet settled, whether madness is or is not the loftiest intelligence... whether much that is glorious...whether all that is profound...does not spring from disease of thought...from moods mixed and exalted at the expense of the general intellect."

I was none his match, but I was beddable. I let him bed me, and then wed me like a gentleman unveiled a virgin. The first night, the second night, and by the last night he'd rendered me serviceable. I'd become a notable renaissance collection of virtuoso foolery, even better than before. I had the stuff Men and Mice fool around with, and could basil him with my new sophisticated mannerisms.

"How could men of such feeble means ever fail society? Be punched out of it like Scarlet wore her letter, when he is none other than a monarch's sheer twin, sun in one hand, mirror in the other, a feast rendering hunger useless, and pain in despair!"

From then on, after he belabored the buffet stoicism I'd used on him, I started calling him the vagabond by his unscripted wish to sleep under the stairs, dining alone, and bedding more whores than the few he introduced me to.

"Long after I'm gone and out of here," he tells me on the last night, "you're going to wish you'd painted within the lines a little more carefully, and been more reserved with your assumptions."

And I turned back to him and mocked, "And yeah, well you're going to be sorry you didn't pass me, now that I've been introduced to all of your whores!"

NOON

my girls

~~

*"There's nothing in the world like a foxhole.
It's where you meet your greatest best friends."*
~~

The truth about it. These were my girls…thru and thru. That's an affectionate adage that gets tagged onto any set of circumstances where a sisterhood is formed and bound by bittersweet hardships and joys.

All of us, the first time away from home, young, barefoot, one in the oven, the other still crawling around on the floor, and as an old saying goes, "not a bucket to piss in, nor a window to throw it out of."

None of this registered with us though. Ask any one of us and we'd tell you we had it made. Especially compared to those back home in our predicament. We escaped the welfare lines, no man, out on the street one day, in a halfway house the next, with the projects waiting for us with open arms.

Not us. So said our one and only favorite uncle, good old Uncle Sam, he afforded us apartments, priority given to military families, a commissary, a PX/BX, a skating rink, bowling alley, safe playgrounds and parks, and each other.

Except for the 15th and end of the month we had no money. That coupled with each of us being so far away from home, and our men, the closest relative we knew, practically sewn to the base, all we had was each other. But we were the pleased, the joyous, the contented grateful…we were the Army housewives.

It was at Gloria's house where we mostly hung out. None of us worked. Not only did we have very little useful skills to bring in earnings that would enhance our circumstances, we really didn't have to. The military took care of its families. The government furnished our apartments. Couch, coffee tables, end tables, lamps, beds, dressers…and we were even allotted one patent leather recliner. 'On the economy', as we referred to anything not directly tied to the military base, also catered to us.

There were pawnshops galore, about the full spread of Rancier Boulevard. And just before payday, like two to three days before, the pawnbrokers would be waiting on us to stroll in with our two to-a-carriage strollers, pawning anything from our wedding rings, on down to our irons and curling irons. The brokers knew we were broke, but promised Uncle Sam they'd look after us, since they knew in return ole' Uncle Sam would be looking out for them.

The Rent-2-Own Centers was another penchant. No credit. No problem. And they meant this…provided we had Uncle Sam's ID card. They'd rent us anything from the latest dinette sets to the pens they used to draw up the terms of our contracts. Mostly, however, we went in for the colored TVs.

To say I loved my new life would be an understatement. I worshipped Uncle Sam like I did the man on the cross. He was my savior, even if I'd rather my girls hang out at my place instead of Gloria's sweatbox.

Forget don't mess with Texas. I say don't mess with Texas' heat! Holy smoking grief that place was hot, which most of my girls coming from Georgia and Alabama were used to hot muggy weather.

Me and Constance weren't. Constance came from New York, and me, of course from Philly. Both of us blew our air 24-7. But the only reason I wasn't thinking about hanging out at Constance's place was because she wasn't either. Neat as a pin she never offered up her place. Probably because she didn't have children like the rest of us. I imagined she was concerned about one of our kids breaking something, likely Gloria's child, or vomiting on her spotless carpet, in all likelihood my son.

But why not my place? I didn't mind having my girls over. I'm guessing the only reason they chose against it was because in addition to how cold I kept the place, I couldn't cook. Gloria could cook. That girl was one mean making a meal from the powder in flour and turning it into sustenance that stuck to your ribs.

Around 4pm, when she got to mixing that flour with hot oil, she used to send all of us home salivating. Our men pulled up in the driveway between five and six, which protocol dictated that we excuse ourselves to spend time with them. Of course what that really meant was feeding them and then doing the other 'f' word with them. Crude and crass, but I'd mislead myself if I tried taking the polite route putting it in any other way. It was literally what happened, though we issued no complaints about it since we had been home all day lounging in the outset of their sweat and hard work.

But for as crass as it all may have been, I'd have to say some of us from the North were even crasser as, speaking for myself, I mostly was just doing the other 'f' thing since I couldn't cook, at least not like my southern counterparts when food was scarce and money scarcer.

I fed my husband, Royce, as best I could…being pregnant again. But the other one, he had to go for what he knew. He could count on a few days before payday having to bring home food from the mess hall due to me not being Gloria. I couldn't make food stretch like she did. Constance I imagine fared better without children and being that her man had more rank than the rest of us. But for me and mines, we sometimes had to tough it around meal time.

Every day, just about, this was our routine. Sitting in Gloria's hot ass oven and beneath her raggedy fan playing spades, waiting to catch a drift of what she was cooking next. She never fed us, not even a crumb, as none of us had that kind of loot, but we did savor many starchy flavors she often had mixing in only one pan.

One day, when I could stand it no longer, the scents just turning my nostrils inside out, I had to get up and get her to show me some of her tricks.

"Girl, what in the world are you in here making now," I asked this one hot sticky day while we were in the middle of playing spades.

And she told me. And then showed me how to take just a pinch of flour and mix it in a skillet with juices from any meat. Didn't have to season a thing so long as the meat had been seasoned. And so there it was, the stuff that stuck to the ribs. The stuff that lasted for days and days.

Phaedra, another southern girl who dropped by Gloria's on occasion, laughed at me for asking. But then I laughed at her when we got back to our game, and started talking about one of our greatest fears… that much-dreaded one-year tour every soldier had to do… unaccompanied.

I could deal with having to scrimp for food, but I didn't think I could deal with being away from Royce for a whole year. I didn't reveal that part of my fear, but did agree with the menacing bleak sentiment hanging in the air.

"I would sure hope he could wait, but I'm not sure he would," Constance told Phaedra who adamantly disagreed.

Now Constance's husband was fairly good looking. He was tall, just about a Staff Sergeant, and shimmied muscles that resembled the façade of someone who'd been sparing in a few rings. No one ever said he looked good, at least not to her face, but with the exception of Phaedra we all agreed with her. "No, Bernard probably wouldn't hold off."

Royce damn well wouldn't wait. He, like Gloria's husband Jerry, needed sex morning, noon, and night. We weren't even going to play around with kidding ourselves. But just in case Gloria wasn't going to speak up and admit it, I said it for the both of us. "Hell no! Won't NO man wait!" It was better stated that way.

Gloria sat there staring into the hand she'd been dealt, smiling gigglishly school-girlish and shook her head in agreement. "I know Jerry won't hold off," she sheepishly admitted. And then she leaned forward, squirming in the chair to squint and add, "Not with the way he chases me around this place."

I watched everyone's expressions as our convictions circling the table grew. Even Tiffany, who had taken the longest to add her input, believed her husband wouldn't wait either. Though none of us were particularly at ease with our convictions, we were just accepting the fact our husbands might cheat on us. It was our way to stay strong, and move on should it become a fact.

Phaedra was the only one arguing the other way. "I know my hunny bunny will wait," she said shaking her head and rolling her eyes for longer than the normal split second eye roll. "He loves me and told me I was the only one for him. And I know he is the only one for me. Neither of us will let the devil come between us."

My eyes connected with Constance's and we sort of locked them together. Both of us were smirking, and not because we had a crush on her hunny bunny, who indeed was far more handsome than all of our husbands combined, but because Phaedra was the homeliest of us all.

If any man would cheat, just based on sheer attraction alone, her husband would have to be the first... even without the one-year unaccompanied assignment. And not that looks added to the equation in a detrimental way, but I couldn't help but wonder if the only reason Ricky married her was so that he could cheat, so he wouldn't have to worry about anyone wanting her.

Body-wise Gloria and Tiffany were solid ten's, whereas Constance and I left a little more to be desired. But Phaedra dragging in last, left a whole lot more to be desired. Mustache and upper extremities aside, she had the worst figure in all creation could possibly create. Long legs, knock-kneed, no waistline…and she wasn't even pregnant, which Gloria and I were, were not selling plaudits. Grant it, she was about a decade older than us, but the long sagging boobs she never put in a bra, the big buck teeth she always chose to smile, and the spray of hair she kept under a scarf at all times, screamed Ricky was a cheater.

The worst part was, the thing she kept tied around her head wasn't cute either. It was just an old rag she tore from the hem of a dress and tied around her head that never matched any of the long floral patterned dresses I could swear her great-grandmother handed down to her.

Sitting in my own space I was too sure I could move her hunny bunny in a corner, lay all of me against him, belly and all, and just whisper, "please…" and up he would rise and down I would go. I was sure of it.

Gloria, Tiffany, and I looked up to Constance, who like Phaedra was older. Where they differed was we considered Connie more worldly, and savvier, being from New York and all. So we left her to try talking sense into Phaedra. Them being in that 25-30 year-old age range, made Phaedra not see us as their equal; one reason she didn't hang around much. We were just babies she said.

"I think what they're saying is that most men have needs that can lead them into temptation when those needs aren't being met," Constance schooled her.

Stop with the sugarcoating, I was thinking. Keep it real. All men cheat! Obviously Connie had pulled her ballot out of the box, even if she still agreed with us, trying to explain man's most basic need the politically savvy way to an unsavvy old maid.

But why-ever did she use that ugly sinful word, temptation?

All Phaedra ever talked about was her relationship with the Lord. Someone sit a purse on the floor and the Lord was going to take all their money. Talk or laugh, or good Lord don't touch a television or telephone during a storm, because the Lord would strike you down. It was a sin to be in the grocery store on Sundays. Don't dare use the Lord's name in vain. And ladies were supposed to be ladies, and men be men, which right there had to be where she skipped over a section getting to the next sin.

"Unt un! No! Not my hunny bunny! Maybe y'alls men will fall to temptation but Ricky and I don't live like that. Our relationship is built on trust, so there is No Way!"

Constance and I locked eyes again while Phaedra got to pacing around the table, sweating profusely citing verses in the Bible and damning us for even thinking it was possible that Ricky would sleep with another woman.

"No woman wants to believe her husband will cheat," I slid in after Phaedra stopped pacing and started wiping her forehead. "But I just know they will."

"And how do you know?" she angrily spat.

I had no proof. There was no way to prove it to her unless I really proved it to her, which looking around the table I decided to let the argument go. Even though Gloria and Tiffany agreed with me, they like Phaedra didn't argue against the Bible. Tiffany's own father was a preacher, and both of them, like Phaedra, were raised by church. I had to accept I wasn't going to win that one.

Come no more than a week later and I awake to this tortured knocking at my door. It was around 10am, quite a few hours after Royce left for work, and just a couple of hours before I'd dress Jude and slug it on over to Gloria's to meet up with Connie and Tiff.

By the panicked sounds of the knocking I thought for sure something had happened to one of my girls.

Because only Constance had a telephone, this was a common way we were alerted when there was trouble. It could have been anyone though; like the woman at the end of the complex who woke up one morning to find her two-year old daughter missing. We told the woman repeatedly to stop letting that child wander around nude from the waist down. Some pervert was sure to grab her, which thankfully it turned out to be her ex-husband who had taken the child.

Another time a young girl who had just moved in with her boyfriend, Broadus, decided she was going to stay out all night since that's what he'd been doing. She went out that night and sure enough Broadus, a brute of an Army sergeant who no one dared to mess with, came pounding on our door at two or three some wicked hour in the morning. That night Royce and I were sprawled out in the middle of the floor in the living room, with the window open in part trying to catch a late night breeze, and in part anticipating Broadus's return home.

Not knowing what to expect, we froze when we heard the knocking. I could tell Royce was trying to decide how he was going to handle this big brute, if in fact it was him pounding, and not his girlfriend bleeding to death. That's when I caught Broadus looking in the window. Scared the crap out of me.

Slowly Royce answered the door and told him he had no idea where his girlfriend was. A few hours later, about 6 in the morning, we hear more pounding, only this time it's coming through the ceiling as they lived above us. There was nothing we could do but listen to the pounding and screams since we didn't have a telephone. The last time we saw his girlfriend an ambulance was taking her away. Hopefully rumor was correct. She made it safely back to Michigan, her hometown.

And so here I go again with this pounding, so symbolic of serious trouble. I almost didn't answer the knock, but ultimately gave in.

It was Phaedra. The first thing that registered was her long face. Longer than usual, her face was swollen and swallowed by tears. Except for the lack of obvious bruises I couldn't make heads or tails out of what happened to her. I stepped away from the door and let her, carrying little Ricky on her hip, inside. Both of them were crying. The first snippet of a hint that it was likely a shut-out. Ricky putting her and little Ricky out.

Phaedra heads right to my couch and plopped down, just after she plopped Ricky down in the same way. Hadn't said two words and she and little Ricky were using my couch as if I wasn't standing in front of them waiting to hear what happened.

"Phae, you want some water?" Not only was it all I had to offer, but it was all I could think to say. Other than maybe asking if it was hot outside, or if she had heard the latest about Broadus and his girlfriend.

"No thanks," she answered in a hoarse whisper, and then lifted her long leg, foot and all, and planted it on my couch so she could rest her chin in the palm of her hand.

Now my couch wasn't nothing but an old beat up piece of pleather. In fact, there was a fresh iron mark that her back covered, but still! To go putting her filthy feet, shoes and all up on my couch was some kind of nerve when I still wasn't sure if I had invited her in.

"I'm sorry for coming in here like this," she finally gushed out in the last of her sobs, while her little boy greedily gobbled the water I handed him.

"It's cool." I assured her, lying to get the scoop on what happened to Mr. and Mrs. faithfully happily married.

"I tried knocking on Connie's door, but I don't think she's home," she continued apologizing.

Apparently I wasn't her first choice, but wasn't her last choice either. She walked right by Gloria's apartment if she stopped by Constance's apartment before coming to me. I still don't know what to say to her. She and I aren't that good of friends. She's older and we shared different views, and that was on everything from wardrobe to religion. And she still has her foot propped up on my couch.

"I think Ricky's cheating on me," she says through eyes so red I actually see Satan telling her how angry she needs to be.

I don't say a word. Even though I always thought it was possible, I am in total shock that she would say 'she thinks' instead of coming right out and admitting he's cheating on her. I can't understand how she would think now, and not have thought last week.

"He didn't come home last night, which he's never done this before. He always lets me know when he has duty and plans to be gone."

"Well, maybe he forgot he had guard duty and couldn't find a way to get someone to tell you."

Phaedra didn't have a telephone either. Like me and many others, the only way we got messages was by someone in the complex delivering the message, mostly Constance. Tiffany and I had it the worst. Our husbands weren't in the same unit like everyone else. If the commander didn't get the news to us, we likely wasn't getting it.

"You really shouldn't think the worst Phae. He could be in the hospital or anything…"

A truck could have rolled over him or he could have been hospitalized from another dreadful accident, and none of this was worse than cheating.

"But someone would have told me that by now!" she spat with the same venom she spat at me a week ago. "He and Bernie work together! Bernie would've…"

Just like that she stopped talking, realizing Constance hadn't answered her knock.

"See…" I said.

Phaedra smiled a small sheepish grin, just as the

evangelist minister Jerry Farwell appeared on my TV. I wasn't sure what the reverend was ministering about, because my stupefaction was on Phaedra's fixation with the anguished pastor, and how I happened to leave the channel on that station.

Too late to change the channel I left Phaedra engrossed in Jerry's soupy scriptures and went to check on my son. I was in my bedroom a few minutes before she slipped in the doorway, weepy eyed with her little boy hugging her around her locked knees. She asked me not to say anything to Constance and the others.

"It's cool Phae…no big deal," I shrugged.

"I'm going to 7-Eleven and calling his unit…"

"Okay," I say, and she left out, leaving me to wonder why she hadn't done that to begin with.

The following day however, she was back. She wasn't beating my door down this time, and neither was she crying. She was asking me to go with her to see a psychic.

A psychic I'm thinking? Do people really believe in that stuff? She wanted to be sure Ricky wasn't cheating. Turned out he did have duty, though she claimed he claimed he told her. She was sure he hadn't because she had fixed his favorite meal; fried pork chops, mashed potatoes, and gravy that night.

That was her convincing proof? But I didn't contest any of this, though I was thinking about how much I could use thirty-five bucks. Hell, we didn't have to go anywhere. I could have told her Ricky was cheating at the door.

We go into town, somewhere very near the most seedy street known in town…"D" Street…and walked into a little wooden building that looked out of place up against the brick specialty shops lining the street.

I wasn't allowed in the red room. I sat out in a cramped crummy front office with Jude and her little boy for about 30-minutes before she emerged from the back wearing the extra-long sad face. She looked so sad I didn't dare ask how things went.

"She told me all about my sister who has cancer, and how I feel closest to her… how she's calling out to me."

I'm walking beside her thinking, huh? I thought she went there to find out if Ricky was cheating. Was that the best the psychic could do? Ask about her family and then tell her which ones she was closer to?

"Well, I told her I had one sister and that I was from Alabama…but she told me about my sister's illness," she argued, obviously against her sensible oasis, since I wasn't saying a word. Intrigued as I was, I just listened.

"She told me she felt I had a heavy burden hanging around me and that I was looking for a friend to talk to…"

…No shit! Who in the world wasn't that went knocking on a psychic's door?

"I just can't believe how much she knew about me," she sighed.

Whadt!?! No Phaedra! You got me to come down here in this seedy district my husband would have a stroke to know I was down here in, because you're worried that Ricky is cheating!

Phaedra suddenly broke out crying. The psychic said Ricky was cheating. She said although he wasn't cheating on her the other night, he was seeing a woman he worked with. Phaedra was sure it was some PFC, a little petite girl fresh out of AIT she had seen him with once before. She was the one standing beside Ricky on their unit photo.

"Crei, come with me to the base. I have to confront her!"

Oh hell no! This was where I drew the line. I hadn't told my girls. I snuck down to "D" Street to see some psychic. And now I was going to the base to confront some young woman who may or may not have been the one seeing her husband!?!

"Phae, my baby is hungry. I've got to get back home. I can't. Maybe you can ask Connie..."

Phaedra's face turned ashy stone cold gray. If she had laid on the pavement, she would have blended in. "No, I can't. I have to do this myself!"

She was right about that because I wasn't about to get involved in a he said, she said scanty relationship brawl where I stood nothing to gain, but everything to lose.

"I'm going to whip that bitch's ass!"

My eyes nearly flipped out of my head. Phae!?! No, not Phae! Not Phae in the granny long dresses with the nylons rolled around her ankles!

"You know, on second thought you may just want to wait until Ricky gets home and just go off on him," I suggested. Why women always went after the other woman was a punk move. It was like stomping on a roach at a time while keeping a filthy house.

Phaedra obviously kept roaches...and Raid. "I want that little hussy first," she spat. "She knows he's married and is just going to push up on him anyways!"

"But how do you know—"

"—No! The psychic said it was her!"

"Phae, I'm telling you; you need to get all of your facts straight and be sure first." I paused, "...besides, what if you get arrested? Who's going to take care of little Ricky?"

I couldn't believe I was having this argument with this once pious woman; trying to push reason on someone so unreasonable.

So, a little desperate, I spun the reason around. The more I kept saying Ricky probably wasn't cheating, the more she calmed down. Gradually the anger and hurt reduced down to freezing his dinner and not giving him any. Ridiculous stuff that told me, not only did she not know what she was doing. She didn't know what she was talking about! No woman who had experienced a cheater would ever use holding out as a form of punishment. She might hold out on him, but it would hardly be for punishment!

"Personally," I added for the umpteenth time, "I don't see Ricky as a cheater."

wish list

~~

"Make Believe: the closest thing to believing."
~~

No one wanted to say it, at least not after learning how brutally Davita was attacked by her husband, but really, she had no business doing what she did. Thank God she pulled through, though.

Come to find out, a whole day later, Davita hadn't been at the educational center, and she wasn't cabbing it around town with another man either. She had been down at the Red Cross lying her behind off to weasel a few hundred dollars out of the government's coffers. And topping matters off, she didn't use the money on food. Nooo, she brought a red leather jacket for herself.

So that was their send off. Instead of possibly getting an Article 15 for the stunt, Keith ended up with a court martial, a dishonorable discharge, and 10-15 years in a brig. And Davita got the boot too. She was booted out of his life and back home to NYC.

"Oool, I think I like this leather jacket," Gloria teased. "What do you think Jerry will do if I brought it?"

I had to laugh. After all, Gloria was about to fight with her life for Davita. "Now you know that ain't right!" I teased, stealing Phaedra's hypnotic one liner.

"I mean, dang Gloria! Are you sure you need all of this stuff!?!" It really wasn't so much of a question as to whether or not she needed all she had piled in her buggy. It was more of a statement. The girl had lost her mind in K-Mart.

We were out, supposedly getting shoes for the kids, before we were to mosey next door to pick up groceries for lunch. But two hours later, with a good fifteen minutes left to pick up lunch before the kids started getting fidgety, Gloria had piled her cart with one of everything K-Mart sold.

Cannon sheets, shams, pillowcases, and two big comforters in addition to bathroom scales, wall clocks, crock-pots, rolled up rugs, Fisher Price toys, a blow-up swimming pool, a sewing machine, and stuff none of us ever heard of. That girl was looking to go out like Davita. Jerry was going to kill her if he came home and saw all that stuff we saw piled in the cart, stuffed in their one-bedroom apartment. Not once had I ever seen her with painted nails, and none of us ever wore make-up, but there was all of Revlon's health and beauty aids beneath the pile up too.

She had to be pushing around a thousand-dollar buggy that increased in worth as we made our way to the register.

"Oool," she cooed stopping at luggage. "I always wanted one of these…"

"Are you sure Jerry will be able to fit all of you in it?" Constance was looking at the price tag dangling from the Samsonite carry-on luggage Gloria was trying to pack on top of the comforters. Seventy bucks for a little itty-bitty travel bag just might fit the lower half of her in it.

Gloria ignored Constance, plopping the carry-on on top of the heap before stopping at a ceiling-high rack of Tupperware. None of us noticed at first, but at the end of the aisle was more Home Goods — vacuum cleaners!

"Oh no! That's it!" both Connie and I said, seeing Gloria make a beeline for the automatic plug-in evidence suckers. We had to stop that madness before paramedics had to be called. "The thought of Jerry using one of them Hoovers to vacuum up the rest of our girl was a hard visual to erase.

"Girl, please! I ain't studdin' Jerry none," Gloria scoffed.

Yeah, right. Whatever studdin' meant, we were concerned…very concerned about what Jerry might do to her that we dragged her and the loaded basket to the register, and then stood behind her. We had to trap her in line so she couldn't turn around and get at any other wares nearby.

Gloria had picked up nearly everything she touched. The only thing not packed in the buggy were the ceiling beams, and that was only because we hadn't passed a ladder... thank you God!

At that point I was curious to see how Gloria was going to pay for her over thousand-dollar shopping spree. I saw Constance intently watching too. Would she be paying by check or cash? Or was she just making a run for the door?

We waited…and watched a stream of transaction tape spill over the register like party streamers. Gloria and Jerry didn't have it like that. They wouldn't have been in the military if they had. At least not living on First Ave like the rest of us…in them one-bedroom heat entrapments sweating it out beneath raggedy fans.

Come to think of it, and I looked between the spokes in the cart to check, but she hadn't thought to pick up a new fan...like one that worked. We had passed some really nice ones too. A whole lot better than that humidifier she used.

"Ugh, wait…" Gloria said to the cashier, grabbing the butterfly phone the cashier was about to scan. On second thought, after inspecting the bottom, she didn't want it. "Never mind," she tells the cashier. "You can put that back."

We couldn't imagine what the inspection beneath the phone was about, since there was no phone service running to her apartment.

"Uh, I change my mind. I don't want this either," she said again to a cashier who was as incredulous as me and Constance seeing all the items piled up on the other side of the register. Surely this had to be a first for K-Mart. A shopper buying so much on one trip. It was a wonder the conveyor belt didn't wear out, weighted down by all that inventory.

Gloria grabbed the next item out of the cashier's hand too. "Uh wait…" and she squinted to look over a hand shovel the cashier was about to ring up.

"I don't think I need this either," she sighed.

Good! Definitely a wise move. She hardly wanted Jerry getting his hands on something like a shovel. Investigators would never find her.

This stopping the cashier sequence continued to the other end of the counter, where she picked through the mountain of merchandise already rung up. Not giving a kitty about spectators, she sifted through the pile.

"…Ugh, maybe I better not get this…and maybe I better not get that." When she finished, standing ankle deep in transaction tape, the only item left on the conveyor was one pair of shoes she originally came to buy.

"We always do that," she laughed after we left the store. The 'we' she was referring to was her mother and sisters. They regularly piled their buggies full with their wish list, and then changed their mind, walking out the door with the one item they had come for.

"Somebody's going to call you on that one day," I said.

"I don't know how they can," she retorted. "There ain't no laws against wishing and hoping!"

playback

~~
"Playbacks & Paybacks."
~~

Never again. That's what I said after Diamond and Jeff almost broke up. After that brawl I promised never to get between lover spats, married or not. They say no when they mean yes, and say yes when they mean no. Truell was right. Too much drama. I got my own yes and no drama. Don't need to sort through anyone else's.

And then came Moxicilla and Keith. Now Keith was the remaining one among us still available... still playing the playboy role, claiming he didn't date scabs, i.e., ugly women (his words). Deep inside we all knew the boy wanted a ball and chain too. Club-hopping and shuffling through women wasn't all fun and sunshine. He knew it, and we knew it...because we'd all been single too.

None of us though, knew exactly what Keith was looking for. Every woman we ever saw him with, was cute, but taken, as in unavailable. The scabs we never saw, but only heard about. So when we, Truell and I, were out trolling one of Keith's hunting grounds (the mall), not stalking him, though we did spot him, we decided to check out the lanky tall scab he hung over a counter slobbering on.

Well, at first we called out, "hey Keith!"

But he threw us shade, giving us a flimsy head nod and eye roll.

Me and Truell were like, 'did you see that!?! Oh, hell no!' We went in!

We rolled in Glass Hut with our big brown bags with one purpose; to get the entail and details.

Keith had no choice. He was surrounded and out-numbered. By group code he was forced to give up the goods.

So he introduced us to Moxicilla, an inscrutable name. Sounded like a tampon or STD ointment. And this woman looked nothing like the women he paraded around our card games and backyard barbecues. He liked knock-out bodies and pretty faces. His hotties with the bodies he'd bring around for a visit or two, before telling us about a psychotic episode that ruined it all. If it wasn't for one of them stalking him, then it'd be one of them inevitably having him jumping out of third floor windows when the significant other showed up. And it was always from that third floor window too... or a higher. Never lower.

Ugly dates he hid, and only laughed about them later... like after supposedly waking up the whole neighborhood trying to make them glow. We never saw his scabs...until now...which to clarify; Moxicilla was not ugly. Sure... she had a long hook nose and eyes spaced further apart than most, but she wasn't so hard on the eyes people had to look away.

"You must be desperate, or going blind looking for a wife in here," I teased when Moxicilla made a trip to the back of the store. (note: she worked there. The blind pun was because this was an eyeglass store).

"Yeah. Pickings must be getting mighty slim," Truell laughed too.

"What? I'ma lover," he laughed, trying to play off what we were witnessing. "All women need lovin'..." he lamely added, face so flushed his blushing hid his freckles.

We left the store tickled. We couldn't wait to run this sighting by the guys. It would be the prevailing joke until Keith found another '10'...or scab.

Except, we'd forgotten the incident by the weekend. Come a week later and there again, in the mall, on his hunting grounds, his turf, was the playboy drooling over the same woman with the penicillin sounding name.

I was alone when I passed the lovey-dovey couple this time. They were nestled in a frou-frou café; Moxi sucking on a straw stuck in a glass with strawberries, oranges, bananas, umbrellas and whatnot hanging on the rim, and Keith hanging on the other side frosting the glass.

All right. What's that saying... 'fool me once...' Shame on Keith trying to pull wool over my eyes twice! I walked right over and re-introduced myself.

"Hiiii," I say, and I'm panning the woman's face so that I catch both her eyes. "I think I met you last week. I'm Crei." And I extended my hand for shaking.

Moxicillan smiled, hesitantly bringing out a thin pale hand she extended over her wilting drink. She was asking Keith's approval, with her eyes of course, but the playboy's tongue was tied, so he couldn't speak.

Keith had sworn, crossed his heart, and now he was just about to die. So I accepted the flimsy handshake and answered for him.

"It's okay," I say to this woman looking more amused than aggrieved. "I'm just a friend, supposedly a really good friend however, who's shocked to find out my good friend," and I playfully nudge Keith, "doesn't think we're good enough friends to meet his new friend."

The woman's roving eyes move. They circle her head twice, while Keith sat there struggling to write the ending of his playboy eulogy.

"Ugh, Crei," he softly replied. "This is Moxi."

'Oooh, so Moxi is it now?' I'm grinning. Before it was Moxicillan...the pharmaceutical sounding name. But I go on and continue entertaining the woman, telling her how she must be 'the one' because it was the second time I was seeing them together. And sure, this was none of my business and not my place to insert this noise, but this was how tight we were. Keith knew damn well he needed help! This girl was 'the one', and he was happy as a kid on a popsicle high I showed up when I did. He knew he didn't want to be single forever!

"Wow Keith," I cooed, using my elegant voice. "You must bring Moxi by the house sometime. I'm sure the guys would love to meet her!"

Next weekend… the very next weekend, after we (the group minus Keith) had been discussing this Moxi business, the blushing new couple dropped by. Normally Keith came by daily. One of us was always feeding him, and listening to his single exploits. But he had to work up the courage to introduce his new 'available' girl to the guys. This was his cold feet moment.

But he had nothing to worry about. The guys were married to us, all tens in their hearts… or at least we hoped. They liked Moxi. She was cool. Down-to-earth. Outgoing. Could rub heads, as in playing Pinochle. And she owned the Optical Illusions store where her playboy was first spotted trying to play a player. Haha!

Next thing we knew, these two were getting married! Honestly, that's when we got a little concerned about our friend. Was he moving too fast? Had he been set up!?!

But Keith was serious. He was ready. He loved Moxi. Was tired of being single. And yada, yada. Yet, what really flipped us upside-down, was when he got to talking about a Beauty and Beast wedding theme.

"Are you sure," we kept asking him. This would be me, Diamond and Truell. We hadn't been to one wedding held in a gym… at the YMCA.

We just didn't get it! Keith, himself, was financially set. And with Moxi supposedly owning the Optic Illusions store, they could have sprung for a church.

But Keith kept saying Moxi wanted the wedding to be special and done her way… referring to this beauty and beast business.

"You'll see," we also heard a lot. According to him, Moxi was really creative. She'd done Pinocchio for her nephew's play. Supposedly everyone was still talking about the production!

"But for a wedding?" He lost me there.

Diamond though, came right out with it. "Keith, you've lost your mind. Do you know anything about that story?"

Of course he knew nothing about the story. He only heard beauty and beast, and saw her and him, and figured it would be alright.

After a while we let it go. Life got busy. Truell had a baby. Diamond wanted a baby. I had two babies... rather, make that three. Point being. We had our hands full. On our plate was a new baby, an in-vitro specialist, and a million small people disputes, to be concerned about any mistakes Keith and Moxi might be making. If by chance the Beauty and Beast production worked, they'd have plenty more chances to f'something else up.

Wedding day came, and all of our men are in this thing. We're not. Thank every aspiring good Lord however. But we told our men it might get a little crazy, but didn't go to the extent to tell them just how crazy. After all, it was their boy who they'd waited forever to get married.

Stealing words out of Jeff's mouth, "don't hate!"

So we didn't. We told them they looked good dressed in the white tails, ignoring their gloating about being up front for all the ladies inspection.

With little Ashley, Truell's baby girl in tow, we inched along, among a huge crowd trying to get into the gym to witness this Beauty and Beast wedding. And man! Were there not A LOT of witnesses! Too many for a bride who didn't seem to have many friends, or for a groom who, despite talking up the wedding, actually getting really selective about who he would invite after the beauty and beast theme grew wings and took off.

There had to be over a hundred people milling around outside the "Y" trying to get in. Diamond looked over at me and whispered, "you know damn well won't this many people fit in this gym."

I snickered, full on expecting a whole lot of laughing.

Finally got in, the three of us already laughing, checking out Moxi and her designer's handiwork. Fake greenery was everywhere; draped over folding chairs, thrown over candle holders ...some pieces even hung from the ceiling. This had to represent the forest.

The altar was jazzed up too. A bamboo chuppah looking creation where the preacher, the groom, his men, and eventually the bride were all to gather, draped over the hand built stage. Not too bad. It could have been worse. Like we didn't need to remind ourselves we were sitting in a gym!?!

Truell didn't want to sit up front, never mind the fact that there were no seats ten rows forward even vacant. Truell's concern however, wasn't about being made a spectacle. She was concerned about Ashley, and the possibility of having to make a quick exit to feed or change her.

So we sat towards the back of the...ugh gym... which surreptitiously provided better cover to closely inspect the beauty and beast theme going on.

"Girl, what the hell is that behind us," Diamond asked fully turned around in her fold-up chair. She was looking at a gray tarp that looked to be concealing the real show we were about to witness.

"I don't know," I answered wondering myself what all Moxi had in store for us. By the look of things I hoped when the tarp was finally pulled, the Beauty and Beast was going to transform into Alice in Wonderland behind us. It would be worth the show if that happened.

Diamond nudged me again, so I turned back around...to face the men who had slipped in and were lined up beside the preacher. They did look good. Chests poked out, arms rigid, jaws tight, clean, shaven, dressed meticulously in all white with the exception of cranberry bow ties. They had to be proud with them tails.

Instantly, as music began to play, the three of us looked up wondering where the sound was coming from. We made out a woman in a pink hat moving her hands along keys on a piano, but the real music, cracking through speakers as it played, included wind instruments…percussions, violins, maybe even a bagpipe, none of which were in the gym… unless…and Diamond cut her eye over at me…unless the instruments playing were playing…and we both slowly turned back around to take another peek at the tarp.

We could have been wrong. Perhaps the bride was going to make that extravagant explosive grand entrance after all. Everyone started fidgeting. All one hundred and seventy-five guests crammed together begin craning their necks and awkwardly twisting around, expecting like us, for magic to hit us from behind.

I see hostesses fanning back guests, to make room for the entrance of the bride's party. Moxi's girls. What looked like every sister who'd ever pledged a sorority, EVER. Old, young, slim...not so slim... swayed in from a side entrance where some had to squeeze in to get through an orange shoe-horned propped open wooden door. It looked bad. It really did.

"Oh Lord," I heard Diamond sigh.

We watched with our mouths open, what looked like fifteen hundred women...could've been more, trail through a side door, which suddenly explained the choke hold by the door. But it didn't explain the dresses.

Beyond the color, an orangey yellow in stark contrast to the cranberry bow ties the groomsmen wore, the dresses were homemade. And while homemade dresses were nothing new, these dresses looked homemade… as in getting snagged in a Singer machine, with the zipper presser foot locked down, and the seamstress, annoyed, snatching the fabric out of the machine to finish the contraption by hand. That's exactly what these homemade dresses looked like…contraptions.

Every bridesmaid that passed by, our mouths dropped lower and lower. Faces and mouths fell so often, we all looked like rugs! Those dresses didn't cry out for help. Those poor dresses just cried. We rolled up our rugs and shook our heads.

There was hope. That tarp still hadn't been pulled back. In this twisted up awkward position we sat in, straining to see behind us, we kept our eyes trained on that tarp. We were so hopeful something so magical and whimsical was going to appear, to restore our faith in fairytales. That they were real and did exist.

All of us sitting right there, and still neither of us could accurately explain what occurred next. Was the tarp hoisted, hand over hand? Or had a conveyor belt rolled it up? It was hard to tell. Between the loud rattling of the tarp rising, and the bride and a man standing at the back of the gym, and I'm talking at the very back of the gym on the opposite end of the court…like beneath the rim…we couldn't make out if we were seeing an open casket propped upright, or if the scoreboard actually read ninety to nothing, in the fourth quarter.

Moxi and a withered looking man stood on a full court, beneath the rim, engulfed by barren nothingness, staring out at the other half of the gym about to rock over on its side we were crammed in so tight.

Everywhere we looked a beast replaced beauty. It was painful, especially being twisted in a position for a lot longer than I cared to be twisted, looking at what I was seeing. Moxi and this old man, who I had no choice but to assume was her father, stood beneath the rim reminding me of Frankenstein and his child bride.

Every step Moxi and her father made towards the handmade altar, another rug rolled out. Diamond and I doubled over. We were through. Everybody say Amen, the wedding was over.

"Who is that?" Truell asked looking around me to ask Diamond about the man looking like something a cat dragged from beneath a rock.

Diamond though, ignored Truell. She was busy nudging me. "What in the freak is that on her head?"

I wanted to tell Diamond she didn't have to worry about letting a curse word slip. We weren't in church. So the question wasn't what in the freak was that on her head, but what in the fuck was that on her head?

We laughed so hard throughout the wedding that the entire back three rows looked as if we were riding a wave. Hands going up in the air, and side to side weren't exactly praises for the officiator.

We laughed even harder during the reception. Finally we got to inspect the thing on Moxi's head. It was a hand-crochet dinner napkin. She teared up explaining how she cried after she finished making it.

"I bet you did," Diamond muttered, and we fell out of our chairs laughing again.

After a while Royce, Jeff, and Leonard joined us asking what we were giggling about. We answered in unison, "Nothing." And burst out laughing again.

"Oh, my, my, my…"

But none of this was the kicker. The kicker came a month later when Keith asked us what we thought of the wedding.

"It was nice," I said. "Not your average wedding, but very classy, if I must say so…"

"Oh really," he smirked.

"Yes, really." He heard about us giggling, but so what. We could have been giggling about anything.

Moxi also asked what we thought. Diamond answered her. "Girl, you outdid yourself on that one." She scratched her brow. "Never saw nothing like it ever. We had a really good time!"

Then Keith dimmed the lights and put in the movie we had come over to watch. It was supposed to be the classic Beauty and Beast film.

Right away we realized we were about to watch the wedding all over again. Now of course this is months later, so not every itty bitty detail was fresh in our memory. The veil, the dresses, and the tarp was most of what came fresh to mind…my mind at least. But the film rolled back and reminded us all, clearing up all the fuzzies.

Caught right there on tape was our every reaction to the events as they unfolded!

After the film Moxi stopped speaking to us, and Keith barely spoke. The film, of course, made it obvious how we felt about the wedding. Pointing and nudging each other, and laughing and shaking our heads in stark contrast to the music playing and others smiling and snapping pictures was a dead giveaway.

But I could have sworn everyone was laughing with us. Guess not. Really funny though, was Diamond holding a camera while we laughed and others clicked away taking pictures. The whole while this camera stayed in Diamond's lap. It wasn't until I pointed at the shoes one bridesmaid was wearing that she raised the camera and clicked, taking a picture of the woman's feet.

I like to have fell out of the chair then laughing while the 'evidence' film rolled. All that stopped me were the expressions on the guy's faces, and of course, Moxi's too.

But, come on now…they had to see the humor. Maybe they should've zoomed the camcorder on them dresses and shoes!

"They'll get over it," Diamond said.

"Yeah… maybe," I replied.

"Well I'm traumatized! I'll never forget that wedding," Truell shrieked.

And we fell out laughing all over again!

hoe' down

~~

"Vanilla and the Gorilla"

~~

But guess what? Moxi's now one of us. And being one of us… she got her revenge. Well, sort of. Our friendship wasn't no written in stone list of rules accord. It's just all of us had our turn to go through something, and took the liberty to either laugh or sulk about it. Life moved on. We could either shake it off, or shrivel up… like when Diamond and Jeff entered the ring… again.

All be a monkey's uncle if Jeff at his old age, all thirty-something great, decided to start working out. Sad thing was, he wasn't doing it for Diamond, or for himself even. He was doing it for the ladies. He saw himself slipping and thought he could catch himself before he turned fifty and fell. That's what was really sad. Nothing could be worse than looking twenty and being fifty.

We laughed when we saw him jogging down the steps with a towel draped around his neck, only to hop in his car and drive to the gym. The gym literally was at the end of the street, located in a shopping center. Of course he was showboating. He knew we were looking out the window.

A week later though, and he had Keith and Royce hanging out with him too. They played ball, though only a few nights a week, which in rapid order turned into zero nights a week. Royce and Keith couldn't keep up. Their schedules didn't permit them getting to the gym by 6/7pm and run up and down a court, to make it in to work by 6am the next day… without the aid of crutches, or a motorized scooter. Jeff was back on his own, which in short order he went from balling… to sparring.

"Don't worry," Diamond ruefully said. "A good hit'll knock some sense into him!"

But she didn't mean this, as well as I doubted it. Jeff was too damn arrogant. The nerve of him teasing Diamond the way he did. "Damn girl, it seems like for every roll I take off, you put one on!"

Some nerve! All a good hit would do for him was knock out the rest of his brains, and maybe leave him with another knot on his head.

But about six months into Jeff's newfound hobby, Diamond told us Jeff had an upcoming 'first bout'. It was taking place at the Astrodome.

We.Were.ALL.Shocked. Me, Truell, and Moxi! All the town's big events were held at the Astrodome. Celebrities performed there all the time. And the place was always packed, regardless of the performance.

So when we looked up on the billboard and read: 'Hoe Down in the Smoker'. Saturday Nite. Showtime 8pm,' we got concerned. Really concerned.

"Jeff hasn't been training long enough to be in something like this," Moxi expressed to Diamond, her eyes making back and forth laps around her head.

"Ugh…Moxi! This is how boxers get their training," Diamond replied, as if it was the mega million time she had to explain such drivel. "There has to be a first you know!"

No one said another word after that. If Diamond was cool with it, then we were cool with it too. After all, none of us would be in the ring.

"…Besides, he's just sparring with a white boy ten pounds lighter than him anyway," Diamond argued.

We did not argue this point either. If the white boy was out of his league, then Jeff might have an easy win. From my way of thinking though, the white kid might've been ten pounds out of his weight league, but I thought Jeff was ten years out of the sports league.

Hoe Down day arrived and just so happened Diamond had to work. She promised to meet up with us after she got off. With Jeff's bout being one of about twenty, she expected to get to the Dome before the fight. But if not, she told us to make sure we recorded it… and took plenty pictures!

"Don't worry girl, Keith is filming it!" That was Moxi. Mrs. Upbeat and Positive. She was rooting for Mr. Big Shot!

Royce, Leonard, Keith and a group of other guys had been bragging too. For sure they would be there. They got ring-side seats, and on Hoe down day were on the floor smoking their expensive cigars while me, Truell and Moxi sat in the balcony. We had a better view though. The guys had to look up into the ring, whereas we got the panoramic cinematic view. In other words, even if we blinked, we weren't missing a thing. We had the bird's eye view.

The fights were surprisingly short. The first five lasted no more than five minutes each, and none where knockouts. Someone at another table in the balcony told us the fights were short because they were amateurs.

"But five minutes?!" Moxi shrieked. She had her camera out and ready for action!

Personally, the beginning was such a bore. Two guys swinging at each other, nothing landing, followed by a bell ringing where the guys retired to corners to have water thrown on exaggerated sweat got old quick. With nothing sticking…or even landing, I could have stayed home and just went to the after party to celebrate Jeff's promised win. Diamond wasn't missing a thing. I hoped she wasn't rushing!

Of course the lively Moxi was mixing on another beat. "Diamond's missing it," she exclaimed, bouncing around and being her extra self. "You'd think after she spent so much money on that robe she'd want to be here to see him wear it!"

"You'd think!" Truell scoffed. She was kind of bored too. Not without mention, she had gone shopping with Diamond for the robe. She also was the one who did Diamond a favor and picked up the garment after it was embroidered.

"Ooo, over there," Moxi goes, hitting and slapping me, directing me to look in a dark area where I have to squint looking for Jeff. He's a chocolate man and it was dim, so I had to squint extra hard to find him.

Finally I see him, or rather I saw the robe; a bright gold shiny cloth with white trim and black embroidery. Against Jeff's Hershey complexion it almost looked like a ghost on a oak tree branch blowing in the wind. I only knew it was him when I saw the JFK embroidery.

"Look at him..." I muttered. I didn't want him hurt...per'say... but hurt a little couldn't hurt.

Jeff flexed and shuffled outside the ring, as trainers pretended to massage his shoulders and whisper in his ear. Jerking his head side to side and throwing neat jabs as if he knew what he was doing, I couldn't help but marvel those that had a hand in building the boxing arena. I'd been to the Dome when it was a basketball court and thought they'd done a fabulous job!

The bell rung and Jeff ducked between the ropes and entered the ring. Not only was he still wearing the robe, but he wore matching gold boxing shoes...with his initials stenciled on them too. Showoff.

"Would you look at..." Immediately I looked at Truell, after he dropped the robe. "Did you help her buy that championship belt too!"

"Embarrassing," Truell sighed.

The fool took it off and held it over his head!

"That's right Jeff! That's right! You looking good baby," Moxi stood up prematurely cheering. "You got this! You got this!"

'I doubt it,' I privately conceded. The scrawny hunched over white kid with the sweaty hair matted to his forehead wore an alarming deadpan expression. It was a big giveaway far as I was concerned. Looked like that white boy feared neither living nor dying.

The bell rung and Jeff, and his ten-pound less, 10-year younger white mismatch came out of their corners, gloves raised, and moved to the center of the ring. Like please already! Let's go! Let's do this! There were wins to celebrate and people to congratulate!

But they circled each other in the ring for a lap or two; Jeff dressed in the fluorescent trunks, and his opponent dressed in dingy white trunks with matted hair sticking to his forehead.

Jeff tapped at his nose. Must've caught one of the pros doing that one. While the scrawny kid gauntly moved around him with his arms practically pinned to his side. Not sure where, if ever I saw that move.

Diamond just might make the fight I thought. Looked like the laps were going to draw out and drag on. Five minutes later and not one jab had been thrown. Beneath the balcony I heard Royce and the guys rooting for Jeff.

"That's our boy! Knock him out Jeff! One hit! One hit baby!"

The guys were talking about the knock out hit.

"That kids' going down!" Royce announced.

"That kid don't stand a chance." Sounded like Keith projecting.

"Look at him. The kid is too afraid to even raise his hands," had to be analytical Leonard speaking.

"That boy is gonna kill that poor kid," someone behind me said.

Sounded like everyone had their money on Jeff.

Meanwhile 10 minutes passed, and I'm looking around for a waitress to bring me a drink.

"Go on and do what you gotta do," someone from down below cheered.

"Don't cut him no slack. Ain't your fault. They shouldn't have put him in the ring," so obviously Royce pumping up the mood.

The waitress brought me the drink. Still no hits or swings, but Jeff continues making laps around the base of the proverbial tree. Jeff was playing with the scrawny kid. Pulling a Cassius Clay on the child. Taunting him. Siking him. Mentally putting the whammy on him.

Finally I decided to take a sip of my drink. I picked up the glass, thought I saw a flicker of white light, assumed it was a camera flash or a ceiling beam had blown a fuse, when I clearly heard "Holy shit!"

Glass in hand, about to take that first sip, when I realized the flicker had indeed come from Jeff. He actually was sailing, airborne, backwards…through the ropes, where he ended up hanging upside down, out of the ring, saved by the shoelace of that one shiny gold shoe entangled in the ropes.

Oh My God. Much as I disliked Jeff for getting on my girl, and betting against him winning this fight, I really didn't expect this. Jeers and laughter rippled around me, none louder than Moxi hanging over the balcony shouting down to Jeff. "You all right Jeff? You all right?"

head of MY class

~~
"Never know who has hiring power."
~~

Shirley Luck. She sat in the second row of my business banking class with her big golden hair and big golden head, and come to think of it, her big golden everything, acting like she wrote, passed, and enforced all banking regulations… international and otherwise. Shirley was a knowaholic.

By the second week of class, everyone in class, to include the instructor, hated Shirley, and the bank where she worked. We hated that her bank put their credits on top of debits. We didn't like that her bank settled their daily journal before 10am. And just who exactly cared that her bank's first batch of work was picked up by eleven…and the second by three? Or that her bank preferred rubber bands to paper clips…because paper clips jammed the counter. We especially hated that she knew all banking policies and regs…better than the instructor. But what we really didn't get, was why Shirley was even taking the introductory banking class in the first place!

By the fourth week, I was so sick of Shirley I wanted to tell her exactly why everyone hated her. I felt this was stuff she needed to know.

Damn it Shirley, the reason why you got the "B" on your test while everyone else got the "A" was because the way your bank does things, isn't the way it's written in the book. Shut up! Get over it! Listen! And just maybe you might learn something!

By the sixth week of class, I thought we'd seen the last of Shirley. Wasn't no way that woman was showing her face after we heard about that super-sized "C" that ended up on her exam. She was mad, mad, mad. She was so mad she let the instructor teach for a solid fifteen-twenty minutes without interrupting. But I heard her behind me mumbling, and turning pages in the textbook, gathering the ammo she was going to use to fire back at the instructor the moment he let us take a break.

And sure enough that's what happened. Soon as the instructor called for a break, Shirley went straight for him, cornering and pinning him against a wall like a soon-to-be ex-wife asking her soon-to-be ex-husband where he was the other night. Textbook out and open, and golden bob weaving and bobbing, she had the adjunct professor's full attention. She wasn't letting that dude out of the corner until her grade was changed. The End!

We strolled out of the classroom humored, none more amused than Ollie, the woman who sat beside me and had a habit of turning around during class to shoot Shirley the daggers.

"Woo, that woman grates my last nerve," Ollie hissed. "How'd you like to work at the bank where she works," she wryly chuckled.

I couldn't imagine. It was hard enough to put up with her for 3 hours every Monday. Shirley was the type person that made me wonder how she managed to get so old being so openly opinionated.

"Like who could put up with that attitude," Ollie was saying. "...And I'm not only talking about the people who have to work with her, but customers too!"

I didn't join in on Ollie's banter, and for more reasons than perferring to avoid confrontation. I just wanted to complete the course, find a job, and that was it, though I pictured Shirley dealing with customers at the bank where she worked. 'Let me see your ID!' Which she'd check with a magnifying glass, her foot in the customer's back while she checked. 'Seal looks fake. The ink is supposed to glow!'

It would not be surprising if she was the most known and hated person, not only at her job, but in her community. Surely whole police departments knew her well. That thick clipboard that hung in post offices filled with wanted profiles, she probably knew every subject because she drafted each profile. Rather than work at a bank, Shirley needed to grab her a desk in the CIA, or maybe be a bounty hunter or something.

By the time the end of the semester rolled around, about a week before the final, I had interviewed with two major banks...and this didn't include the instructor who offered me a job at the bank where he was the president. That was a nice compliment. My prospects in banking, and this class, looked promising.

Ollie and I, as usual, met up outside the classroom in front of the vending machines. We chatted about some of our prospects, along with topics covered in class, and of course Shirley. Ollie couldn't stand Goldilocks, and not that I liked the woman any better. It's just Ollie's disdain for Goldilocks was rawer...and so much greater that whenever Shirley passed by, Ollie never forgot to snarl and lend me her thoughts.

"It would be so just if he flunked that woman," Ollie sneered as Shirley passed by. "I would give a mint to see her fail the final and watch her face reading her final grade on a closed locked door!"

I chuckled, though I hardly wanted to be standing anywhere near Shirley, with major fault lines running under my feet when that woman got earth shattering news.

"I just hope I get hired before the semester ends," Ollie sighed. "That would be my cherry on top."

I had been hired by a major bank, but neglected to share the news with Ollie. Truth was, this wasn't the time to be boasting. I'd gotten quite a few offers and didn't see this as the time to be elaborating on the how, where, why and when.

"I interviewed at this one bank," Ollie went on. "...but they told me they hired someone else."

"Oh really," I replied, more so obligatory. I had nothing against Ollie. Other than this class... and our passion in banking, we had nothing else in common.

"Yeah," continued Ollie. "It'd be nice to know who they hired and why."

This was odd. It never crossed my mind about who companies chose to hire over me. "Aww...I'm sure something will come through," I offered. It was a big city, I learned, mined with many other banks, I also learned.

"I sure hope so," replied Ollie, just as Shirley was about to pass by us again. Only this time, before Ollie could do her famous eyeroll, Shirley stopped beside us.

"Weren't you just hired by FIB," she asked me.

I was, which Ollie frowned. "You were," she asked surprised.

But Shirley cut Ollie off, before she could share this was the bank where she had interviewed, but was not hired.

"That's where I work," Shirley exclaimed. "When I saw you come in for your interview, I told Leslie you were in my banking class and would be a really good fit..." and she laughed, "...yeah, I told her you were the quiet girl who sat at the head of MY class!"

...a plug out of some chick's diary

~~

"A good place to vent."
~~

I've decided to heed my father's warning and steer clear of autobiographies that reveal it all. Although it might not matter much to me what others think of my travels, I have to consider the feelings of others. Except, hold on now! My father said nothing about sharing a few plugs out of some other chick's diary.

...with flashing caution lights here's what some chick writes...

Monday...

Here it is, or rather here it goes. Monday. The absolute worst day of the week. The day when all the crap starts all over again. Should make one wonder, particularly those fond of jumping on bandwagons, hating Mondays to hump over Wednesdays, leaping to Fridays, just to get to the weekend where the cycle starts all over again. Like, why rush the inevitable?

So, I choose to lay here and write a few lines in full view of the fact that I should be preparing for Tuesday. That's because I'm saying to heck with Tuesday. First I'm going to write about Monday. Why not? Especially when I think about Bad Monday, and Black Monday, and Blue Monday. I'd bet anything it was some awful Monday that formed the words to those lyrics. As sad as a sad day may go, sadness still doesn't have to equate to destitution. Folks capitalize all the time off of misery and pain. That old man who comes in the bank to preach to me is right. Folks have a choice. When the day is going bad, you don't have to go with it.

At any rate, today was a real doozy. To begin with I was four minutes late, but otherwise the day started out good. And then I was smacked in the face with my boss's sour attitude. Dee, my boss, flatly stated that I couldn't take vacation on the date I needed. I couldn't believe it. My sister's wedding is over a year away. And to think that I thought I was being considerate by letting her know a whole year in advance.

But Dee says I'm not allowed to write in the vacation book until three months prior. And only after all of those with more seniority fill out their vacation requests first. According to Dee, which she so eagerly pointed out, this means there are four people ahead of me, which one of the four (Ms. Franklin) will be celebrating her 25th anniversary in the same week as my sister's wedding. Now, Ms. Franklin... and I have nothing against the clean cut woman... but she has celebrated TWENTY-FIVE anniversaries with her beloved Mr. Franklin! That is 2 5... a whole lot of anniversaries! My sister on the other hand will only have ONE wedding!

But I got over that hurdle. I don't care if all thirteen of us take vacation in the same week. If any bank should stand out and set a precedence closing its doors for reasons known in advance, I think it should be our branch. I was just trying to be thoughtful. Hell, I could have waited until the week I planned to leave and say I have a family emergency, leaving them all stranded for teller help. Although I realize I am replaceable, it's no secret I am one of the best tellers in town!

Yet no sooner than I cleared that hurdle was it when Mable's wobbling tail walked pass my teller station and scowled in my ear, "Smile!"

I really wished I could hurt this old lady. Not physically of course. I just want to do something to teach her a lesson about telling me to smile. She doesn't even bother to ask how I am feeling or is everything okay at home. She instead elects to snarl, "Smile," in my ear every time she passes me. Sometimes I'll even have my back turned, or will be in the middle of counting someone's cash when she jumps right in to point out the fact that I am not smiling. And what is even worse, she isn't smiling when she says it. I think that woman is full of evil, like the devil. Her eyebrows have corners like horns. And her pinched pencil lips look like they flew off a witch and landed lopsided on the other side of her face. And she acts clairvoyant too. One day last week she walked up to me and told me that she could read my mind through my facial expressions. I doubt it. Most times I am off in another world viewing the bottom of an endless hole. And when I'm focused, I'm thinking about what to fix for dinner, or wondering if I gave a customer the correct cash back, or hoping my husband doesn't find the receipt to the latest whatever I've bought, or just plain thinking about how sickening it is that Mable, one of the part-time tellers never balances. Frequently she is the cause of me having to stay later than I plan, waiting for her to find her balancing error. She truly is one of the few people that make the hairs on the back of my neck rise. I mean, to think that some qualified person is without a job. So I looked at this woman squinting out of those beady eyes and said with my own eyes, 'woman, you can't possibly know what I'm thinking because I don't even know what I'm thinking!'

And sure enough, right in sync with my foul Monday, I got off a full 40 minutes past the time I was supposed to leave. Every bit of gratitude goes straight to ole' Mable and her countless smiling mistakes. I can just imagine her giving away extra 10's, 20's, hell 100's, with that big simple grin smeared across her face. Or maybe, and it's a bad thought, but someone's got to think it, but just maybe all that smiling business and her old lady appearance is a cover up for some shady shenanigans going on. Luckily for her however, she must know someone 'on the inside'. Ain't no other way that woman wouldn't have been FIRED long ago! So much for Monday. Hopefully Tuesday will be better. Good night.

Tuesday...

Got to work on time, thank God! I don't know what it is about me and this adrenaline I have for a great rush. Seems like I'm not at my best until I'm pushed. Anyways, I get to work...and get this, Dee asks me to walk with her to the vault. I thought, "oh hell, now what's up?"

In the vault Dee starts off by saying, "I hope I can get through this without crying..." and then burst into tears.

Through sobs I made out that someone had complained about the FYI newsletters she regularly sends out. Oh My Goodness. I couldn't believe what I was hearing. Just yesterday she got all snotty about my vacation request and today she is wiping her nose all over my shoulder. Through the sobs and tears she dropped another ball on me. She asked if I knew who complained. I absolutely, unequivocally, could not believe that she did not know which one of her comrades to distrust.

Wow! The one person she would deny vacation time, was the same person she knew hadn't sold her out. Funny. A part of me really empathized with my boss. She couldn't help that good ethics didn't run in her genes. Only an unethical person not apt at connecting moral dots would distribute so called FYI newsletters to their staff instead of simply telling the affected individuals to their face what they were doing wrong. I think the little cute girl, who worked on the platform out front, was offended by the newsletters. Dee worded the complaint something like: 'service representative who are clearly visible to clients, and expected to bring in new business look unprofessional wearing stretch pants.'

Even though the grammar read a little off, the letter overall didn't read bad at all. That was one of her better letters. But the letter still bothered someone who took their offense to corporate, who in turn called Dee. Corporate demanded she immediately suspend further newsletters, which I happen to agree with.

Putting those types of observations into writing and giving it to people you see every day is a cowardly thing to do. The situation warranted no more than pulling the three or four culprits aside and telling them to dress it up.

NO! Wait! One of the girls who worked on the teller line, Trish, actually needed to be taken out back and dealt with for crawling into polyester the way she did. The little girl on the platform was actually the lesser of all the evils. She always appeared professional, both in mannerism and appearance. Plus she was slim, attractive, and decent! That's why I thought it was she who took the matter to corporate.

Anyway, maybe now this will be the last of the bitch session newsletters. Perhaps, and hind sight is always 20/20... but I could have been honest with Dee when she whined on and on about how this person went to human resources without first consulting her. I should have told her that if she had gone to them first, the matter may have never reached human resources.

So what. Call me naïve too. And then again. I'm not the boss. Bosses are supposed to be example setters. But the corporate world is funny like that. They enjoy confrontation without being confrontational. I'm just surprised she never addressed me in one of those newsletters. And then again, she probably did. Of course I won't know it until she tries to revoke my annual 6% raise!

And YES!!! No Mable today. I got to go home on time... for a change.

...Wednesday

Another great day, even though Mable didn't balance!

The day began with a surprise conference with Dee and Trish. Trish is the Merchant Teller who was ready to quit one day last week over some bullshit. I had to tell the chick like I saw it. The nexus of this incident actually happened so long ago I had nearly forgotten about it. It happened, of course, when Dee was off and Trish, as usual, was trying to play boss. It kills me how everyone wants to be the leader, especially those with no vision. The extent of their foresight is being up front telling everyone what they 'need' to be doing. Trish was this type. She had to make sure every customer knew she was in charge, and her favorite words were my trigger words: "You need to…"

This was why, on the offending day, when Trish jokingly said, which I of course didn't know was a joke at the time, else I would have kept my big mouth shut, "I need to make Crei crack all of this coin, since it was her customer who brought them in here," I BLEW A FUSE!

Yes, I, one of the many women gracing this great green earth, who can't keep her mouth shut to save her life, snapped back. "No! You need to do your job!"

I know it's the wrong approach to have the 'it's your job' attitude. I just get so tired of miss lower case work ethics, who thinks she knows so much, with her nose pointed in the air like someone told her she was Ms. AllStar Intrastate, throwing her hair and arrogance all around the bank.

Needless to point out, but I will anyway, I missed the joke. And the reason I didn't get the joke was because one: I've been working for the bank a long time. A lot longer than her anyway. Yet, she talks to me like I started the other day. Reason two: Not only is she the Merchant Teller, but she is the vault and chief teller too! Reason three: The coins I accepted and sold to her came from a merchant customer who was supposed to be in her line (with all that coin) to begin with. In actuality I was helping her and her customer. Reason four: I was not given a storage area to hold all of that coin. That room was reserved for the know-it-all Merchant Teller!

Reason five: She should have put all of that coin in the vault since she knew good and well that the three of us---me, 'Ole Uncle Tom Jr., and herself, were all the tellers there were on the teller line that day. If the three of us focused on coin cracking, there would have been no one open to focus on the customers.

And reason six: It was 3:30 when she decided to do this coin cracking stuff, a full half hour before I was due to close and go home. Trish with all of her banking knowledge knew all too well that the specialty window, my workstation, needed extra time to balance, and leaving on time was crucial to the Specialty Teller!

So sad, so sorry, but she was 100% wrong! There wasn't no, 'a right and wrong' making two wrongs. She should have quit. Except get this…

The woman went crying to the branch manager. This chile, oh yes she did, had the nerve, no the audacity, to be sittin' up in Uncle Tom senior's office talking about team play! Just like a patriot! And not too surprising---the two Tom's (that would be the branch manager and the little goof ball teller who helped her cracked all that coin... what's his name Yazz'em) jumped on her side. Simple-minded people. Just too freakin' simple!

Well, I didn't hold back. Yep. I kept my foot right where it belonged. Stomping and jumping up and down, all over her feelings! I told the branch manager, Jack (what a name), he could do what he needed to do, and I was going to do what I needed to do. In other words, he could go jack off! That's how the mess ended up back with Dee.

When Trish finally returned to work today, I guess after recuperating over her damaged feelings, she went straight to Dee, her chummy in-cahoots friend who incidentally thought she had dimed her out, and ran down what went down. Yep, hot pants bled her case all over her 'untrusting' cohort. And Dee, who evidently had forgotten about her suspected backstabber, otherwise she wouldn't have locked horns with the polyester abuser, went out on a limb to maul over my problematic attitude with this bitch!

You see, their team play, in my rustic opinion, amounted to making special arrangements for Trish to take classes during work hours so that she could get her degree quickly, while ignoring the fact that I obtained my degree outside banking hours. I didn't benefit from the princess treatment. While Trish's polyester covered cheeks hung off the side of chairs in class, during working hours, my tail was at work team playing. That's right! I was doing my blasted job... and HERS!

Needless to say however, if Dee hadn't thought she had a case against me, she would have never pulled me into the office. The woman must have thought, even after letting her cry on my shoulder, she had me. Trish probably had the whole story laid out like an atlas for 'ole Dee. And Dee went for it.

During the conference I sat across from the tag team, and looked directly into their sulking... we got this monster in the bag faces, and made clear my team play theory. Other than my voice, there wasn't another sound in the conference room. Daft and dafter sat glued to their chairs looking conspicuously dumb-founded. I couldn't believe they actually forgot. It never cross their small minds how I got my degree while working normal hours at the bank, not to mention, how I accomplished this while also taking care of two young children and a husband, something neither had.

But Trish had comprehension issues, or else she just didn't care. She came out of her corner with her dukes raised. The chile' had the nerve to tell me she was thinking about jumping on me. Wooo! This heffa was thinking about whipping my ass. Now that really would have been dumb. Just when I thought the girl couldn't get any dumber she said that shit. Yes indeed. Today was my kind of day.

Thursday...

Today I got to work four minutes late but in the end actually found a real reason to smile. First thing I see this morning is Mable, sitting in the hot chair beside a livid Dee combing through a snow bank of transaction tape. Poor Dee. The woman can't catch a break. Bossing ain't easy, the ONLY reason I commend Dee to begin with.

Apparently Mable hadn't balanced, again... and Dee was looking for the paperless error ...again! Things certainly didn't look good for Mable. It was written all over her unsmiling face... and that pink slip laying on top of the heap of paper.

I wanted to make a light-hearted, but sincere comment, but ultimately decided to leave it be. I knew the fluffy plus-sized old white-haired woman was getting fired. Dee had too much transaction tape on her desk, not to mention the pink slip. So I headed on to the vault to start my day. It didn't stop me however, as I prepared my cash drawer, from thinking about all the days Mable tormented me with those phony auspicious smiles. Something real mean started stirring in my heart. I could feel it. I was smiling, stealing little peeps at Mable's upside down smile. Before I knew it, I was standing before the bubbly sized woman, with her upside down smile, and my right side up smile. I had the biggest grin on my face as I looked down at tunnel faced Mable and said rather loudly, "SMILE!"

I know it wasn't right, though Dee did peek up and smile too. Ms. Franklin turned around and smiled as well. Both of them knew that old wobbling tail had been purposely tormenting me. Payback was a bitch, which I was still petty enough to not let nobody forget.

I think that was the worst thing I've ever done to someone... who admittedly deserved the reminder. Mable lost her job, and I didn't care. But why should I? She didn't care that I was standing on my feet taking care of customers, while she was mismanaging hundreds... maybe thousands, and while Trish was sitting in somebody's class, covering a whole chair with her funky fleshy flabby ass, returning to work at the end of a long workday bitching about team play! F-that! I stand with the customers. Everybody wants to smile!

Oh well. Maybe I burned a bridge. So be it. If it was a bridge not to be burned, God will make me repair it. And, of course too, if not, then at least I won't have to cross that one again. Say Cheese!

Friday!...

Yay! The day every worker who watches clocks pines for.

Forget being my customary 4-5 minutes late. I set a record. I was 15 minutes late. Started to call in sick, but reasoned... why use up a sick day on one of the best days in the week. I worship Fridays. And I love my job!

Nevertheless got to work and felt a little sluggish. Thank goodness it was Friday though. Usually it's the fastest day of the week...none more so than end-of-the-month payday Fridays. We get lines wrapped around the bank on Fridays. It's also when robbers like to visit us, and a whole smor-gasbord of other quirky stuff goes down. Once we were held hostage, for ransom! I'm pretty sure that happened on a Friday, too!

But what I love most about Fridays, and my job, are my Veteran custom-ers. They are full of wisdom, great company, and funny as hell. I even got one World War II customer that melts my heart. He don't talk much how-ever, but one day I had to really go to bat for him. The powers to be have us now, 'so called educating' our customers not to visit the bank. They want us to exile OUR customers, and then take our jobs as a reward. The damnedest thing ever!

At any rate, this one World War II customer was one of the commodities the powers to be wanted 'educated'. Of course they don't care that he walks with a cane, can barely see, and don't know or care a damn thing about banking in cyberspace. He just wants to do his banking business in person with people he can hear, see, feel and touch. Sometimes it takes him almost 30 minutes or more to help him through his transactions, which is a lot of time to spend with one person. We often service up to three hundred customers, SIX days a week ...a piece!

But there aren't many customers in the shape this veteran is in, why it behooves us to use sensitivity and common sense when helping customers like him. Of course, many...even those working in banks... don't have a lot of this stuff. Common sense, that being. One day I had to hear one of our slower tellers 'educating' this veteran on filling out his deposit slip. The man could barely stand up straight, and trembled like a leaf, yet she was practically forcing him to fill out this slip by actually guiding his hand! I wanted to scream. But didn't. I minded my business and tried not to look.

Lo and behold and all be damned if not a customer later a really snotty bitch... so it was a woman, far younger than the WWII veteran, with no obvious disabilities...well other than her entitled behavior, didn't approach my window and demand I fill out her paperwork. It was as if she knew about this radical policy and came to specifically test me. Well, it was either that, or God had entered the building. I was like, YES MA'AM! I am here to service you!

Politely I told the heffa to fill out her own slip. The winch snapped back, "NO!" And she flicked her paperwork towards me. And I, politely, flicked it back. She grabbed her shit and ran to the opposite end of teller stations where all the Heads were. I still heard them. 'I treated her badly' and 'the bank didn't tolerate MY behavior' and 'they were going to have a word with me...' and yada, yada, yada.

I waited. In fact, I couldn't wait. I kept my back turned, as if oblivious, and then let loose on the two little Heads that eventually showed up. I shut them down before they got to their second word. Next morning the real boss was in. She told me to meet her in the back room, BEFORE opening my teller window. I was about to be fired. The only reason it didn't happen was because I coolly described how OUR WWII 'black' veteran was treated. Unlike the teller who held the veteran's hand, essentially forcing him to fill out his own paperwork, the boss knew good & well what would have happened had I attempted to 'TOUCH' and do the same with the white winch. BAM! Discrimination all up in the bank's face.

So, I kept my job. And the old vet was assisted with future transactions. And as for the white disgruntled bitty who wanted me fired... she stopped wanting me to help her. Good! She got to be treated to one teller, more to her color preference, who ended up taking checks from the back of her checkbook. One day, probably a Friday, the winch came running into the bank crying about 'the bank' stealing her money. Turned out it wasn't the bank (per say), clipping her, but the teller she thought more of. The old bitch got her money back and the teller was fired, but served her nasty ass right… and I'm referring to the time she put a big nasty booger on one of her deposit slips she shoved it at me when her only choice for getting service was me. Karma is a bitch!

But back to today!

So, this Friday it was a Vietnam Vet that strolled in. Mr. Sanders stood at my window talking his nonsense, naughty stories that Dee (and perhaps a few others) don't particularly care to hear. But me. I can laugh with the man all day long. He only has one working hand…he said he lost the other one inside some pu'na (lol) when he was in Da Nang. Okay, maybe not so funny, but we were horsing around like this when Dee interrupted our social. This time it actually was a good thing she did. No sooner than Mr. Sanders stepped aside, incidentally in the opposite direction of where Dee asked him to go, was it when a customer drove right through our double glass doors!!!

Sounded like a planet had entered the building. Never heard a noise so deafening, and I experienced F-16s diving towards the ground right above my head! Besides the sound, it was the shaking ground, reminiscent of the Loma Prieta 7.1 shake that shook me too. I really thought a bomb had detonated. I'm so glad Mr. Sanders stepped aside when he did, and in the direction he did, because when I turned around and saw that 4 door sedan parked no more than 3 feet away from my teller window, it was but a stroke of His grace and mercy that Mr. Sanders wasn't killed.

Of course I couldn't pass up the opportunity to slip in a teaser, especially since by the grace of timely mercy no one was sitting in the lounge or otherwise hurt. "Next please," was my humor attempt. "How may I help you?"

That incident was the highlight of our day. I don't think our insurance carriers, and for sure not Dee who had to call them, thought it was so funny. Aside from the robberies and hostage threats and incidents like Dee's little annoying newsletter, this was the third time a customer rolled into the bank. Corporate has to be so tired of hearing from Dee. Hahaha!

Nevertheless, boarded up doors and all, I ended up with a 117 transaction count and balanced to the penny, within 6 minutes! Now that makes a great day! It's the other reason I love my job!!! It is fast-paced, pushes me to the limit, and I get to meet a variety of interesting people. The same day never happens twice.

I was up in the clouds, on my way out when Dee called me back. She said I had a phone call. It was my daughter, informing me she didn't make the squad. I looked over at Dee, looking at me swallowing this bitter pill. The woman appeared to be smirking. She was enjoying my pain. Note. Can't help but blame this woman for my hardships. Guess, it's supposed like this way. It's taught on every job. You're not supposed to like the boss.

So head down, Dee smirking, I left the bank not feeling so great after all. I'm talking a swift kick in the tail and going six feet under. For the 20 minute ride home I pictured my daughter sitting in the bleachers watching her friends who probably made it, jumping up and down. Even though I tried like hell to think positive, I couldn't help going back to destructive feelings, like wondering which one of her friends had made the squad. I even blamed myself. That's what I got for smiling in Mable's face I told me. I questioned God too. Like, why punish my child? Why was she mixed up in my karma?

At any rate, I pulled up in the carport and my son comes running out the house. "Did you hear!?! Did you hear!?!" He was so delighted to shove this karma down my throat. But that's how he and his sister were. Competitive. I passed him my bags and sucked in the last bit of fresh air, preparing to spend a long weekend consoling my child. When I entered her room, that's what I was about to do... rub some motherly wisdom on her. But just as I leaned over her, she suddenly sprang up! "Sike Mom! I made it!"

My kids! That's all I could think. They never failed pulling these type heartaches on me. So my Friday, after all, wasn't so bad... until I got to thinking about Dee and that smirk! I can't wait to go back to work! First thing Monday I'm rubbing this one all over her face!

Saturday...

The funniest thing happened at the post office today. I watched a dozen or more people tug on a door that had been locked for 10 minutes or more.

I know it's the craziest observation, but someone, somewhere is seeing to it there is not a dull moment for me.

I don't know. Perhaps these people were not paying attention. Or in a gigantic hurry. Perhaps they were trying to be funny. Who am I to judge? I had a problem too. I was overly focused on the fact that the Post Office closed at noon on Saturdays. The hours of operation sign was right there glued to the door. Had been there for... oh I don't know... the past half century. Me, and about five others, made it inside in just a nick of time.. There was a clerk who locked the door right behind us. That's why when I saw the figures that came behind me, one after the other, all tugging on the locked door, I figured that there had to be somebody seeing what I was seeing. But nope. While everyone seemed mesmerized with what the clerks were doing inside, I amused myself with the side show happening outside.

I watched vehicle after vehicle dash into a vacant parking spot, which was clue number one. Rarely were parking spots this available at this particular Post Office...when it was open. Yet, patron after patron pulled into the wide open spot, and jumped out of their idling car, to rally around partially drawn shades and a big sign on the door that read: Closed. And one after the other checked their watches before grabbing hold of the door. Guess they didn't believe their watch. Some seemed livid the Post Office didn't know they were on their way. Others, a few passive ones, pressed their faces against the glass, perhaps to see if there was an hour's of operation sign to their liking posted somewhere inside.

And yet, the four or five that came in with me were even more baffling. I watched each of them tug on the door too. One after the other, they all yanked on the door, to get out! It went something like this: The clerk would unlock the door, let a customer out and move a trash can maybe a couple of feet. As soon as the trash can was in place there'd be another customer yanking on the door as if there was no oxygen inside. The scene was repeated at least a half dozen times. I could swear each customer was not trying to be funny. They just weren't paying attention. Simply amazing.

I'm just glad I finally got to mail off photos I promised to send my family weeks ago. We haven't seen each other in quite a while. Hopefully, however, the package will arrive in one piece. The postal clerk seemed really annoyed that I couldn't distinguish between first, second and third class mail. All I wanted to know was, how third class mail was delivered...if first class was flown, and second class driven. What, was it walked, or dropped kicked across the country?

Welp, never got the answer. Instead, I ended up with a mini lecture on much policy garble, which confirms my belief that people in the customer service industry really should become better mind readers. The clerk should've known any customer that starts off with, "I just want to send this package 'regular mail,' definitely don't care how long it will take to get there. They just want it TO GET THERE!!!

And so, one mother sums up her Saturday.

Washed 10 loads of clothes. Stopped on the 11th load to rush to the Post Office about to close. Made it inside and got to be entertained by a novelty side show. Then managed to tick off a postal worker who may, or may not, deliver the photos I raced to send off to family who haven't seen us in a while. Now, I sit on my sofa cradling my diary, as my husband who is away for the weekend on military duty, and my children who ran off to celebrate with their friends, have all left me in here alone with these thoughts. This is, as Ann Crittenden, so eloquently laid out in her widely acclaimed book, "The Price of Motherhood".

...Sunday

Today I took my butt to church. I had to thank God for my children, my husband, my family, and for the numerous questions I asked Him over the past few weeks. I also needed to get on my knees and ask for forgiveness… and the continued wisdom to understand the mean stuff that creeps into my heart. Just like we wash the outside, I believe we should wash the inside.

My only trouble with church today was the preacher, or rather the sermon. Maybe both?

Seemed like this man, with the Adam's apple and booming voice, but dressed in a robe kind of like one I saw Jesus wearing in a photo, was trying to make me feel bad. I hate when flawed mortals point at other flawed mortals. And I don't care if the mortal is a preacher. That man stood behind that podium in that pulpit staring me straight in the face, pointing out as many sins as he could pack into a two hour sermon!

Look, I don't think I know that jackleg preacher from Alabama. I'm positive I've never been to that church before either. The whole reason I went to that church was to avoid running into anybody I might know. So, it got extra creepy real quick looking at this bootlickin' preacher looking straight at me. I mean, even some of the congregation kept looking over at me!

WTF! I started to collect my children and make for the exit, but didn't want to cause a scene. By the way this preacher was talking…and looking… it wouldn't have surprised me if he didn't disrobe and really call me out!

Hey, I know I'm flawed. But isn't it written in the Bible 'let him cast the first stone'? See, that preacher did not want to get into a biblical scrimmage with me. I was not the average church-goer. Heck, I was not even a church-goer. I will fight back. And nobody there probably wanted that. Just sing, which the choir did do. I love a good choir. Music, especially good gospel music, has the majestic power to draw on energy that cleanses and fixes the heart. It might not even be a bad idea for churches to move towards all music and meditation since, speaking for myself, the last place I want to hear about how derelict I am, is the one place I go to get a vision of eternal peace.

The choir really sang this morning. 5000 pound voices strong, God's people rocked the house. I kept still though, fearing a discotheque might've jumped out of me. When they were done, I turned my purse upside down and inside out. I dumped it all in the collection plate. Ok, so it wasn't much, but it was all I had. Amen.

…now back to Monday.

early bird

~~

"…of course gets the worm.
Cut that up and spin it any way you please."

~~

Get your ass up and be first! Someone should have told Mr. Smothers this. What propelled him to hanky-panky behind his wife's back, let her find out about it, then lie and say he wasn't when everyone clearly saw him walking out of Motel Six with the 'other' woman…in broad daylight no less, and then laugh about it telling his wife of twenty-five years that maybe if she brushed the chip off her shoulder and wrapped her legs around his neck, he would be home more often.

Mr. Smothers sure had some nerve, and ultimately got everything he deserved…or rather didn't get everything he thought he deserved.

Pulled into the parking lot around 8:35am and the first thing I see is Mrs. Smothers pacing around the front door. I looked at the clock, knowing I was late, but hoping I wasn't that late, and hissed beneath my breath. Sometimes customers like her needed to get a life!

The bank opened at 9am, which according to both clocks, the one on my wrist, and the clock in the car, Mrs. Smothers probably didn't realize the bank wouldn't open for another 20-25 minutes.

"Hello Mrs. Smothers," I spoke approaching the front door. "You know we don't open until 9am today," I smiled, hoping somewhere between that time and when we opened she might find this other life.

"That's fine," Mrs. Smothers answered a little tersely. What else was new? She never was in a good mood. Although Mr. Smothers was the biggest flirt, I sometimes couldn't blame him. I didn't even live with the woman and found her attitude just as difficult to tolerate. And she could call it how she wanted. No one understood what she was going through, because she'd be right. No one didn't know and didn't want to know.

I went inside leaving Mrs. Smothers sort of stewing and smoldering around the front door. Every so often a co-worker and I would look over at the door and laugh about the way she was dressed…old wrinkled housedress, curlers, house-slippers; just the typical portrait for why husbands sometimes looked the other way.

Nine am the branch manager opened the doors and in flew Mrs. Smothers, like a bat out of hell. She rushed right in and bustled straight over to my window, throwing her purse on the counter and demanding all of her money out of the bank.

"…And I want it all in cash!"

So early in the morning I didn't feel like fighting, but the law was the law. Seventy-five thousand dollars I could not give her in cash, even if I wanted to. Please Mrs. Smothers, let's not make this transaction any harder than it has to be, I almost sighed aloud. I wasn't the one who woke up on the wrong side of the bed, and I as well don't have that kind of cash in the bank. I'd be lucky if I had ten dollars in all five of my accounts combined!

I looked at the woman knowing she was a fuse away from blowing up the city and told her as calmly as I could everything I could do for her. I had no problem closing all of her accounts and quickly typing up cashier's checks as fast as my fingers could type. I might've suggested opening a single account, had it not been for the fumes I saw jetting out both her nostrils. She was on her way to Acapulco and wasn't coming back. At least no time soon.

"That's fine," she retorted. "Just make the check out in my name only!"

…And trust me, I had no problem with that request either. In fact, she didn't even have to tell me. I wouldn't have made out those checks any other way. It was clear what she wanted the moment I saw her pacing around the bank.

After drafting withdrawal orders, and ducking to get out of the way as she swung the metal safe deposit box around, clearing out that drawer as well, we laughed about the 9am morning visit. That woman was pissed. Really pissed! We surely would've had to call in the FBI had that morning gone any other way!

That's what made it funny when about noon I looked up to see Mr. Smothers standing at my window. Now what exactly did he want? He wasn't wound as tight as his wife, but the grinning and schmoozing was out of line after my experience that morning.

"Ugh…how can I help you Mr. Smothers?" I wanted to add, 'because baby, you don't have any more vested interest in this bank.'

But a part of my job required I be professional at all times.

"Yeah…umm…" he waffled, struggling to appear cool but coming off a little frazzled, as if he'd been up all night fighting with Mrs. Smothers. "…umm, I need to close my accounts," he finally weaseled out after a little hemming and hawing. I guess he was embarrassed, as if I might guess why he needed to close his accounts.

Pretending as if I couldn't tell the difference between Mrs. Smothers and Motel Six, I looked up his accounts, pulling his signature cards right out of the closed accounts file, and told him with much objectivity in my voice that all of his accounts were already closed.

"Wha…what?! What do you mean my accounts are all closed!"

Couldn't say what I wanted to, but if I could've, after slapping him upside the head, I would've told him. "Who in the hell comes in the bank high-noon fashion after scorning a woman he promised to faithfully love, through sickness and health and for richer, or poorer!?! WHO!?! Who does that shit!?! Was he out of his friggin' mind!?!" Mrs. Smothers was probably thirty-five thousand feet in the air, halfway to Acapulco by then!

trick or treat

~~

"Peek-a-boo… where were you…"

~~

No glove, no love. He was an engineer, and I mean the real mathematician engineer type. The type that worked with the absolute and resolute, and not nebulous philosophies…if that, then this.

With the thick black-framed glasses, Orthodox haircut, cotton-twill dress shirts with the Sears pin-striped neckties, penny-loafers…he just had the whole math-collar preppy look defined down to the scientific gray matter.

The first day he stepped foot in my door, I read him like the book he followed. Nice, pleasant, but a prudish nerd. I didn't even fool around with a flirtatious dialogue. He wouldn't have understood a thing I said, or so I thought.

His business with me was having me to hem his trousers, or replace broken zippers, or sew on missing buttons… little stuff unmarried mathematicians didn't usually tend to. He was one of my best clients.

I had a few other regulars too. Most worked for the same agency however, like the bubbly young woman with the bright green eyes and red hair who told me about a Halloween party the whole department was hosting. She asked if I wouldn't mind making some of the costumes for the party, which I humbly accepted.

I only had a wedding dress on my plate and several pairs of jeans waiting on zippers. I had plenty time to work on a dozen or so costumes.

Within the first week a few people came over to have costumes made. There was a red devil, a jester, a playboy bunny, and a few more along the adult theme line.

"Man," it crossed my mind… "…this is going to be one swinging Halloween office party!"

The following week a few more clients came to me for costumes. There was a vampire, a pimp, the belly dancer… and then there was my favorite client who told me he would have to describe the costume he wanted me to make.

He pulled a poly/cotton broadcloth blend of fabric from a bag. Natural in color, it looked like the type of fabric sold in bulk, though he only pulled out what I'd estimate was eight yards worth. He'd likely have the more exact measurement.

It was quite a bit of fabric, but he was a tall man… about 6'5"- 6'6". The way he traced his hand around the fabric showing me how I was to cut the fabric, I quickly picked up the costume was to cover him from the top of his head to his feet, plus there needed to be extra fabric left at the bottom to roll up a few inches.

By the puzzled look on my face, he felt that it would be better if he drew the costume he wanted. I agreed, handing him pencil and paper, to watch him draw what looked like a baby's bottle. It was exactly what he traced on the fabric. Still puzzled, mostly because I couldn't understand why he couldn't just tell me what he wanted, like everyone else had, or maybe brought me a pattern, I just smiled and thanked him for giving me another job.

The drawing was sufficient. After all, he was a man known for precision. The design wasn't much trouble to handle at all. In fact, his costume was the easiest to make. It only required making sure he had two peepholes to see out of and a tip at the top, with a few inches of fabric left to roll up at the bottom. The only kicker I couldn't get out of my mind was the stress he put on making sure there was that tip at the top.

A couple days later everyone picked up their costumes, to include my favorite client. He smiled when he saw what I'd done for him. It was exactly what he wanted. He even left me a tip, and turned to thank me again.

A few weeks later my super bubbly client stopped by. She was dropping off jeans to have zippers replaced, and eager to ask how I felt about making my favorite client's costume. His costume apparently was the life of the party.

I didn't know what to say…other than I enjoyed working with the mathematician. He was a super nice man, always so polite…and of course, I was very excited that everyone enjoyed his costume and what I'd done.

She looked at me, as if she was waiting for more. But I had no more to say. I couldn't tell her I thought it was really strange with the way he handed me the job. I wouldn't have dared mentioned a word because he was my favorite client. So long as he was polite, brought me work, and paid me, he could provide me with instructions any way he saw fit.

But that wasn't good enough for my super bubbly client. "Do you know what it was he had you make?"

I had to be honest. I really didn't know. "No, he never told me," I said.

And she laughed loud, just as bubbly as always. "He came dressed as a condom!"

ms. murphy

~~

*"All work and countless distractions
makes for an untenable itinerary."*
~~

Sweetest woman in the world! All of us thought so.

"Honey, are you cold?" And she'd give you the sweater off her back.

"Baby, are you hungry?" And she'd share her lunch.

"Sweetie, what's wrong?' And she'd listen until you ran out of air.

Never judgmental or gossipy. She could keep a secret forever. She loved everything and everyone. But honey (her lingo, and my opinion) she could give it to you Dirty Harry style and be as genuine and sincere as old-fashioned homemade apple pie. Mess with her money was one way to find out how.

Fool around and mess with Ms. Murphy's money…and honey chile…Houston could have more than a spaceship problem. Discovered this after some real hellaciousness happened at work.

Up until this event I only knew Ms. Murphy as the loving mothering grandmother …with a super quick tongue. She never got riled up about stuff, even if she was cussing someone out in her tongue. All of us in the front office still laugh about the time Lana returned from a restroom trip, talking about some business a woman was taking care of in one of the stalls.

"Who reads a book at work while sitting on the toilet," Lana, one of the career snitches that worked in the executive suite, asked with her nose turned up.

Now I was thinking, who in the hell peeped through stall slats…pervert! But Ms. Murphy beat me to the punch.

"Lana…baby," began the loving grandmother, using her soupy sappy happy syrupy mentoring tone. "Maybe the woman needs a laxative." …And she pulled one out of her purse. "Did you ever think of that? Baby, go on back in there and see if this will help the lady. Tell her it's mild."

All color drained from Lana's face, and continued draining as we…me, Gloria, and Brea fell out laughing. From then on, when Lana went into the restroom we'd extend our hand pretending we were holding a laxative. "Here Lana baby…" we'd tease. "Take this with you. It's mild honey…"

Now anyone who happened to overhear us, would think it was Lana who needed laxatives. We never corrected them, though Lana always tried.

But that's how Ms. Murphy was. Always sincere. Not putting on, or trying to derail someone's career. All her love came from a genuine effort to help others.

So when I saw Ms. Murphy rush by my desk one mid-morning, face contorted as if she was about to whip up on someone, I got concerned.

Good Lord, I hoped it wasn't one of her children, or her husband, or some other drama she had brewing at home. Ms. Murphy had a big family and lived in a dicey neighborhood. From time to time the stories she shared convinced us she wasn't all fluff and fold. As she liked to laugh in her rich grandmother voice, she had one of every type in her family… from pastors to killers. It was hard picturing this if you ever saw her, looking like Little Lotta from the bottom down, and mother of the church that collected the tithes and offerings.

This is what made Ms. Murphy a valuable travel coordinator. She was trusted. Executives had complete confidence in her to get them where they needed to go… in the fashion they were accustomed to, and not break the bank. She could sweet talk anyone into anything and make the next to impossible happen. Once she held a plane for three hours. The airline caught hell, and almost went out of business reimbursing 153 passengers, but she kept her job, and the sales director made his flight… and pitch…and got us another contract!

This was what Ms. Murphy was doing when I saw her dash out of the office, and storm back in. She was in the middle of making travel arrangements for a director. She started working on his travel when she arrived, and by noon, when I caught her running one way and 30 minutes later the other way, she was still working on those arrangements. Because I'd never seen her this frazzled, or her workload resembling a pile up on one of JFK's tarmacs, I asked Gloria, "what's wrong with Ms. Murphy?"

"Somebody messed up her money," she dryly replied.

Messed up her money? I couldn't fathom it. Ms. Murphy was not only good with her dollars and cents, but the company's money too.

We teased her lots, fussing with agencies over discounts and vouchers clipped from dubious sources. Don't let her catch an Ad or code promising a savings on a trip somewhere. She loved to travel and seemed addicted to saving the company money.

She was like that with her bills too. Once she had me crying laughing after her cable service was interrupted, for a scheduled maintenance, which lasted an hour. Ms. Murphy went to bed irked, and woke up irked, and came to work with the cable company on her mind. In her Bible, which she carried everywhere, she calculated the cable company owed her 28 cents. During her lunch break she pulled out the Bible and went to work on the cable agent, whose name was Jane, and who was unlucky enough to get her call. Jane disagreed, and Ms. Murphy kept that woman on the phone for her entire lunch break! Over twenty-freaking-eight cents!

And better believe it. Ms. Murphy was on first name basis with everyone she talked to. It was the first thing she got when she picked up the phone. Name and time of call. She'd jot it down, slip in her Bible and used it like a coupon to prove everything. Hilarious!

At any rate, people were stopping by her desk all day, nonstop, asking about their airline tickets. One had to leave at two and needed their ticket in ten minutes. Another one wanted to know if she'd been able to get them a discount. And then there was this director, Stephan, who wouldn't leave Ms. Murphy alone. He circled her desk like Jaws the Revenge. His daughter was getting married. If he missed the wedding his wife was going to cream him ...whatever that meant. He had to have a direct flight because he couldn't risk any leg of his flight getting delayed, or canceled. If he wasn't back by Monday he could lose his job.

Panic and long sob stories hung all around Ms. Murphy's desk. I wanted to help but my abilities went as far as making copies of all this madness, which of course, given Ms. Murphy's distractions there was little to copy. At one point I heard her tell Stephen if he didn't back up, she was sending him to the Netherlands!

"But I have to be in Cincinnati by six tomorrow," he insisted. "Actually, before then," he corrected.

Ms. Murphy sighed. "Shugga, you need to settle down. The only thing either of us need is air to breathe."

The director had to catch his breath to recover from that comeback. "This is not going to work," he said shaking his head, and looking around for other help. Gloria was a viable option, had she not been flashing the lashes and waving her hands in midst of negotiating another director's travel. She was too ghetto for him. He couldn't have forgotten the last cussing out she delivered him when he barged in on one of her calls. Brea was an option too; had her chair not been empty. He glanced Pica's way as well, but just as quickly looked away. It would take them until six the following day to figure out what each other meant. Last resort, he looked right at me. I was sitting at my desk not doing a single solitary thing but watching events unfold. Open invite looking right at him.

Except Ms. Murphy hung up the phone. "Alright Stephen. Check your inbox. Tanya sent your tickets."

Stephen hurried off, back to his office, and an hour later we saw him leave the suite. An hour after he left, we all left. Turned out the lights. Locked the doors and enjoyed one weekend doing what we normally did on our two days off.

Monday morning we were back in the office, turning on lights, making coffee, and checking email when I heard Ms. Murphy gasp… "Good Lord!"

"What is it now," I idly joked. "Stephen missed his return flight and now wants you to book him on Air Force One?"

"Oh no, baby…" Ms. Murphy sighed. "For some reason Stephan is in the Netherlands!"

testing… testing 1-2-3…

~~

*"Sometimes things don't come around.
They go around."*
~~

Another back-to-work doodle. "Hey Ms. Murphy, how was your weekend?"

This was a different weekend. A three-day weekend to be precise. Memorial Day landed on Sunday that year.

"Not long enough," replied Ms. Murphy, sounding like her normal self, between cool and lukewarm.

However we, or I, saw her at work, her family was another story. She had a husband who was less than ideal, and children, grandchildren and neighbors consistently taking her good nature for granted.

"Awww…" I cooed. Though I couldn't do her work, I could act like I cared…the same way she did with all of us in the office.

"Baby…got home and it looked like someone had pulled my house apart. Almost didn't recognize it," she started explaining. "My son had his girlfriend over, and they were in there just ransacking the place. They tore up my bed and was working on my drapes."

"Oh my goodness," I gasped. "But what were they doing in your bedroom?"

"Chile, fighting," she replied like it wasn't the first time this had happened. "I couldn't tell if I was in my bathroom, kitchen or the damn zoo!"

"…but in your bedroom," I repeated again.

"Honey, from where I come, every room in my house is mines!"

I laughed. Where I came from, that's how it was too. "Yop," I agreed. "My mama always said she paid the costs to be—"

"—and my money was a mess."

Oh, Lord. I stopped talking, knowing whatever happened, I was in for an amusing anecdote. Last time her money was a mess, Stephan ended up in the Netherlands. So I simply asked, "is everybody okay?"

"Oh, everybody's doing just fine," she replied, coolly spraying Lysol over her desk. "I told my son my grandbabies could stay, but he and that girl had to go," she continued, shaking the Lysol about to spray her keyboard, the phone, her plants; basically everything in her cubicle. That was another thing about her. She was a white glove lady. Clean as a whistle. Like her Bible she carried a can of Lysol everywhere, and pulled it out the instance she detected filth. Every time she went to the big boss's office she whipped out that can. She claimed his office was nasty. So, before she touched anything in there, she sprayed it… to include him if need be.

"…Now my neighbors…they might be a little mad with me," Ms. Murphy went on. "…But they'll be alright too," she chuckled.

Casually she continued her story, and I patiently waited. She was my kind of storyteller, rarely letting me down. My all-time favorite Ms. Murphy story happened a few years back when a guest of the *old* big boss, Rita, passed by her desk and got to admiring her collage of photos. Nobody kept as many trinkets and photos on their desk as Ms. Murphy. She had been everywhere and had a mess of grandbabies. According to her, 33 in all. And they lived all over the world.

So of course the guest, a Chinese National, like most noticed. "You have a beautiful family, and very big too," the woman said.

Ms. Murphy was thanking the woman when Rita added her one cent, talking about her daughter in-law's side of the family…since she only had the one grandchild. I caught some rolling their eyes. Rita was already the boss, but had a greedy need to dominate in every situation. "Well, do you know any of your ancestors," she asked Ms. Murphy at one point.

Gasp. A big collective gasp too. People working on the third floor probably gasped too. Rita's remark hit below the belt, coming from a woman whose own ancestors prevented many of our ancestors from knowing their origins. But we wanted to keep our jobs, so we acted like we hadn't heard the insult. Ms. Murphy didn't.

She whipped her head around and looking Rita up and down replied, "please! What do you mean, 'do I know my ancestors'," she parodied. "…You probably don't even know who your daddy is!"

Gulp. That quip definitely reached upstairs, and almost got Ms. Murphy fired, and did get Rita fired. The controversary got so big that for months casual conversation in the office was banned. We even stopped greeting each other. For a long while we walked on nails. Only Ms. Murphy could get away with her stories.

"…Chile, I didn't want to do it," Ms. Murphy sighed, going back to what happened over her three day holiday weekend. "…But when I heard, 'testing, testing, 1-2-3…' I was like, not today Satan!'"

I wanted to burst out laughing, but kept my lips pressed tightly together. I couldn't wait to hear the spin on what happened next.

"…Crei, I looked out my bedroom window and

do you know them niggas had boom boxes strung up in their backyards?"

"Boom boxes," she emphasized, looking at me like I had asked her to spell supercalifragilisticexpialidocious. "Crei…there were two parties going on," she said, her voice low, near a whisper, contradicting the shock on her face. "…One in the house next door to me, and the other in the niggas house that live behind me."

I knew what she was talking about. I'd been to many block parties where Busta Rhymes and Method Man could be heard for three or four city-block miles. But this is usual life for the city. Ms. Murphy herself more than likely had been to many of these parties.

"…It was like they were partying off each others music," she continued, speaking in this daze. "…And I was trying to pay my bills."

And here we go. I wanted to HOLLER!

"…Crei…I'm getting old," she sighed. "I had to take that utility pole out. I'm just glad one of them niggas left their car keys in the ignition. The police understood. I just hope they don't try to take my license away."

I was done. Capital D O N E!

Picturing a woman…fully gray… barely five feet …big bulging Lucille Ball eyes hanging just below the steering wheel, doing doughnuts in an 80's style Cutlas Supreme trying to take out a utility pole is a sight I'll never unsee…regardless of how many eons go by.

Ms. Murphy had lost her everlasting mind!

emergency! emergency!

~~

"One plus one, and under any and every circumstance, always equals two."
~~

The government told us to Watch out! And Beware! 'The world is a mess and at an all-time height of terror. So, watch your surroundings. And if you spot or see something suspicious, Report it!

...Except, report what to who?

NO ONE was beyond suspicion. Not the weirdo next door who never spoke. Not the kid who wore all black with the 32 face piercings. Nor the religious zealot touring the country swearing up and down the end was coming. Or the child that turned in the violent essay, parodying 99% of books published, feeding off a media inspiring paranoia every time it rained.

Fear had blossomed to a pancreatic foreboding consternation, none more so pronounced than one concerned citizen named LaWanda Payne.

"911, what's your emergency?"

"Yes, this is LaWanda Payne here."

"Ma'am, please go ahead with your emergency."

"Ah yes, I need to report some strange men digging on our street."

"Ma'am, did you say strange men are digging on your street?"

"Yes I did," LaWanda confirmed. "Strange men are out here digging on our street. You need to hurry up and send someone over here, before something gets blowed up!"

"What's the address please?"

LaWanda didn't care for the operator's tone, but provided her address anyway. "I live at 1501 Dammit Street, but the digging is on Main Line, between 101st and 18th," she clarified.

The operator mumbled, trying to line up the input she received; digging, strange men, Main Line and caller calling from Dammit Street.

"Well, what were these strange men wearing?"

"Blue jeans, t's, hard hats, and... the men are all white and wearing sunglasses," described LaWanda.

The operator stopped typing. She needed a sec to get her head in the call. It wasn't the first time a spastic petition came through the call center.

"Umm, ma'am, there's probably work going on in your area," the operator eventually said. "Did you see any city trucks around?"

LaWanda was tired of this operator taking her call for granted, so she copped a little attitude herself.

"I wasn't looking for no city trucks," she snapped. "All I saw was strange men digging up the street."

"Ma'am, this line is for emergencies. You—"

"—This is a damn emergency! There are white men out here in broad damn daylight, wearing sunglasses... in the middle of our street digging!" Like how in a samclusky was that picture so hard to get!

"Ma'am, this—"

"—would you stop calling me ma'am! I know who I am!"

"Ma—ugh, " stuttered the operator, scrambling for the right words to reach LaWanda and not get fired. She settled on reading a line from her operator protocol manual. "...You could be held criminally accountable for misusing the 911 system."

Not shaken LaWanda argued back. "Who died and left you in charge of deciding what constitutes an emergency?! Your job is to dispatch fuckin' help! That's it! Nothing Else!!!"

It didn't occur to LaWanda that she was being recorded, not that it mattered. "Where's your boss?" she demanded. "I want to speak to the fuckin' boss!"

"Ugh, ma'—I mean...I'm warning you. You're on a Federal line. You are being recorded—"

"—and I hope I am," LaWanda shot back. "My president told me to call and report any suspicious activity, and that's just what I'm doing! I saw something and I'm saying something!"

—Click.

A few minutes after the click officials dressed in suits and SWAT gear showed up at LaWanda's door. Pads out they got to asking questions and taking notes.

LaWanda was asked to describe the strange men and activity she witnessed.

"Sir, all I know is I was on my way to work when I looked over to see about four or five men wearing these hard hats and sunglasses digging in the middle of the street."

"Un huh," the lead white guy on this assignment hummed, head down and holding the pen in a way that said he was waiting to write more.

"Look," LaWanda pressed on. "Long as I've lived here, I've never seen any white men wearing sunglasses on our street."

The white detective flipped his pad closed and sighed deeply. It only took him a second to look up, but this pause in response seemed like days had passed before he addressed LaWanda.

"Ma'am, we really do appreciate your call," he began, his words delivered at a steady pace. "We looked into those guys you saw and determined they were city workers authorized to check the city's gas-lines, but..." and he paused, reaching in his breast pocket "...if you see any more suspicious activity... or white guys in your neighborhood, I encourage you to give us a call," he said smirking, as he passed her his business card.

collinsberry lane was such a street

~~

"Obnoxious, Arrogant, and Ignorant
is a debilitating Jungle Juice."
~~

Growing them up. Kevin Ubanks was the typical college graduate embarking on a new career. Like so many of them before him, he too was one we had to grow up.

At first sight of Kevin, I didn't care for him. I instantly detected smuggery, proven as I listened to him flunk the first part of the test all recent graduate should know. Never underestimate anyone, from the janitor to the lead secretary. Obviously the top brass, new recruits learned to respect. It's kind of intuitive to appreciate who signs your check, unlike understanding the rank and file of perceived underdogs. This kid needed to grasp the concept of the 'last man hired'.

Kevin walked in disputing a service engineer — this would be a janitor — about how to get to Matador. Barry, the janitor, was telling Katy, one of the lead 'technical' engineers working a fiber optics contract, the best way to get over to Matador. "It's three stop lights after Collinsberry Lane," he explained.

"Ugh…that street has since been renamed," inserted Kevin, in a tone far too disrespectful for my liking. He turned to Katy, as if Barry was the stuff on the bottom of his shoe, and took over the conversation. "Ya' might want to Map Quest it," he said.

Now Katy really didn't have time for map questing. She needed to get over to Matador quickly, or 'we', that being the entire damn company, might lose the contract. Yet and still she said, "I think you're right." And she politely smiled at Barry before excusing herself from the situation.

See, I hated those types of exchanges. It told me

Kevin's day was soon on its way. I just didn't know how soon.

About an hour later I got instructions to go see if I could lend Kevin a hand with getting 'his' proposal out. This was a proposal similar to the one Katy had taken to Matador. Kevin's proposal was complete and only in need of preparing to 'get out'. This meant sending the document to one of the deluxe printers and hand delivering to the print shop to have thirty-five copies made. Kevin, being the new man on the totem pole, was given the smallest task, the more manual administrative task. A task most admins usually handled.

I've seen this job done dozens of times. It sounded easy, but there were numerous loops and sink holes that could obliterate the job. Deadlines had been missed, and as result contracts lost on account of these plot twists. Jobs were lost as a result thereof. It was the primary reason I'd been asked to help. Directors who've earned their stars and stripes knew this.

I poked my head into Kevin's office. There were stacks of papers covering his desk and his officemate's desk. I knew better. Regardless of Kevin's rank with the company he still qualified for being respected. This was incumbent of everyone hired.

"Kevin, can I help with anything?"

"Have you ever worked on a red team," he asked first, sniffing as if his nose was running.

I answered him honestly, "no," knowing he was clueless as to why I was there.

"Well then, I'm not sure how you can help," he curtly answered, dismissing my help by turning his back on me.

I started to be nice, and tell him how I'd been directed to help him. But instead decided to let him figure it out for himself. The janitor's position, like mine, were fixed. His was not.

Back at my desk I returned to my normal routine,

answering calls, taking messages, checking schedules, and assisting recent graduates with completing tasks as the one Kevin was assigned.

A few minutes later another engineer was standing over me asking if I had been by to help Kevin. I told him I had, but that Kevin said he had things under control. I didn't tell him Kevin questioned my credentials, but did let him know he might want to let Kevin know how I could help him.

One delivered message later and Kevin was back at my desk asking my assistance. If I could just help him print and organize the materials he would appreciate it.

Turned out I needed to make adjustments to the document, and as well the copier, to get the inserts to print properly. It was nothing Kevin would have figured out on such short notice. He'd have to have worked in this place for more than a week to know each printer's social hang-ups.

That done, I organized the document and prepared it to send to the print shop…what would be the real job. Again, nothing Kevin in his wildest nightmare could imagine. Just a tidbit I learned after being on board for longer than a week. Kevin however, tie loosened and a little sweaty, did tell me I was quick, and thanked me sincerely.

"Let me know if you need anything else. I also can take care of getting them printed for you," I offered.

"I think we can handle it from here," Kevin said back in his fearless voice. He was getting it, but still hadn't gotten it.

That time I was at my desk for a couple of hours. It was almost four o'clock when I caught Kevin's red team members swiftly walking back and forth mumbling his name. I ignored them, too busy making evening plans. I got off in another hour and a half.

Suddenly Kevin comes running over, looking particularly wild-eyed and panting. "Those assholes in the print shop haven't even started the job!" he yelled. "I told them I needed the job by 3pm, which they confirmed they could do. But when I went down there the job hadn't even been started!"

"Okay, well let me call downstairs and see what I can do," I said meeting his ire with ice.

I'd dealt with the print shop many times before. I knew the assholes he was talking about. These were people who got last minute rush jobs from the time they arrived at work in the morning, until the time they left. Nothing was urgent to them anymore. Unless a director's name they liked was stamped on a job, or it was a name they respected, his job could easily end up sitting on the tarmac behind hundreds of other rush jobs.

I really felt bad for Kevin. He knew none of this. Like the day when I arrived, none of it made any sense. Some had even quit their salaried positions over those assholes in the print shop. Those assholes, like me and Barry the janitor, had fixed jobs. Hundreds of corporations were looking for manual laborers...people who hadn't completed college and settled working at our wages. And so long as there were fresh-mouth college graduates like Kevin, eager to look down on unimportant employees, we'd always be in high demand. It didn't matter if every toilet and sink bowl in the world disappeared, there would always be jobs beneath someone's call to want to do.

Soon Kevin, provided he lasted in the company, would understand this economic social dynamic...the lesson he likely missed. This was just one simulated test to show him how to handle a Boeing jet when it had 375 passengers onboard and was flying with no nose gear and one engine. That time his landing was quite bumpy, though he landed safely without losing a passenger. The next time, provided he learned from this test, his landing might be a whole lot smoother.

He shook my hand, and I wished him luck.

lazy

~~

"Study long, study wrong."

~~

It doesn't get any better than being lazy. Except, who's calling who lazy? Because you run a stair master to the point the people next door hear your heart beating, and work 8-to-5 without realizing an increase in profit, no production, consuming mostly imported goods, don't mean you're ahead of the man (or woman) who doesn't exercise.

I say most people are lazy thinkers. Think about it, if you aren't too lazy. If people exercised the thought muscle, like they exercised the biceps, all of us would be in tip top shape…the epitome of brains and beauty… since that is the end objective, right?

Tally it up, again, if you aren't lazy. This mentality of getting rich quick…lazy. Wanting more, faster and faster, younger and younger…real lazy. Assuming …lazier. Skipping pages in books…the laziest. Keeping busy for the sake of just looking busy…OMG, this has to take the trophy for being the summa cum laude, grand Poo-Bah lazy.

In defense of both, thinking versus the treadmill, each exercise exerts equal energy, except one is less destructive and much smarter. If you don't mind my thinking, it has to be mindlessly asinine to run a treadmill when you can spare your knees, and the rest of your joints and ligaments, to achieve the same goal, plus be less ignorant. But sssh… this is my less known secret…

…I put on display the day I was tasked to ship

a dozen binders to a satellite office five states over. Though not for this particular company, I'd done the task hundreds of times over. However John, who sat a cube behind me, the real office laze, so obviously hadn't. He was one of the ones who thought wearing out his limbs got jobs done.

When I was tasked with this shipping project, he called down to the receiving dock, and no I didn't hear the conversation…I am assuming, though assuming correctly, that he called his buddies in receiving, telling them about lazy Crei 'who thinks she can get stuff done sitting in her office chair.'

I know how stuff works. That's because I'm really not so lazy. Been there, done that.

He obviously told his buddies how I thought (and do watch that word), I could waltz into the office brand new and get things done without knowing 'the game.'

Now, don't get me wrong. Resources are important. But leveraging resources is far more important.

So, I ignored him, and just went on and did what I had done so many times before. I packaged the binders …right there sitting at my desk, slapped shipping labels on every one of the boxes, and had a courier…pre-hired and pre-paid …to take the binders to receiving.

Meanwhile, both my superior who had tasked me with the project, and the satellite office, were inquiring about these boxes. "Have you sent the binders? And, have the binders been shipped?"

"Yes, the binders are in receiving and should go out shortly," I replied to all. Unless UPS had a mishap, the binders were scheduled…according to my receipt… to be shipped and delivered the Next Day, before 5pm.

No sweat, small potatoes. Though, on a non-lazy hunch, I called receiving to re-confirm.

Well, be damned! John and his networking buddies were down there in receiving doing a very foolish thing, trying to teach me a lesson.

At first they wouldn't pick up the phone. When they finally picked up the phone, they didn't know where two 24-square foot boxes were. Was I sure I brought them down?

Oh, so they wanted to play games with the office laze? Thinking quickly, something lazy people never do, I got busy.

In a few keystrokes I emailed receiving, and copied my superior and the satellite office about the missing boxes, and attached the receipt the courier handed me.

And lo and behold, and what do you know? Miraculously, before the email made it by the first socket, the boxes were found. But because of what likely was to happen next, I also called UPS personally, something that had never been done in this company's 100-year span of doing business, and (apparently against protocol), had UPS go directly to receiving to pick up the boxes. This move cost the company an additional forty-five bucks. But too-shay, too bad. You wanna play. Let's play.

I smiled. Task completed, even if I was pulled into the boss's office to explain the extravagant extra forty-five bucks. Nothing came of it however, given I had receipts with time stamps. John and his buddies almost went down in one day on that one. They were only spared by the boss realizing what happened, and deciding to, (a week later), give John the same task.

Interestingly enough, I didn't know what was about to go down. Far as I was concerned, I thought the boss was in on the shenanigans. How could she not know? A blind person could see what John and his receiving cronies had been up to. But apparently, perhaps, just thinking out loud here… she decided to see how the stair-master would fare handling the same task?

So, a week later John was charged with the task I had coolly handled. No sweat. Or so John thought. He exercised. And he knew people, though what he and I both did not know was due to last week's fiasco, some personnel changes had occurred in receiving. His scheming buddies had been transferred. But no problem. John knew lots of people. His networking, socializing, bullying, intimidating and groupie skills were second to none.

Before even packing the boxes John got up from his desk, jogged down ten flights of stairs to receiving, and in addition to learning his scheming buddies had been transferred, he got the skinny on proper protocol for sending two 24-square foot boxes five states over within proscribed time limits.

The new people in receiving told him what he needed to do. 'Do this and do that,' and by the time they finished the tutorial... and schmoozing anew, the clock on the wall said there was no way the boxes would arrive in time.

Concerned, but not yet frantic, John dashed back up to the office, all ten flights running, sweating and panting, and pacing. What should he do? He couldn't think. All he knew how to do was run and schmooze.

Desperate to follow the status quo, what he called protocol, and oddly believing he was going to defy that looming already missed deadline, he first threw the binders in boxes...and I do mean threw. By the time he finished taping the boxes, not only did he end up with more than two, what he taped looked nothing like the boxes I had packaged... you know... neat, orderly and actually shaped in real squares.

Oval and oblong boxes sealed, he next hoisted them bad boys and threw them on a dolly. Funny. The dollies was his greatest hook-up. That's what helped him get the disheveled boxes downstairs in one trip.

In receiving he decided to asked a favor, his best thought yet. 'Could they pretty please send the boxes and waive the rush fee.

DENIED.

So he ran around the building, about a track field

and a half worth of running, trying to schmooze everybody he knew. After begging and pleading and literally crying a bucket of tears he arrived back in the office
physically depleted. He looked a wreck, especially from
the neck up.

He looked over at me, face so wet I honestly felt
sorry for him, and sighed. All the exercising in the world,
wasn't going to get those boxes any closer to crossing
one state, let alone five! "Don't worry about it," I told
him. "I called the satellite office and was able to get an
extension."

visiting dr. klein

~~
"Drug Lords & Health Junkies."
~~

Kraup & Klein. As a favor for a neighbor I was taking
her father, Mr. Kraup, to visit his doctor. He seemed alright to me, but then I wasn't a doctor.

"This sure is a beautiful building," I was saying
to Mr. Kraup as we passed a sprawling manicured lawn
draped around a castle-like structure. I could only imagine what it must have looked like inside.

"They all look like mortuaries to me," Mr. Kraup
huffed. He wasn't as keen on knowing what his blood
pressure read, or what his prostrate looked like. He had
gotten by eighty-five years without one day in all those
eighty-five years ever having heard mention of either
one.

But it was true. On second glance the place did
sort of resemble a mortuary. It just sat up a little taller
than most mortuaries. And instead of the placard over
the parking garage reading 'mortuary', it read Helens-
dore Hospital.

I helped Mr. Kraup out of the car, which didn't take much. Making it out of the Korean War with only one nip in the buttock, he got around better than I did.

"I'm sorry my daughter is making you go through all this trouble. There's no reason for us even having to be here!" Being bitter about being there he didn't want my help.

"But you want to make sure you're okay," I teased him.

"Why!?!" he wasn't in a laughing mood. "You think these people can turn me into what I was thirty-forty years ago? You think they really have that kind of power?" The long brisk strides he took to reach the door indicated his anger.

And still, I loved people like Mr. Kraup. He had so much vigor left in him. Over the years he taught me much... like how to feed a cold, and starve a fever. That I should always wear a hat in cold weather. How I should know my body. "The moment you feel a change, take note...and work on a fix. Wait a couple of days for the problem to disappear. If it reappears, watch what you're eating." If I had an apple when I hadn't eaten apples in years, I should consider this. My body was my temple, and I should know it, and be in charge of it.

A doctor didn't need to tell Mr. Kraup a thing. Unless he had some sort of virus, or encountered some sort of tragedy, like a car accident, a doctor couldn't do a thing for him but make him sicker. That's how he got to be eighty-five without ever having seen a doctor.

I noted as we navigated our way around the hospital looking for room 304, every face attached to a body wearing a white coat looked mad. Mr. Kraup said it was because they were sick of dealing with sick people! Not one doctor spoke. Wouldn't even acknowledge us with a head nod. They instead sneered and rolled their eyes. I wouldn't want any of the faces I saw to take my temperature, let alone prescribe me medicine.

Poor Mr. Kraup. His daughter making him go through all this trouble to, as he pointed out, add five extra minutes to the tail end of his life.

But I said not a word. Had I spoken up, we would have been back in the car, and perhaps I, one less friend. His daughter may have never forgiven me. So, all I could hope was that the face attached to the white coat that would see Mr. Kraup, would be a friendly face, and hopefully a nice person too.

We got to room 304, where the lobby didn't look too bad. At least it was clean, even if it looked nothing like how I expected it to look from the outside. The receptionist handed Mr. Kraup papers to fill out and told us to have a seat.

Mr. Kraup took his time placing the clipboard on his lap and right away started grumbling.

"What brought me here," he scowled annoyed. "My daughter," he protested, fussing as he read down the list... "Alcoholism, Anemia, Allergies…" he sneered before pausing. "How would I know this?!"

"I think they just want to know if you've had any of these things. If you don't know, just leave it blank," I told him.

"No," he objected. "I'm checking them all. If she's so sure something is wrong with me, (speaking of his daughter), then doggonnit, we're going to check them all!"

With that, he checked every condition listed. I didn't say a word. I only laughed to myself. Whoever this doctor is, he sure is in for a treat today.

A few minutes later an assistant came out and escorted us into a small office in the back. I asked Mr. Kraup and the assistant if I could sit in the examination. Not that Mr. Kraup couldn't take care of himself. Quite to the contrary. It wasn't every day to come across people like Mr. Kraup...very alive and animated...and spoke his mind. I imagined the doctor might need my help!

Dr. Klein zipped in the office, head down as he whipped around his desk and plopped in a chair as if he'd handled these visits a zillion times.

"Hello Mr…" and he squinted, reading from the medical chart trying to pronounce Mr. Kraup's name.

"…Kraup!" snapped Mr. Kraup, gripping both armrests, braced for a fight.

"Oh," Dr. Klein said, looking up surprised. He tried to impart a smile but noticed neither of us smiling.

"Well, hi there," he continued, appearing un-fazed. "I'm Dr. Klein," he said without stuttering, almost pronouncing his name with pride.

When he got no response that time either, he went on and asked Mr. Kraup how he felt, as he glanced over the medical history form Mr. Kraup had filled in… purposely incorrect.

The same way Mr. Kraup read down the list, was the same way Dr. Klein read back the list. "Breast cancer …cervical cancer…infertility…" he muttered, growing more alarmed. Abruptly he looked up. "Uh, Mr. Kraup, you can't possibly have ovarian cancer!"

"I've had experience with them all," Mr. Kraup snapped back. "Those things are in my history."

"Yes, but we want to know about your personal history," and Dr. Klein shook his head, again revisiting the list. "Like breast cancer…and postnatal depression."

"Why, men have breast," Mr. Kraup contested. "They can get cancer in their breast too. And each time my wife gave birth I got depressed!"

Dr. Klein desperately looked over at me. But I looked away…down at the floor.

Pleading for help Dr. Klein point blank asked, "have you seen this!?!" He flipped through the survey, fascinated, and flipped to the cover page before turning the clipboard around so that I could read what I already had seen.

"Do you understand what we are looking for?"

With as straight a face as I could keep, and without leaning forward, I told Dr. Klein that Mr. Kraup wanted a thorough examination.

"Well, in order to do that I need to have some idea of his medical history."

"I told you," Mr. Kraup loudly interjected. "I can speak for myself!" And then he looked at me. "See, what good are these doctors!?! I shouldn't have to tell him what's wrong with me. He should already know!"

I wanted to tell Mr. Kraup that he was a doctor, not a psychic, but feared his response. I saw him going through the roof.

"Okay…take pregnancy…" Dr. Klein interjected before taking back the thought shaking his head. He must've known Mr. Kraup was going to bring up his wife again.

"Well you've checked deafness too, and it's clear you're not deaf!"

"I used to be," Mr. Kraup argued. "I didn't have anywhere to put it on the paper, but I was in the Korean War. Got shrapnel right here," and he lifted his buttocks and pointed. "The blast was so loud I was deaf all day."

Dr. Klein stared out at Mr. Kraup, ultimately making the decision not to give in . "But blepharospasm?" he asked. "Do you even know what that is?"

And right on cue Mr. Kraup started blinking. "Now why would there be something on that paper you people don't know what it is!?"

"Mr. Kraup, we want to know if you've ever been diagnosed with having these conditions." Exasperated Dr. Klein sighed loudly. "Sir, are your health records kept at the VA?"

"I don't know why not. But I also don't see how you can call yourself a doctor and not figure all this out on your own. Nobody shouldn't have to tell you a thing about my history!"

"That's not the way medicine works sir—"

—and why did Dr. Klein ever mention medicine. Mr. Kraup cut him right off. "Do you know how old I am!?!"

Dr. Klein glanced down and quickly back up as if he misread the chart, expecting to learn Mr. Kraup was Jesus Christ's oldest brother.

"I am ninety-five years old," Mr. Kraup growled, rising from his chair and planting both knuckles squarely on Dr. Klein's desk. I wanted to tap him and tell him he was eighty-five but didn't dare. Not with him leaning on the doctor's stethoscope, bending it the way he was.

"You son, are used to people who drag from hospital to hospital, with a bag of chips in one hand, a cigarette in another, asking doctors to tell them what's wrong with them," Mr. Kraup growled. "But I don't like drug pushers! And never have," he argued. "I am not a junkie! I never have been, and never will be!"

Honestly, I felt a little sorry for the doctor at this point. It looked like his last concern when he left his house that morning, was the possibility of the hospital running out of prescription pads. Surely, that one, never crossed his mind, though here was Mr. Kraup, calling him out.

"…Young man, I want you to know, I have never taken more than an aspirin in my entire life, and never will take more than an aspirin. I am ninety-five years old and that's all what's wrong with me!"

NIGHT

She could have worked anywhere. But she chose to work there, because she loved customer service.

Number One Pet Peeve.

~~
*"Nothing is worse than taking a job you do not love.
Go ask a prostitute."*
~~

Have to love it. Absolutely love it. People watching that is. It started a long, long time ago for me… with these paper dolls I created… hundreds of these little urban whole-bodied characters… like over three hundred miniature hand drawn people… each one distinctive of the other, going by first, middle, and last names… and each with their own story… their own personalities and nuances… a story I internalized and memorized like I knew myself.

This is the impetus behind almost everything I write. People. I simply love to people illustrate, which leans into my number one pet peeve. Lousy customer service, fed by another pet peeve. Sarcasm.

Sarcasm annoys the hell out of me, and yet I do it all the time. Hope that doesn't get too annoying. My sarcasm that being, especially since I think I'm really good at it. But a whole lot of us are little more than a sarcastic pack of cynics. Got a smart-ass comment for everything. And though only probably a few of us ever look inside, come to find out, we don't know diddly.

…overlooked a simple syntax, or missed a critical word that meant all the difference from sounding intellectual versus coming off like a total jackass. It's like passing a homeless person sitting on a park bench and stopping to chew the person out for not getting an education, only to learn, oops, that was Professor Einstein Smith. You do know homeless people come with stories too, don't you? I didn't, though I do now. But I've got another fave you're gonna love even better than Professor Einstein Smith.

Well, and then again, maybe not so much the hopeless cynic. But a mild critic will.

Take this clip. A young man rushes into a hat store where he's spent thousands of dollars. Proof be; Mr. Manager's brand new Merk is parked out by the curb, just bought a home in the hills, and he has hat stores by the galore... one on Swiss Street, one uptown, one downtown, and one even out there in some place called Sicily.

So on with the hat story, to Mr. Thousands of Dollars who rushes into a hat store... the one on Swiss Street... sweating and panting, "Oh good golly gosh gee, guess what just happened to oh golly gauche not me?"

The wind kicking up a storm blew his hat off his head. Now his hat is outside parked up in a tree. Yes, he heard weather reports. Called for a tornado, yet a low-grade hurricane came skipping along instead. But why should any of that matter now that his brand new hat had rolled off his head and had clear been snuffed up in a tree.

It was awful, but what could Seven Bucks an Hour say? It wasn't like it was his store... or his hat... and what's more, what could he do? —Hold back the wind? Seven Bucks wasn't paid to climb trees and contain wind. Seven Bucks was only due one thirty-minute break... which ... and no pun intended, it wasn't to be used for running down hats and stuff like that.

Other than breaks, there were only two rules Seven Bucks followed. The first and the last rule: "Had better (absolutely) nothing leave the store Scott & willy-nilly pumpernickel free!"

Mr. Thousands of Dollars wasn't having it. Meeting or no meeting, "go and get Mr. Manager and tell him DAMN IT, I need help... to come out here QUICK and Help save my HAT DAGGONIT'!"

Ticked and annoyed... face just as scorned as a

hot red chili pepper; jaws drawn tight, lips pinched tighter… Mr. Manager stops his meeting to look up at Seven Bucks apologetically waiting.

"At seven bucks an hour you go back out there and tell Thousands to call the fire department, or the SPCA. If neither works, then Thousands might want to go on and just call the number on the back of any milk carton."

Hell it wasn't Mr. Manager's fault the damn hat got blown up in a tree either. Didn't Thousands know any better; listened to the news? Read the papers? Watched TV? Served his dumb ass right. People like him shouldn't be allowed to buy hats anyway. In fact, Thousands should be banned from entering all retail outlets—hat or otherwise. His picture should be posted in the post office. Wanted: Dumb Ass Hat Wearer.

Moving right along. Thousands wasn't happy, especially when he knew good and cheery windmill well, fifteen blocks over to the left there's this other hat store where another hurricane, almost-like tornado, had whipped along and took another hat up in a tree.

Mr. Business operated that store. And he wasn't anything like Mr. Manager. Instead of dismissing him, he came out of the back, and went right into appeasing his customer. "Oh golly, oh gee. Thousands let me tell you I am so very sorry. Now let's see how we can help make you happy!"

Mr. Business retrieves the hat. All Ends well. Or the hat ends up lost and never found, and all still ends well, for Thousands will be getting a discount on the next hat he purchases not so free.

None of this stuff is brand new. It's all relative to economics 101 or 102; supply and demand. Ignoring the people quotient to cash in on hot commodities such as… increased security, which only drains expenses since it doesn't put a dent nowhere, no how, in revenue. Let's face it, SHOPLIFTERS and crooks weren't going to buy nothing no way… exactly where my paper doll pastime and pet peeve meets and picks up. Just kickin' back watchin' the people system communicate…

And please believe me. I have nothing against technology and a secure infrastructure, or cats and dogs and other living things that more than likely hate people attributing their point of views, to their point of views. I'm just more for communicating with systems I get, and they get me. Building safe user-friendly communication systems and networks are best served by investing in, and leveraging, people systems primarily.

But be warned in advance: if you do not like people, or have anything better to do, and that means anything at all… such as pulling out your hair until one strand is left, or ringing enough doorbells until you have a down payment to hop on the next shuttle heading out into space, I suggest you go on and do it.

But if you're satiated, love people, and especially love yourself, then I guarantee you'll enjoy the following discourse that none too ironic takes place in the perfect setting. The customer service department in one of the most upscale Federated Stores.

Proof in the Pudding.

~~

JIMMY

~~

Everyone picks their own peace. Jimmy Chung wasn't saying this. Someone else was. Jimmy was making fun of lazy government workers. In his estimation he thought government workers would rather kick, yell and scream, and raise all kinds of taxes before they'd hike it a flight or two up the stairs. Laaazzzzeee!

But who ever said government work had to be smart work? Everyone knew unless a government worker was a part of a scandal, they always started their day at ten, Monday through Thursday. And every other Friday at eleven.

And don't even think about finding any real loyal government worker in the office past fourish, or beyond noon if it was an official. By that time all the elevators, escalators and any other apparatus riding up and down would be permanently grounded... until it had slept off sixteen hours too.

Zoey started to throw in a plug about holidays, but then Jimmy beat her to the punch. "Holiday's! Are you kidding? Don't even start counting all the holidays they observe..."

Jimmy got to counting on his fingers using his

index finger several times. "…Washington's birthday, Lincoln's birthday, King's birthday, Ash Wednesday, Groundhog Day, Leap Year, Work Man's Comp Day, Sprained Ankle Week, Ten Snow Flakes picked up on a satellite in the middle of Africa…"

Jimmy laughed, "…they get them all!"

"Yeah, whatever," Jordana smirked, peeved at Jimmy, Zoey, and the dark haired girl from the Dong not doing much talking, but a lot of grinning. Shucks, she had a government job, which unlike whatever their main hustle was, at least her job held security. Hell, who wanted to work (like Zoey), four or five part-time jobs and one full-time job, while raising a slew of children alone, real hard? What was her angle? Shucks, everyone had mouths to feed, but they didn't have to work around the clock to do it. What? Was she working real hard for the thrill of it? And what about a pension…or one day RETIRING!?!

In all those years, Zoey had yet to come by a gold mine. And the world hadn't gotten any better either. Same old world, with the same old problems.

Jordana rolled her eyes and slid next to Lillian, a woman she vibed with better. She liked Lillian's huge roving eyes and mad with the world expression pulling down both sides of her face making her jaws jump. Kind of reminded her of her grandmother, especially when she got to dishing out the animated insults.

"Y'all doggin' government workers when all of us still on the same plantation," Lillian rowed back. "White, Black, Blue, Purple, like my daddy used to say, if you gotta work, you a slave!"

"Unt unn. Not me," Jimmy contended. "I don't have to work. I want to work."

"Yeah, right," Lillian chuckled. "So, I'm to believe you want to pay rent too?"

"Gotta stay dry," Jimmy shrugged. "…And I like taking showers once a day too," he laughed.

"Boy, hush up," Lillian playfully scoffed. "...Before you find yourself back home in one of them real slave labor camps!"

Jordana fell over laughing, especially when Lillian got to comparing human life, no different from ants ripping and running around carrying crumbs on their backs, one foot assault away from amusing some kid looking for entertainment.

"Look, I have no problem admitting I'm caught up in the rut-rut. Found out I like to eat," she laughed in her quacking duck echo.

"Me too," dittoed Zoey. "But I like the feel of earning what I make," she added.

"Oh, so you're the noble ant," Lillian clucked. "...Running around here with the mountain of crumbs on your back."

"Aww Miss Lil, and you're the pot stirrer," Zoey shot back.

"Pot-stirrer," Lillian asked, as if Zoey had been following her little ant parody. "Ants can't stir. They —"

"— They just keep shit going," Zoey filled in.

And this was the general flow in the customer service department. Cracking jokes. Teasing. And sometimes complete dysfunction and insanity. There were 19 different personalities working in a bay no bigger than the average home hallway. This factor often tripled the point of views and tsunami of attitudes.

Factor in customers... and throw in a diversity of cultures from around the globe, plus age and gender ...and things could get as bizarre as Lynne's 870 credit score (inside joke).

...Case in point.

Town Marshall.

~~

MARJORIE

~~

Marjorie was on this night. The night shift called her Town Marshall. But she wasn't a seasonal part-timer hired mostly to wrap gifts. She was full-time. The Big B was her real and only job.

The hefty bright-faced, red-head woman came straight from a small college in West Virginia to the Washington Metropolitan area to search and search for the perfect career opportunity, and whaala! On the corner of an extremely busy intersection she happened to notice the Big B.

A few years later she was promoted to supervisor and her very first Christmas in her new role became Town Marshall behind her back.

But she could care less what the night-crew found so funny, hovering around the mouth of the storage room cackling like bumbling buzzing bees. She had a job to do, and intended to do it well. She treated slackers no different than shoplifters.

Fact to the matter; the Big B, one of the top auxiliary retailers in the retail industry, was where the most prosperous from all over the world shopped. They came looking for Kooba, and Miu, and Jimmy Choo, and Fcuk, and Bvlgari, and Escada, and all the finery one could wear between there and someplace like Neimans, William Sonoma, Crate n Barrel, or God forbid Macy!s or JCPenny!s.

Rules were made for a reason. To follow. When a rule was broken, it created a domino effect. A heap of confusion would lead to one dissatisfied customer, a missed sale, a drop in transaction count, and Naomi jumping on her when her sales quota hadn't been met.

This trifling galley of helpless help was taking food off her plate. Were they deaf or what? She had to have said it a dozen times: "We need to make sure the storage area is clean and the shelves are stocked."

But no one moved. They all sat there, all five of them, on boxes containing wedding paper (barely out of view of the customer service counter), as if they were waiting on her to pull out her grandmaw Peterson's double-barrel shotgun.

Marjorie had that kind of temper. Got it straight from her grandmaw, where she also got the red hair. In other words, these slackers were messing with the wrong red head. She might not have had a cigarette voice, and she never got around to finding a polka dot dress like the one her grandmaw was known for standing on the front porch dressed in, double-daring poachers to cross her line, but she learned from the best how to keep ahead in hard times. Don't get mad with her because she came out ahead.

Zoey though, mused about the ukulele chiming edge to Marjorie's voice. Though she always looked as if someone had stolen her lunch, at least her voice wasn't irritating. But "we" she muttered. And she tapped at a spot at the back of her neck that didn't itch. She did that when telling herself to keep her mouth shut.

"We need to defrost my fridge," she snickered loud enough for only Lillian to hear. Shucks, she wasn't no pushover, but she wasn't no fool either. Acting tough paid no bills. She needed her job…especially easy money like what the Big B was shelling out, just to wrap gifts, and shoot the breeze with an otherwise good group of coworkers... between customers.

"Yeah, I got her 'we'," laughed Lillian in her serrated tone, loud enough for everyone to hear. "It's floating out on the Potomac."

Marjorie didn't hear her. She had already stormed away, back to her main post — Register Number One, the one furthest from where the seasonal help huddled.

Instantly Jordana started laughing. All Lillian had to do was open her mouth and she would fall in. Lillian was one of them ahead thinkers who always said whatever was ahead of her…like when three old ladies appeared at the customer service counter and asked for gift wraps.

Lillian got up to help them, since wrapping gifts was her specialty.

"Miss, we'd like to have our presents wrapped in wedding paper," the smallest woman in the center said. She was the one wearing a leopard fur pillbox hat cocked to the side, and bright red lipstick.

"Sure thing ladies," Lillian smiled, before turning away to clear a space for the ladies' gifts.

That's when the lady on the left, standing somewhat behind the lady in the pillbox hat, spoke up. "Well aren't you going to take our things?"

All three ladies turned and looked at one another, in a 'isn't this a shame… what is the world coming to,' expression. Lillian wasn't being hospitable. She hadn't informed them on what she was doing. As far as they were concerned, she was on her way out for a cigarette break. See… stereotyping. Lillian didn't even smoke.

So Lillian turned around, just her head though,

not her whole body, and gave the sugar ladies one of her 'don't mess with me looks'; a look that had Jordana scrambling to the storage room, trying not to spray her drink in the little old ladies faces.

"Well!" The lady on the left huffed.

And "some nerve," the lady on the right hissed. Lillian ignored the well and hiss. She came with her own story. She wasn't about to let three old women put her in her place, just because she accepted employment that had her standing between two 15-feet counters handling returns and exchanges, and wrapping gifts and making change for floor associates. Her granddaddy said it best. "Kick a mule in the ass, and it'll kick you rat' back." Other farmers used to catch the devil of a time getting their mules to cooperate. But not her granddaddy. "Miz Molly always took good care of me, jus 'lak I took good care of her," he also used to say.

"That's rat'," Lillian muttered aloud, her back turned on the women. "Treat sales associates like crap, get crappy service. Calm the hell down and not only can I help you, but I WILL HELP YOU!"

Other kinfolk in her clan as well learnt her on addressing this hostile behavior. Like her grandmother, Ma Tedda, and her Aunt May. When she was little girl she tagged along with them to help clean white folk's homes. An old woman who lived at one end of the block treated them decent. She'd greet them heartily. "How ya'll gals 'doin' today?"

Ma Tedda, the proper type, greeted her cordially, "jus' fine Miz Ruby. How's you?"

But her Aunt May was different. She was loud and spirited. She'd greet Miz Ruby back with, "Gal, we's all be smiling, so how you think we be doin'?"

Still, Miz Ruby opened her front door wide, grinning wider, and welcomed them in. Her house was beautiful too. Polished pine wood floors, raised ceilings, oil paintings, and antique furnishings passed down from her papa. The whole house looked royal. Nick-knacks were everywhere. It would take hours to put a spit shine on the house. Miz Ruby lived good, reflective of how she treated others.

Now Miz Ethel who lived a few doors down, was another story. They only had to be told once they were expected to enter the house through the back door. Sometimes they had to wait nearly 30-minutes or more for Miz Ethel to come to the door.

Just so happened, Miz Ethel's back door didn't provide protection from the weather. No matter how suffocating hot it was outside, or whether it was storming cats and dogs, Miz Ethel always took her time answering their knock. And they weren't allowed to knock hard either.

One time a neighbor's dog had gotten loose, and was coming after them. Aunt May panicked. She got to banging on the back door real hard. She didn't make no dents, but May was no small woman. And her aunt was deathly frightened of dogs. So when Aunt May got to pounding on the door, she was really pounding. Lillian ended up fending off the dog by throwing her shoe at the dog. Hit the dog dead in the eye. After that, the dog took off running, back to where it had come from.

When Miz Ethel finally answered the door, some many minutes later, she scolded them something awful. She threatened to take them to court for her door too, and that was after she made them work that day without pay.

Miz Ethel was a mean one, and she hardly lived like a queen; not with poison ivy rubbed over her bed linen, and floors washed with fish oil, and a pantry full of food that had been messed over.

As Lillian began wrapping the gifts for the little old trio, she mused to herself about them days. Taking her sweet time, clearing counter space for the special gift-wrap she still had in mind to do, she heard one of the ladies mutter something, but ignored them. She couldn't tell these women apart from a pair of blue suede shoes, but she knew their attitudes well. They had nothing to worry about. She loved wrapping gifts and intended to give them her best. Customers fawned over her gift wraps, often requesting her by name, waiting in lines for her to tie the fancy 'one of a kind' bows on their presents. It pissed some of the lower hunchos off, like the register hogger, but the Big B wasn't complaining. It was hard to argue against a positive revenue stream. One time she overheard two women in Macy!s talking about taking "Barbara-Ann's gift over to the Big B to get the 'signature wrap'." "...Oh yeah, you have to! Miss B does a fabulous job!"

Yes she did. Lillian actually heard that... standing right there in Macy!s!

But the little old trio knew nothing about Miss B. When they handed over their precious purchases, they had no expectations. In fact, their expectations were so low that the lady wearing the pill box hat held onto her bag as if Lillian was about to rob her.

So Lillian shrugged, assuming all the gifts that required wrapping had been accounted for. She turned around to start working on wrapping the gifts when a little indignant clattering crawled over her back.

"Well aren't you going to do this one too!?!" It was the pill box lady, still clutching her bag.

Lillian didn't miss a beat. Gaily she turned around and in an exaggeratingly buttery voice declared, "Why Miz Ethel, yes I sure am."

The lady on the right, with the huge sacs resting on her cheeks, and even huger emerald jewels dragging down both earlobes, eyes' shot wide open. "How did you know her name," she asked startled.

"Oh, as soon as I saw her, I knew her name was going to be Ethel," Lillian smiled. "She just reminds me so much of someone I know."

Jordana was in the stockroom, laughing so loud Marjorie looked over. Ms. Ethel however, was not impressed, but finally decided to relinquish her bag.

"I'd like to have this put in one of your bigger boxes," she said, gingerly pushing the bag over the counter. "And please be careful. I don't want it squished."

Lillian looked in the bag. At first she thought it was one of the plush bathrobes shaved off a goat she had seen in lingerie, on a trip to the restroom. But it wasn't. Inside the bag was a good size furry white bear.

Reaching in the bag and looking over the counter at Ms. Ethel still eyeing her with suspicion Lillian gingerly lifted the bear out of the bag. "Oh, don't you worry about this teddy," she said stroking the bear like she would a pet. "Oh no, don't you worry about a thing. I wouldn't dare stuff this precious little teddy in a box the way our slave masters stuffed us in slave ships!"

With exception of Jordana who burst out laughing, there was only a collective gasp in the bay. And it was louder than the gasp the three ladies made.

On cue Marjorie unhooked herself from the first register, headed Lillian's way, when she was stopped by a woman storming into the bay demanding a manager!

That's all that spared Lillian...that and the fact the woman hurled her big brown bag over the number one register. "I want to return this!" she snarled.

Marjorie peeked in the bag. It was houseware merchandise; a $275 serving set.

Under no circumstance and over her cold dead body was she associating her employee number wih this return purchase. "I'm sorry, but you'll have to take this to housewares—"

"—I've already been down there and they told me it was over their limit," spewed the customer.

Marjorie called downstairs to Housewares and got the same story. The associate she talked to couldn't process the transaction, even if she wanted to.

So Marjorie spent 20 minutes calling all over the store trying to find a sucker to return this purchace on their store number. And call after call each employee gave her the big fat NO. If no one in Housewares could approve and process the transaction, then it was on customer service to deal with it.

Now she could have called the store manager on duty, but nooooo, she wouldn't dare make that call because whoever was on duty would've told her the same thing, and then reported her to Naomi for not following the rulebook she knew inside out.

Marjorie's face grew red and redder. She couldn't find a pigeon, and this woman was getting tired of waiting. "Where's your manager!?!"

"I am the manager," Marjorie replied...ahem lied. She was a supervisor, and dead wrong in this instance, the very reason she was dubbed Town Marshall. It was going to take an act of Congress to pry a refund from her cold dead hands.

"Well, you're going to have to contact corporate because I cannot help you," she told this woman starting to fissure into two.

"Look! I'm not walking out of here tonight without my money!!!"

And right then Town Marshall went for her hip and started firing off shots like Wild Bill. 'The best she could do was give her a rain check...or call security!'

Was she serious!?!! The customer went for her hip too. Instantly the seasonal help stood back and started placing their bets. Two Wild Bills?! It was on! The red head trigger happy Wild Bill might've been good at shooting and not known for reloading, but the blue in the face Wild Bill had the advantage. Marjorie needed to revisit the first page of her employee manual. The customer was ALWAYS RIGHT.

"I'm putting my money on old Wild Bill," Jimmy stated, rooting for the customer, and co-signed by all but the contrarian — Lillian. "Ain't no way a cent is coming out that cash drawer," she laughed adding. "Not without a real gun!"

"Aww…that woman is getting her money back," Zoey said sucking her teeth. "Big b don't play that!"

And guess what? For a while Wild Bill hugging *her* register and plucking on that six-shooter looked like she stood a good chance of winning the OK corral gun battle. Looked like the customer was near to throwing in a towel.

But then Marjorie got to talking about how the register wouldn't balance and Tracy would be mad, and finally, her fatal mistake. She said NO CUSTOMER was above Big b's policies.

Apparently the customer was a pro at returning stuff. She left the bay, prompting Lillian to prematurely celebrate. "Toldja," she chuckled. "Sookie ain't lettin' nobody in that register while she's in here."

Except a few minutes later the customer returned with the real McCoy — Big Bad Beatrice!

Not Today Satan.

JORDANA

Town Marshall was again working the evening shift and she wasn't happy about it.

Normally she worked days, but Naomi decided to teach her a lesson for her gun-slinging handling of the bay. And she accepted, begrudgingly, committed to fast-tracking it to the Ms. Big B title.

But moaning, to the point it sounded like she was being dragged through the evening, she complained bitterly about this group of seasonal workers. They were the worst she'd ever seen. Jordana and Lillian causing her the most pain.

So she arrived to the bay flaming hot, and started frying and crisping up when she looked at the schedule and realized it'd be another agonizing 5 hour night putting up with them and their mouths.

But she wasn't the only one curled up over having to work together. When Jordana looked up and saw Town Marshall punching keys on the number one register, she got to scoffing from that moment. From her field of view there was more to hate about Wild Bill than her six-shooter and behind that swaggered like a cowbell. She had fat ankles, and who in the hell wore Birkenstocks in the dead of winter — with socks! And white sweat socks at that! The Big B blinged style, taste, class and pizzazz the most. And here this red-hot mess was walking around with a six-shooter, wearing flip-flops in the dead of winter, with white socks!

"...Somebody betta' tell her, cause I'm telling y'all straight up... the ho' say two words to me and I'm knocking her out the plastic slide-ons. It's that simple," Jordana pouted.

"Girl, you need to calm down, damn!" That was Zoey, who while Jordana loved laughing at Miss Lil, she full on respected. "You actin' like somebody makin' you come in here...which the season is almost over anyway!"

Only Zoey could talk to her like that. No one else was allowed in her feelings; not the aunt who raised her, nor courts that ended up emancipating her at sixteen. She was the boss of her, starting from her father's disappearing acts, and her mother's subsequent death. Six grueling years under her aunt's preachy rule with a man friend who repeatedly molested her, she had seen too much, brought into the world kicking and screaming, raised like a pit-bull, armed to the teeth to fight.

Had anyone but Zoey said she was blessed to have a *fun* job and a *real* job, she would've told them exactly what she told her Aunt. She wasn't blessed because her mother drank herself into a coffin after her father ran off with another woman, leaving her and her siblings in the care of relatives and strangers. Having a roof over her head, food in her stomach, and clothes on her back was supposed to be the norm. That wasn't no blessin'!

Hearing that ukulele chime definitely wasn't a blessin'. The cow was working her last nerve.

'Why hadn't someone refilled the bridal wrapping roll?' Because they fuckin' didn't feel like busting out a kidney or a spleen. That's why, bitch! Shit, despite the offense, she actually had bothered to read her agreement. It SAID, 'Be Able to Lift UP to fifty-pounds!'

"Sheeit…" she continued pouting. "Somebody's gonna have to call somebody to lift that thing if they expect me to put that thing up there. I ain't bustin' my gut to do it. And I ain't buyin' no extra insurance for them to do it either!"

Jimmy wasn't touching the roll either. "Equal pay for equal work," he laughed when Marjorie was out of earshot.

And who were the slobs living in the pigsty? Did anyone ever open the microwave in the office? Zoey said it smelled like fried nasty ass in there.

Vince, though, strolled in the service bay and slid his slim tail on a crate in the holding bay. There was no way in an el barro tornado he was disgracing his new slick look after his father had scraped his knuckles in the dirt to bring them out of the city of no gold—Jalisco. He hadn't been hired to be no janitor, nor no work horse lifting more than a comb to keep every strand of his hair in tip top place. "Yo, people be tripping around here yo."

Everyone was fussing, but none more so than Jordana. "Who in the heck are all these people getting married in December anyway?"

Someone could have handed her a million bucks and she still would complain. It wasn't enough, or it was too much, or why hadn't someone thought about the homeless, and why did she have to pay taxes on a gift. The girl couldn't help herself.

Marjorie heard the griping, and on cue, hellbent on proving she had the chops, pulled out the six-shooter. "The new roll hasn't even been replaced," she said looking at Jordana sideways.

"Well, ya'll need to call somebody for that. I ain't no man," Jordana said turning away and leaning into Zoey to whisper her disdain for Wild Bill.

"Well, you need to get Vince to help you because we need the roll up now," Marjorie ordered, talking to the back of Jordana's head.

Jordana didn't bother to turn around. She played with a piece of string on the counter, chosing to ignore the gun-slinger. And Marjorie left her alone, be it due to the memory of the other night, or knowing Jordana was more than likely to make good on her threats.

She wobbled over to Vince, her backend moving like a raft in the middle of an ocean. "Can you help me get that tube of paper up on the roller?"

Now Vince had already said, beneath his breath albeit, he wasn't lifting anything heavier than the cell-phone he happened to be looking at, but didn't repeat this to Marjorie standing over him. He did give her the finger though, after she turned and headed back to the tube. And he also pocketed the phone and helped her hoist the 60lb tube on the roller.

Jordana laughed as Lillian chided him about his pants falling off his tiny hiney. "Child, you need a belt! Nobody wants to see the color of your drawers and two butt cheeks!"

"Unt un. Miss Lil, that's how the guys wear them now," Jordana laughed. "They won't fall off because they get 'em fixed to their briefs," she giggled, looking Vince up and down, liking what she saw.

"Well, when I see someone's ba'hind, all I think about is spanking it!" Lillian stood back and looked at the back of Vince, up and down too. "You want me to spank that butt," she cackled, kind of laughing along with Jordana near to the floor.

Vince didn't reply, as he and Marjorie struggled securing the tube on the roller.

"If you don't have any change on you, you can always grab some of these hangers lying around here to hold up them britches," Lillian continued.

Jordana shook her head. "Miss Lil still calling

drawers, britches," she said, speaking to Zoey. "People was talking like that a hundred years ago!"

Lillian handed Jordana a wedding gift to wrap. "They's britches from where I come from." And she looked over at Vince, "and they's certainly britches by the way he's wearing them! These kids are so lost!"

"Miss Lil, you a mess. I bet you was something back in your day," Jordana continued laughing, clumsily handling the gift box.

"My day?" Lillian looked at Jordana, pointedly looking her up and down, ignoring for the moment the crappy job she was doing wrapping the gift. "I probably got you beat by what? A day or two?"

Lillian hated the way the new kids dressed. As much as it got on her nerves seeing Teresa wearing the haute couture dresses, with her nose up in the air, she'd rather see people covered, than uncovered. Actually, and to tell the real truth, everybody and everything got on her nerves.

"And how can you wrap anything with them nails?" Lillian scowled.

"Unt un. I've been working with these nails since acrylics became the thing," Jordana chuckled.

"...And it looks like it too." The scowl hadn't left Lillian's face.

"You can be a crabby old lady," Jordana snarled.

"You don't tie a bow like that!" Lillian stopped and watched Jordana trying to make a loop... seemingly without injuring her nails. "Look at how you taped the paper. We're not making quilts!"

Jordana giggled, leaning on the gift exposing her ample cleavage. She really didn't care. Not even about Miss Lillian's up and down mood. She lost interest with the things going on around her the minute she arrived. Nothing Lillian said riled her. She liked, or rather craved her motherly attention. "They're gonna rip the paper off anyways," she giggled more.

Lillian couldn't help it. She had to rescue the gift from Jordana's precious nails, and vulgar cleavage. Though she loudly proclaimed her love of Christ and the recognition of His birthday as the reason she so loved Christmas, it really were those surprises she got to wrap for why she loved Christmas. But just as she reached up to tear off a sheet of wrapping paper, Marjorie stepped between them.

"Ugh, that needs to be rewrapped. Customers do care," she supplied. She was becoming Ms. Big B, even if it got her killed.

Jordana stepped back and gestured towards the gift, in her estimation only missing one more loop to the bow. Marjorie could go on and play with the bow all she wanted. The bow was going to be the first thing ripped off, and probably using somebody's teeth.

Marjorie coolly pulled a sheet of wrapping paper off the roller. "You're supposed to fold the paper to the center of the box so that the ribbon will cover the seam." She gracefully demonstrated, turning the paper full of busy bulb patterns over the box.

Intrigued, Lillian watched. Marjorie couldn't do a thing for her spiritually, but she loved following her hands magically moving, making the bulbs line up and match, and the tape totally disappear. Her movements were so graceful, like synchronized swimmers. Jordana, however, wasn't paying a bit of attention to the demo. She missed the entire production. Marjorie lost her at "that needs to be..."

"Ooo, look!" Jordana interrupted. "We have a customer," she giggled.

"I'll take care of them," Marjorie told Lillian, turning around and bringing a hand straight to the hip.

Lillian and Jordana exchanged the same knowing expression — the smirk.

"How can I help you," they heard her say.

Jordana snickered. "You can feed my dogs."

All night long, from one elbow to the other, when Marjorie wasn't bossing, or reading customers the rites from the customer service handbook she selectively read, she hung over the register checking her sales. She'd ring up three gift checks, and she'd check her totals. One gift card, and she'd check again. A gift-wrap, and she was back punching buttons to check again. Now she was hogging the register to tell a customer she couldn't take his check.

"That's such bullshit," Jordana fussed. "When did this shit happen?"

"That policy came out about a week ago," Jimmy replied. He was speaking of a new rule to stop taking Big B credit card payments; the easiest transaction to process. Took less than two seconds. All of two keystrokes.

"But if you think about it," Jimmy continued, "it really helps the customer."

"Un huh," Lillian huffed. "Heppin' 'nem out, huh? My granddaddy always said nothings' free, especially help!"

Marjorie didn't care how anyone felt, particularly seasonal help. She had a job to do, and that was the long and short of it. She slipped in the office and placed a call to the store manager on duty — Beatrice.

"I can't deal with them," she explained. "All the laughing and swearing and things they're discussing is totally inappropriate."

"I'll be right over," Beatrice said. And minutes later there she was, in the office standing in front of Marjorie guessing why she was there. When she walked in the service bay she saw nothing amiss.

"Well, who are we talking about," Beatrice asked partly annoyed. Already she was not okay with what went on the previous night, and it was not the seasonal workers that gave her the most concern.

"Well, it was the bla—" and she caught herself. She was about to say 'black', which was one of Beatrice's arc concerns, and not only because she happened to be black. She had a problem with Marjorie's inability to communicate effectively with a diversity of people.

"I'll speak to Naomi," Beatrice tersely replied. "In the mean time I'll talk to the employees."

Beatrice marched to the bay and Marjorie sighed. It was a proud moment. Instead of calling Naomi and complaining, she stood up for herself.

Out in the bay Beatrice waited for a lull in busyness before speaking to the group as a whole. She stood by watching LIllian's signature wrap, and listening to Jimmy explain to a customer the convenience of paying his bill at any register. She chuckled at Zoey using the Purell between customers, and of course took note of Jordana's nails. Her hands were beautiful.

"Can we chat for minute," she asked when the bay cleared of customers.

Instantly Jordana and Zoey cut their eyes over to Marjorie who clearly was not a part of the 'we'.

"You know this is a professional environment," Beatrice began. "But we're getting complaints about the personal conversations taking place in here," she coolly explained. "We really don't like having to let people go, but we will if this continues…"

Beatrice left out, and Marjorie stood her ground, as if she didn't know their jobs had just been threatened, or that they didn't know she was the snitch.

Jordana turned to Zoey and flat out said, in an open unmodulated voice. "I'ma tell you like this…the ho' betta' not say one word to me. From where I come, we kill rats!"

"Just be cool," Zoey softly said.

"Well, I'm just warning you…" Jordana said.

"…And I'm warning you," Zoey tossed over her shoulder. "It's not worth it."

Mr. Big b.

Hue was hotter than red bricks keeping a campfire lit. He was so lit up that all the lights in the store could have been turned off and everyone still would have been able to see.

With his campfire face good and lit he spat, "I don't give a rats' behind if you have the cure for brain cancer! If you can't get along with the team, you don't belong here!"

Naomi knew better than to speak. Right or wrong the boss always got the last word. And in Hue's case it was pointless to dare try. His disposition wasn't a straight line. He was all over the place. A bad leader in her view. So she kept that opinion to herself… since the boss, like the customer, was always right.

"I want a thorough investigation done into what happened last night," he spewed, sitting lower than the average size man behind a mahogany wood grain desk.

Before this meeting Naomi was through with this person. Now she was like an overdone steak still on the grill, still cooking. Normal rationale was gone. Had abandoned the building, and there were three of them staring back at Hue. Beatrice to her left, and Faye, the HR director, on her right. The Big B was an 'at-will' employer. They hired 'at will' and fired 'at will'…and didn't have to say why, given the Big B's high DEI score. Within the store, her department set the model. She did not discriminate. But right was right, and wrong, wrong.

"I want a summary report on my desk by the end of the week," he bellowed, having lost his cool when the greasy slimy Jarad, Harold and Epstein called, trying to blindfold him and tie his hands behind his back, blackmailing him about a basic fact. Africans had been stuffed in ships! What was so bad about that!?!

Naomi had no idea what was going on in Hue's head. From the outside it looked like a lot. He probably ran into issues buying hats. If the fabric wasn't made out of knit, it likely didn't fit.

"I want a statement from every single employee on your payroll," he waged on. "I want to know what they feel about the supervision going on down there, and I want complete employee files on your supervisors, on my desk no later than the end of this week.

Naomi only had one question, besides wondering why Faye was sobbing. Who in the hell did he expect to conduct this investigation? Was he bringing in outside investigators? If so, why was he holding them hostage?! Did he honestly, with a straight face think his directors, managers and supervisors would incriminate themselves…asking people who had other real jobs, how they felt about people who made the Big B their main priority?! If so, he was wasting the Big B's money.

The meeting was going nowhere fast. They let him vent; Beatrice taking notes, Faye quietly sobbing, and her staring at a little man talking assed backwards at them, because he felt he could.

The previous store manager he replaced, wasn't like him. Neal was an old-school thought leader. He was tough, but sensible. Not once in his 50-year career with the store had he ever called a mandatory emergency meeting where he sat on a soap box and talked out both corners of his mouth. He didn't spend his waking hours barking about change and regurgitating buzz words at people he barely knew.

How dare he chomp on her girls who, overall, were doing a fantastic job. Contrary to his myopic view, there was more to the job besides managing people who cared more about their 'real' jobs. Besides being first to address the store's daily concerns, they managed the store's 1798 registers, and were piloting his cataloging division! Dealing with seasonal attitudes and wrapping gifts was a snippet of what they did each and every day, 7 days a week.

But the new kid on the block was in his moment, leaning into his boss. So, she kept her thin lips zipped, and fat ankles quietly crossed, listening to Beatrice's nasally breathing, and inwardly laughing at his toupee moving across his forehead unassisted, and wondering why Faye was sobbing. The meeting was a joke, spared by the fact she was soon due to retire. In a few short months she'd be the last of a dying breed. She could put the Big B up on a shelf and celebrate change starting with changing her drapes along with the seasons.

Quite a few times though, she ached to ask Hue if he was still chummy with his barber. Looked like his type of change involved changing barbers weekly. Each time she saw him, his toupee looked worse than the last time she saw it.

"Has everyone seen the video?"

Huh? Naomi frowned, and looked over at Bea, since Faye was still sobbing. They were in charge of new hire orientations and training.

"You mean the sexual harassment video?" Bea asked.

"Yes," he snapped. "The video that teaches employees how to behave and treat each other!"

Naomi shook her head. Manners was learned at home. No one training could teach cultural polemics to an ever changing culture. By accident though, she rolled her eyes, and he saw her. Fortunately he caught the faux pas after Beatrice followed up his response, reminding him of his budget cuts to new hire training.

He waffled. The man's voice actually buckled. He mumbled something about how they needed to get creative.

Oh! She was so glad she was soon retiring! If he had a beef with her, she had an even bigger beef with him. Watching his magic carpet going up and down, back and forth, his hairline disappearing and reappearing at odd intervals, periodically readjusting itself without input, she mused on the entertainment for her retirement extravaganza. She'd invite everyone, her girls and customers foremost. And for sake of the dunk tank and the piñata, she'd especially have to invite him.

Oh, the games she'd play. Pin the tail on the donkey. Yep, he'd be the donkey. Duck, duck… yep, he'd be the goose. Crack the whip… again, he'd be the caboose. And wall ball… where (of course) there'd be no way she wouldn't replace him with the wall.

Listening to him and watching his magic carpet, she fought the urge to pick up one of the darts off his desk and nail that sucka' still. At the rate the rug was moving, by the end of the meeting he just might have one ear muff.

Suddenly his phone rang. He held up a finger and Naomi looked over at Beatrice, staring down (and she had some huge eyes) at a notepad lying in her lap, while Faye closed in on another tissue.

A minute later he ended his call and quietly placed the receiver on the cradle. "I need those statements, ladies, by the end of next week," he said. It was hard to tell but it sounded like he had just gotten off the phone with bad news. He had pushed the deadline back.

But good. The meeting was over, or so Naomi thought. She started to rise when he sneered, "where are you going!?!"

'Really, Hue?' In front of her colleagues he'd do this? Treat her like this? Beatrice's eyes looked like they were about to cartwheel out of its sockets. She had them big ole' eyes good and plucked open, and with her protruding teeth pushing her lips apart, braced to hear what was coming next.

But he was interrupted by Faye springing from her chair. Hand covering her mouth she fled out of the office.

"What's wrong with her?" he asked, his nose crinkled and his 'do' pushed back to no avail.

"Her husband is dying of cancer," Beatrice ruefully spat. "Brain cancer," she added.

The Inquiry.

~~

LILLIAN

~~

Don't start with her. It was too early in the morning, and it was Saturday. Plus, like something else her granddaddy learnt her, "she hadn't seent a thing!"

She had no desire to talk to Tracy, a skinny little bleach-blonde who looked nothing like an investigator, but more like a beauty pageant contestant whose only talent was wearing heels and a bikini. Unnecessary. Maybe. Stereotype. 100% Not!

"Well, I have to turn these forms in first thing Monday morning," Tracy said. "We don't have an option. It's mandatory."

'And'...Lillian thought, almost aloud. Like, what was she going to do? Try to drag her big old whole self into the office? Cause that's what it was going to take. She had no plans to move away from the counter until it was time to leave. God help her if she had to use the restroom. Shoot, that counter was the only thing holding her up. Well, that and wrapping gifts...the one thing that literally lifted her up off the sofa and drove her to work.

To her good fortune a real life-sized Ngo walked

into the service bay at that moment. He was tall, dark and handsome... and staring into Tracy's translucent eyes, and she was staring back.

Good. Lillian slid over, towards the storage archway, dubbed the holding bay. "I'm looking to have a few gifts wrapped," said the Ngo, in a deep chocolatey voice. He sounded Caribbean. "I've been told to ask for Mizz Bee."

"Who," Tracy asked, who mostly worked in the office, so she knew nothing about the whole Ms. B thing.

"Do you have a Mizz Bee here?" asked the perfect picture of many women's dream husband.

"I got 'chew," Lillian said.

Tracy looked over, hesitated, was about to speak, but decided to turn on her heels and head to her cave.

"Thank you so much," the Ngo says in that carnivorous tongue, lifting several bags over the counter.

"I thought you said a few," Lillian scoffed, jovial albeit. "This looks like a whole lot more than a few!"

"Ooo! Let me help you," Lynne offered, drawn into the conversation by Ngo's heavily fragranted scent.

"I don't need your help," Lillian said. "I got it!"

"Oh, that's okay," interjected the Ngo. "I like the idea of two ladies helping me."

Lillian's head swiveled around. First of all, she was interested in his gifts, not him... or those gifts! She was far too mature, and clearly uninterested in adam's apples and abs. But in case he didn't catch her drift, she asked if he preferred his cast iron Calphalon frying pan in a box, or upside his head.

Lynne giggled. "Aww...Miss Lil, don't hate."

"I'm not hating," Lillian snapped. "I just need to know how he plans on leaving out of here today!"

"Yeah, right," laughed Lynne. "But did you see that watch?"

"What watch?" All she saw was women's things laying on the counter; pieces of strings with dangling lingerie price tags attached, and an assortment of items that belonged in a kitchen but could also be used as weapons.

"...That Movado sapphire steel watch," Lynne whispered. "Girl, that man got it. Whoever his lady is, she is a lucky woman!"

"Ump! Seems to me she's about to find herself barefoot, pregnant and stuck in the damn house!"

"Aww, you just a hater," Lynne giggled.

"Child, just hand me some tissue paper before I pull off my pantyhose and stuff them down this vase!"

Lillian was no hater. She had a man. Well, not any more. But once upon a time she married a beautiful man. For 42 years she experienced the touch of a man who loved dancing and showering her with praise. He gave her five wonderful children. And brought them a modest, but lovely 4-bedroom home she still lived in. They traveled all over the globe. And up to his death they enjoyed many late nights playing Scrabble. She wouldn't trade that experience for any other man in the world. So, Lynne was dead wrong. She was plenty satisfied, thank you very much and praise her God.

"Ooo, what's that I smell," Zoey chirped entering the bay.

"Sssh, better keep it down," Lynne said. "Tracy is in today."

"What's she doing in here on a Saturday?"

Lillian and Lynne didn't answer because the girl from the Dong, whose name was Emanuel, but asked to be called Emma, walked in. "Woo, smells nice in here," she noted too.

Lillian scrunched up her face more. She hated women falling over pretty boys. Everyone of them she knew were either single...or dead! The nightgown Lynne drooled over, she would've torn up and used to patch her bathroom curtains. The Pink by Nanadebary... after a quick sniff she would've put it in her pantry, behind the Lysol. And that entire Calphalon set… she would've cooked him in it. She would've eaten a whole year, without having to buy one piece of meat.

But Lynne, Zoey and the girl from the Dong fell all over that man, and his cheating lying behind grinned and grinned.

"You have a lucky lady," Lynne had the audacity to say. "I bet she's pretty…"

She wanted to kick the girl's shins, and almost reached for the mane on her head… to mop up the leftover Christmas mess on the counter. Like why would he say his woman was ugly?

"All women are beautiful," replied the dirtbag Ngo. "Beauty is only soul deep," he lies.

Lillian was highly irked at this point. So she kept facing the other way, wrapping his gifts with a heavy hand. No matter what, he was getting her signature wrap. He just wouldn't know what she was thinking when his beautiful woman opened her gift and asked why he bothered to wrap orange scissors!

"Ugh sir, which wrap did you say you wanted for this one," she asked over her shoulder.

Ngo glanced up at the wall and then lowering his voice replied, "I didn't." A suave grin followed. "I'll leave it up to you. Let you decide…"

"…Ugh!" Lillian closed her eyes and snatched a foot of paper off one of the rollers.

"Unt un," Lynne squealed, "Do number thirteen. That's prettier. Plus it's luckier."

Lillian looked at the paper she snatched off the roller. It was a yellow print, scattered with butterflies, figs, oranges and other fruits. It was the Big B's Easter print. "But I was going to change the bow," and she added. "For luck."

"I bet you were," Lynne smirked, leaning into Lillian. "You just mad 'cause he got it."

"Girl Please! That man don't have nothing I don't

already got! Now, get off me so I can..." and she pulled extra hard on both ends of the ribbon, using every muscle in her jaws to tighten the bow.

But no sooner than that one left out, his brother from another mother...and father... walked in. "Hey...hey...psst," hissed the brother from the ugly side of the family, leaning way over the counter.

Lynne turned around, since Lillian didn't answer to hissing men. "Can I help you," she smiled with her lush candy red apple lips, showing off about 20 to 23 huge glossy white teeth.

"Com'mere for minute. Lemme rap to you," said the other brother.

Lillian didn't completely turn around, but cut a lazy eye over at Lynne. "Girl, if you go over there, I'ma whip your behind right here and right now."

Lynne giggled. "Aww Ms. Lil, we're in the help business. This is what we get paid to do."

But Lillian was serious. "You wanna see Thumbelina times ten?" She was speaking of Jordana, who quit after the Beatrice exchange. It was why Tracy was in on a Saturday, collecting statements...supposedly.

Lynne ignored Lillian's warning, since there weren't many choices. The hissing guy started causing a scene. "I got some cards I want you to pass around," he said, holding up what appeared to be a pack of playing cards.

Lillian gave this guy her full attention then. She decided she wasn't about to let nobody lose their gifts, socks and shoes playing three card monte in customer service around the holiday.

"Look! I don't know what you're selling, but you are in a store that got its own shit to sell," Lillian began. "You in the wrong place for that buddy."

Everyone stuffed in the bay laughed. And there were at least a dozen customers in there, plus those working on the opposite side of the counter.

"But don't you care about what happens to you after you die?" asked the hisser, fanning what turned out to be hand crafted insurance business cards, copied word for word from an ad in the Yellow Pages.

"No," Lillian replied, glaring the hisser straight in his dull colored sclera.

"Aww...you don't really feel like that," insisted the unhealthy hisser. "You wouldn't want to leave your loved ones with all of your debt, worrying about how to pay for your funeral."

"Listen Brown, if my loved ones love me, they'll take care of me while I'm here," Lillian snapped. "Cause anybody sittin' around waitin' on me to pay for my own burial, to hell with them!"

She turned around and there was Tracy, eyes opened wide and pulsating. "Umm, I really need to speak with you," she said.

Bad timing, but she meant every single word. She would give anything to see her husband when she got home, especially after a day like this. It was the only reason she chose the seasonal work. Wrapping gifts in a holiday atmosphere was so perfect. But if they couldn't use her anymore, there was always Macy!s. It would suck, because she had come to like the group, and of course reveled her fame, but she wasn't changing for nothing or nobody. And not because she didn't want to, but because her God told her not to.

Looked like Zoey shrunk two feet, and she was only five feet. Speaking of death, another part of the vibe that kept the service flowing was about to bite the dust.

No Help!

The flirt had one thing, and only one thing, on his mind. Women. And he loved, loved them all, especially the way Tracy's lips moved when she said his name. Nice and slow. "Kareem..." Ooooo, she said it with just the right pauses between each syllable. So sweet, like blowing him powdery kisses.

"Have you ever worked with Marjorie?"

"Huh?" Hearing that name was like a jolt and a sting zapping him off screen. He flinched and frowned until he opened his eyes and realized she was still there. Then he smiled.

"Kareem..."

He was out of it again. Hearing the moos... her purplish Burberry lips blowing him the Yasmine Bleeth-Penelope Cruz kisses.

"Have you noticed anything out of the ordinary going on in the bay," she asked.

He must've failed her little test because next thing he knew, Naomi was questioning him. Ooo! Her breath smelled like cheese. Fresh aged Sicilian cheese.

Next thing he knew, he was back in the bay extracting flowery scents clinging to Emma's long strands of beach bum auburn hair. All the way down to the small of her back he followed the slinky scent. He didn't want to marry the girl, he just wanted to lift her sweater to see if he only imagined a cleft at the small of her back permanently scarred by the tattoo of a dragon. An earth dragon, or water dragon probably.

Emma stepped aside jerking around to face him, her slinky mane swishing across his face. "Do you need to get over here," she asked.

Embarrassed he had been standing so close, he pretended an exaggerated stretch. Emma looked like the type who only dated Wall Street types, or during times of desperation, corporate execs. She never dated black ball players, no matter how rich, or intelligent. She certainly wouldn't fool around with third-year undergrads who weren't sure if they were black or African. If he wasn't Carnegie, Walton, Sir Newton or someone with a real name, then he was struck entirely off the availability of women like Emma.

So, he eeny, meeny, miny moed over to Vita and Lynne. Which one would it be? Vita with the dark eyes, or Lynne with the large plentiful suckable lips?

He chose Lynne. He loved her ashy Madonna voice. "Hey, you okay?"

Of course she was okay. He was the one standing out in the cold in need of a ride home. "Have they asked you about Marjorie too?"

'NOOOOOOOOOOOOOO!!!' he screamed out loud …in his head of course. Why did all these beauties keep saying that name!?! All night long he kept hearing that name. Were they trying to hook him up with her? To teach him a lesson about his raging hormones …or for so-called having a one-track mind? He wouldn't 'hook up' with Marjorie if she was the last hole on earth!

"They've been asking everybody in there about

her," Lynne went on. "I hope Jo-Jo sues the bricks off that place. I know I would! We're always the last hired, first fired!"

He agreed, but wasn't really listening. His radar was honed in on tails, visualizing squirrels chasing nuts.

"Everybody's talking about it," Lynne chattered on. "Dominique said..."

...and off he drifted, until he opened his eyes for real and recognized nothing but pitch black. "Where are you going!?!"

"Don't you live off Route 7," she asked, her eyes barely open, and not because she was high or sleepy or the cross-eyed type. She just had them sexy Asian eyes.

"No, I live off Route 28," he said annoyed. They specifically discussed this prior to pulling off the Big B's parking lot. They spent 10 minutes discussing it, in fact. He stood out in the cold freezing his ass off waiting for the friend to give her directions to his house, which was supposed to be near where he lived.

That was the part that annoyed him. This friend she was going to spend the night with! But then Lynne was a complete ditz.

"Oh, we can get over there from here," she replied. "All I have to do is make a right at the next light."

Not true. She needed to make a left. "Are you trying to drive me into the woods to make out with me," he teased. Might as well kick up the heat. He still had his ears to thaw out.

"Boy, I ain't making out with nobody," she said like she might change her mind… one day.

"Why not?" he laughed. "So, you're one of the ones...not into foreplay?"

"One of the ones," she huffed offended.

"Damn!" Did he just mess up? Quickly he regrouped. "Well, I kind of always fantasized about getting raped and dumped in the woods, you know..." he carefully said. "I was just hoping you might be the one."

"Boy, you are sick! Can't no girl rape no man anyway!"

"If I let you, you can…"

"If you let me," she shrieked. "That ain't rape!"

"Unn hun…yes it is. If I say it is. No means no," he playfully argued.

"Boy, you are crazy! Where do you live?"

He looked around. Or tried to look around. He saw not a damn thing. "Not out here," he chuckled. She had made the right, so he didn't know where they were.

Lynne squinted and scooted up to the steering wheel, stretching her naturally slinky eyes as far apart as she could to see through the fogged up windshield. She couldn't see a thing. Not a house…a car…not even a street lamp. She could barely see the road! It was just the two of them in complete and useless darkness.

She got serious then. Real serious. "No, really," she said. "Can you see anything? I think we're lost. I don't know where we are."

Plot twist. He turned right, his head first and then his whole body, looking something like a twizzler. He had never been to this crevice of the DMV. She was on her own. He had zero advice.

"Damn! I can't believe you don't know where you live! You got me out here in the middle of bum-fucked nowhere…lost as fuck," she fussed. "I don't do woods. I'm from the city! I've got to see some concrete."

"Look, don't panic," he said. "How about you let me drive—"

"—Why would I do that!?! Why can't you just tell me where you live!?!"

"But I told you," he said. "I said I live off 28. This is not 28!"

He changed his mind. A girl like this would drive him mad. She was proof cute wasn't everything… and that there was a cure for horniness. Meet Lynne: 'She will dry up your insides, and frankly piss you off!'

"Wait, it looks like we're at a dead end," he said peering out into no-man's land from the passenger side window. "Let's turn around and drive towards lights."

That time she did as instructed. Neither spoke much throughout the ordeal. Forty-five minutes later, after two-hours criticizing the dark, he arrived home... unharmed and unmolested, but scarred for life. Lynne was the worst 'possible date' ever, and he had many. Naomi's breath was better. At least it had a sense of humor. Even if he was desperate to get laid, he wouldn't waste his time on that ditz!

Next morning he awoke; cold, sweaty, and smelling parmesan cheese. He got up, splashed water on his face and picked up the phone. Lynne might've forgotten about the other night, or thought it no big deal, but he hadn't. He couldn't go back in there.

But Dominique answered, club style. "Hey babe, you calling out? Got a tummy ache? Sore throat? A cough," she teased.

"Umm...no... is Naomi there?"

"Oh sweetie, she's not here today," Dominique sang. "Are you calling about that investigation?"

"Actually no," he replied. "I just need to talk—"

"—You need to talk," Dominique sighed, climbing into her sexy voice. "Why you want to talk to her," she said switching to her pouty voice. "What's wrong with talking to me?"

"Well..."

"Tell you what," she came back with New York speed. "I'll call Nae and have her call you. Is that okay?"

"Okay..." he replied, sounding like a two-year-old little boy looking for his mommy.

Truth was, he thought about Dominique a lot, but she was scarier than Naomi. This loose, fast-talking Brooklynite cougar wasn't like the Lynne types, girls he could play with and feel like a man. He had more growing up to do before playing in this field.

"Do you need my number?" he gingerly asked.

"Babycakes, I got your number," she replied. "Give me a sec. I'll call you right back."

She might as well had told him not to wet his pants, she'd find his mommy in a sec. Five minutes later his phone rang. It wasn't Naomi though, it was her; the Marine vet who'd been around countless blocks.

"Hey! Just talked to Nae. She can't put nothing else on her calendar today, she said in a hurricane clip. "...But I'm sure anything you want to tell her, you can tell me," she coyly teased. "I keep secrets too..."

"Oh... okay," he dragged out, moving checkers around in his head, much too slow for the city dweller.

Sensing his hesitation she wasted no time clearing up his fuzzies. "You wanna talk in private," she asked. "I can drop by your place if you'd like?"

What in a 'Miracle on 34th Street' was going on here? His verbal quit notice somersaulted over Naomi and into an arena outside the stadium. In a span of one phone call lasting no more than a few words he found himself running around his apartment tidying up. He flushed the toilet, kicked everything on the floor under the sofa and bed and showered all inside 10 minutes... the exact amount of time it took to get to his place from the Big B, precisely the amount of time it should have taken Lynne to make the same journey.

Dominique showed up looking like she was on her way to a strip club, with all of her clothes on.

"Hey handsome," she smiled devilishly, arm up and resting on the door frame, posed like he had called her, and not the other way around. "...Feel like a drink?"

"Now?" he asked panicked...and like he'd just flunked 1st grade. It was 10 in the morning!

"Yes now, silly," she chuckled, inviting herself inside. "You're so cute," she said, running her eyes over his small living space as she lit a cigarette in his non-smoking apartment.

"Well…I was thinking maybe we can—"

"—Aww, come on dude. Lighten up," she said kind of edgy. "I like to sip and talk," she chuckled like the hardcore Marine Corps warrior that made it through boot camp and one overseas desk assignment.

"Ok…" he replied. Forget flunking 1st grade. He now was securely back in his mother's womb.

"Well…I have to get dressed. I wasn't expect—"

"—Oh, come on now lova' boy. Why we getting dressed. I've got to get back to work!"

Don't Ask Me Nuttin'...

No one wanted to participate in the investigation. None more so than Zoey, and with good reason.

Truth was, though no one knew the whole story, Zoey knew the most. Jordana never touched Marjorie. She did, however, exchange words with her, in the parking lot, which there was some name-calling, albeit all on Jordana's part, though not what she told lawyers who she indeed contacted for representation.

Minus the giblets and gravy, Zoey only had three car payments left. This gig with the Big b would put that pink slip in her hands by the 1st of the year, provided she minded her business and stayed in her lane. She planned to do just that. She had no idea what was going on corporate-wise at the Big b, but as God her witness she was bringing in 05 on a good foot. No major bills but rent, food and gas.

So when she saw Tracy coming with the pen and clipboard she turned to Kareem, who happened to be standing beside her, and muttered… "better not ask me nuttin'!"

But sure enough Tracy walked right over to her. "I need to speak with you…in the office," she said in her rice paper kitten whisper.

Zoey tapped the back of her head, something she did when trying to stuff her own foot in her mouth. "Umm… do you mind if I finish helping my customer," she replied.

The girl had no manners. Zero. She knew nothing about 'Yes, ma'am. No, ma'am. Please. Thank you. You're welcome. Excuse me. Standard stuff. Pleasant stuff. Mannerable stuff. Decorum taught shortly after birth, proven when she turned to Kareem.

"Do you mind finishing up wrapping this gift," she huffed at him, as if the customer was a mild inconvenience.

She got in the office and followed Tracy to a rear corner where Naomi's closet she called her office was located.

Being polite and on her best behavior, soon as Tracy opened her mouth her hand went up. "Please do not ask me about nobody no longer here. Honest to goodness, I don't know nothing, haven't seen nothing and don't want to talk about nothing."

Tracy looked at her, upper lip turned up, like she might look at mating goldfish. "We're actually looking into concerns our seasonal workers might have about supervisors," she said.

"Oh," Zoey said, her foot already wedged where it needed to be. "Well… I got nero for you there either…"

A minute later Zoey was back in the service bay, a lot more surprise than when she left. She didn't think the tender-face ice-cube had a heartbeat at all. On the way in that morning she passed the half pint of a girl hanging around foundations, as if she really needed to pile on more gook and gumption. Their eyes connected, but when she started to speak, the tin-face powder-blue tartlet looked away!

The bitch didn't even try to part her lips to speak. And yeah, it was possible she didn't see her. It was cold out and she did have her coat on. But she also had a shirt on, which she still had on, not without mention, she was wearing the same face. What? Tracy didn't do her speaking until after she punched the clock?

But it was all good. It was cool. Zoey had enough admirers who spoke to her, on and off, the clock... none more so than Shoehorn Sammy!

"Unt un… and you too! Gotta stop you right now before you get going," Zoey chuckled with the hand raised. "Don't come in here asking me nothing about Jo-Jo. I don't know what happened. Don't care where she is... what she's wearing...who she's seeing... or how she's feeling!"

Everyone knew she knew Jordana outside of the Big b. She and Jordana were neighbors. She used to watch Jordana's little girl. She also braided Jordana's hair. And although they didn't hang out, it was Jordana who told her about the Big b's customer service opening. Also, Zoey was in the parking lot. She had seen and heard everything.

"How you know what I was about to ask—"

"—Cause I see Jo-Jo written over your face," she said rolling her eyes, bracelets jingling as she went for the Lysol.

"Oh, so now you about to mace me," he laughed.

"Look Sammy, what do you want? And Jo-Jo better not come out your mouth!"

"...Whoa...whoa champ," he playfully laughed, grabbing the cross pendant dangling from a thick gold chain he wore around his neck. He brought it up in front of his face. "Get back Satan! I got something for your Lysol!"

Zoey ignored him. "Boy, you cashing in more of them stars," she chuckled. "Somebody need to be investigating you. I bet them things are counterfeit."

"What you wanna bet," Sammy playfully baited. "You wanna put a biscuit on the table?"

The guys, Jimmy and Kareem, burst out laughing. Coughing and clearing their throats and whatnot.

Stars were kudos (gold stickers) customers gave employees who went above and beyond. Sammy racked them up, above and beyond every associate employed, past and present, and likely future. He was a fast-talker, a womanizer, worked in the shoe department, basically a salesman ...a top Big B star! A GOAT.

So his making dozens of trips to the service bay throughout the day was as routine as salacious.

"Naw...we need some change," he finally said, pulling a twenty and ten out of his pocket.

"Boy, I can't believe Big b also is letting you walk around here with their money stuffed in your pocket." It was bad enough they allowed him to cash in, sometimes $300-400 worth of stars, a day. Each kudo was worth a dollar. Do the math. Especially on the days when he got more kudos than sales.

But he never was checked on it. Everybody in the store knew Sammy, and the females adored him. He was like their postman, pimp, priest and sometimes, poppa. Ask anyone in the store, 'who's Sammy', and the answer invariably came back some form of, 'the slick playboy'!

When Huong walked in the service bay, cute as a button with the little flat spongy face, no taller than the longest arm and eyes like black marbles, fixed and staring straight ahead, on cue Sammy zoned in on her.

"Hey Huong, how about you?"

Her eyes opened wide, "Huh, how me what?"

"Did I ask you about Jo-Jo,' he laughed.

"Who?"

Zoey turned around. "Jordana," she sighed.

"Oh," Huong only knew ghetto girl. She smiled, waited, stared blank-faced, and when nothing else was said she slipped in the office with her grass jelly drink.

Sammy leaned into Zoey and whispered, "go in there and ask her what she's doing this weekend."

"Oh please. You better leave them young ones alone. Don't want you to hurt yourself," Zoey laughed.

"Well what about you then?" He laughed, cocking his head to one side to give her the up down. "You ain't so young."

She narrowed her eyes. "Boy, don't make me jump over this counter and go all out Jo-Jo on you.

Jimmy, and Kareem too, encouraged the diatribe on, snickering and laughing.

"We should get a bet going," Sammy suggested, his wide mouth stretched open eager to take on Jimmy and Kareem's egging. "How about we see who in here gets to butter your biscuits first!"

Zoey narrowed her eyes again. "Bye boy! Take your change and get out of here before I turn you in!"

Jimmy and Kareem exchanged a glance, just as the diva, Dominique walked in, bumping into Sammy.

"Heeyy Sammy!" she cowed, hooking him in a neck embrace by one arm. "Mmmwaw!" — the noise she made planting a tight closed-lipped kiss on his jaw. "What 'cha know good baby!"

Sammy slid away…to get a look at her from the rear, headed for the office where associates stored their coats and purses. She was wearing the leopard tights. "Girrrl… you better watch it kissing on men like that!"

"Ha, Ha, Ha," she cackled doing the Zsa laugh. "I'm not worried. I see the collar around your neck."

"Unt un," he called after her. "I am available. A-VAIL-LA-BLE," he emphasized, lowering his voice when the office door opened and out stepped Tracy.

She was always doing that. Checking. But she never got far with her checking because everyone did just what Sammy did. Stopped talking. He didn't mess with her. He knew better. She'd walk them little strawberry blonde size three feet all over his final exit.

They huddled near the storage area, furthest from the office and drifted into guess-a-gating.

"So, you don't know anything," Kareem asked Zoey. He found it hard to believe. She lived right next door to Jordana. Plus, she was in the parking lot.

"Like I said. My name is Hess. Not mess!"

Kareem knew the deal. "Well, I just wanted to know if she was okay," he said.

"She's fine," Zoey replied. "I saw her the other day getting her kids things off lay-away."

"Lay-away?" Dominique shrieked. "Who's—"

"—Wal-Mart," Zoey slid in. "They still do lay-away in there."

"Damn!" Dominique shirked her eyes. "I haven't seen lay-away in a thousand years!"

"I guess that explains the pants," Jimmy teased.

"And I guess it explains all these bibs in here," Dominique quipped back.

Kareem tucked his head and chuckled.

"But I kind of like getting a bet going," Jimmy said, the joke sailing over his head. "I mean, we could bet which one of us gets Wild Bill to leave... might be a good way to make a lil extra Christmas cheese," he shrugged.

"Umm. No. Sounds more like a good way to end up doing 6-to-life!" —Zoey.

"Yeah bro, you talkin' jail time," Kareem agreed.

"Not necessarily," Jimmy insisted. "Okay, check this out..." and he dove into describing a dream he had after being inspired by a short film, 'Bank', where he had practiced an eight palms old qi six-thirty focus, white brows, no gloves and all fists, Feng Shou, gouquan, fu jow pai no thumbs night deposit switch. He'd have that till switched in no time. "All one of us has to do is be the one that lures her away from the register."

"—And turn out all the lights in the store and wear a ski mask too, huh?" —Zoey.

Emotional Wreck.

~~

VITA

~~

Not that anyone took Jimmy's plan serious, it was a limp one if he couldn't deny something he 100% did not do!

No hello, good evening, or how are you, Vita marched right up to him and accused him of trying to set her up. "It was you! You! I knew it was you all along!"

Her eyes looked like glowing eight-balls turned inside out getting smacked around with a cue stick. For such a pretty face, she looked terrifying.

"Why did you do this!?! Why did you put this in my pocket!?!" She shoved a small piece of paper into his chest, poking him with her bony knuckles.

He looked down shocked and confused at two bony fingers stabbing him in his chest, and a little 2x3 yellow post-it note stuck to his knit sweater. He started to speak, but before he could open his mouth, she was all over him again.

"You're going to pay! You're going to really pay for this! You shouldn't be touching people's things! How dare you! My husband knows people. He will contact them and have you arrested!"

Vita wasn't a big girl, but looked like a giant standing on her tip-toes pushed up to him. Never, in his life, and he attended some pretty rough public schools where he was the only Asian American, and lived in a home with a father who could spit fire, and this was by far the angriest anyone had ever been with him. Like, what did he do? His frantically roving mind desperately wanted to know.

But these stone cold killer eyes and razor sharp teeth scissored him apart with no explanation. Kind of reminded him of a metal dragon. Her venom was so hot she breathed dry ice, instead of fire… accusing him of schmoozing each and every short skirt, and having oil slick grimy gothic hair, and behaving like a know-it-all arrogant American. "You think you're going to get away with this! I am a married woman! If my husband had seen this, it would be serious trouble! There would have been consequences!"

She rambled like this for a good fifteen minutes or more, before storming off, headed to the office where Tracy was working.

Gosh. Never a smooth night. The others were right. He'd never get away with sabotaging Marjorie, and she deserved it. Really, all of them were some fuddy-duddy nuts. Everybody in there had issues. Funny, though. He thought for sure he left these individuals in kindergarten. He couldn't wait to finish school and get on with the rest of his life. People who built things, like tech enterprisers, weren't emotional wrecks. Like what did she mean by his 'slick gothic hair'? She had the same kind of hair. And touching her personal things, to leave a note? Why? He didn't even know shawls and scarves had pockets!

Like Holy smoke…what was next? He peeled the note off his chest and started to read it, but tossed it in the trash instead. He didn't care to read it because he hadn't put it in her pocket, or pocketbook, to begin with.

From the bay he heard her in the office, going off in the same manner as she'd done him. Complete ape shit crazy screaming to the top of her lungs at Tracy.

"I know it was him! It was deliberate! No one else would do such a thing! Only him!" Every word she yelled ended in an exclamation. And it didn't help that her voice erupted like black lava. Smooth, but forceful. She had a distinct husky sound. A noise that hung in the air and pounded on his chest.

"He didn't even try to defend himself," he heard her vowing to Tracy, also adding for the manyeth time since the dramatics started, how she wouldn't stand for it. 'His look made her sick. He didn't even look at the note. Guilt was written all over his face. Her husband would have been really upset if he had seen this note. He didn't trust American men. They showed no respect for themselves, dating any type of woman outside of their kind. They had no shame or respect for anything, always wanting and taking what was not theirs.'

"Take! Take! Take!" she bellowed loud and clear.

Emma walked into the bay and looked over at him. 'What is going on' was written over her face. She was headed to the office to store her things, but brought them into the bay with her.

"Is someone getting fired," she asked.

He shrugged. "Dunno. Not sure."

And he didn't know. He couldn't see Tracy, looking as perplexed as he had been. According to her, and Naomi as well, Jimmy was so sweet. A harmless puppy, always so polite with everyone. There had to be some mistake. He received lots of compliments from customers, far more than Vita, who on the other hand got far more complaints, almost as many as Marjorie who received the most.

Vita was just too excitable…emotional… or how Naomi explained her; a wreck. She was so quick to point a finger and 99% of the time be wrong. If she would just calm down for a second and let her try to figure out what was going on. Couldn't she see that she and Naomi were still dealing with the Marjorie brawl?

But nooooo. Vita was not calming down. No one else would do such a thing. This was deliberate! Only him! "You all think he is innocent, but he's not. Don't be fooled!"

"Alright…alright," Tracy said, her voice so calm and creamy that the only reason he heard it was because she had opened the door attempting to escape. "Let me talk to him and—" and she didn't get to finish. Vita shot past her like a bullet.

"No! I'm going upstairs to report this!" Those words vibrated through the air and traveled around the corner, into the fur department and disappeared.

Tracy looked at Vince, as if she'd just seen a horror movie.

And Jimmy raised his hands. Both hands. "I swear, whatever it is, I didn't do it," he chuckled.

"Ugh," Tracy sighed, about to return to the office when the voice, like a traveling parade, turned a corner and picked up volume.

The three of them; him, Emma and Tracy stared, waiting for the unhinged Vita to reappear. They could hear her, but not yet see her. One thing Tracy, and Jimmy too knew, there were no stairs or escalators in Maximillian. That department was purposely stationed at the back of the store, in a dead end, at the encouragement and blessings from their insurers.

Suddenly there Vita was again. All 5 feet some few inches of her, still yelling. "No, you must understand," she screamed besieged, directly into Tracy's pale white face. "I was up all night long worrying," Vita raved.

"All night that note was buried in my purse. I found it when my husband asked for my checkbook. I was lucky he didn't see it!"

According to Vita, she was so worried, all night long, that she burned the mashed, fried the peas, and "Oh God! Dinner was a disaster."

The explosion flabbergasted Tracy. Vita's rage was off the chart. She wasn't able to get in a word herself either. But she tried. "There must be an explanation because Jim—"

"—You think I don't know!?! Hear it!?! Them talking about what I eat smelling up the office! How I'm not smart, and don't know my job! And I DO TOO LISTEN! I hear it all! You are all two-faced backstabbing creeps. I should report you all. God have mercy on your souls!"

Tracy extended her hand, again attempting to calm the truly shaken woman, to no avail. Vita snatched away. She had only returned to retrieve her things. She had forgotten them. But thank heavens she remembered. The miscreant (a word both Tracy and Jimmy mistook for Hindu), could have left another note!

"You don't understand how it is for me! My husband is not American. He would not have believed me!" She grabbed her coat and purse, the whole while Tracy holding the door open, as she hurtled by for what would be the final time. "All of you are going to pay for your wrongdoings! You'll see!"

"No wait," Tracy said, trying again to prevent Vita from running off in this blustery squall. It wasn't good for the bay. They'd be short-staffed that evening. And it certainly wasn't good for corporate optics. Hue was going to pitch a fit. But mostly, it wasn't good for commuters. Vita could end up picking up a homicide charge herself, attempting to drive so out of sorts. She was more dangerous than a person with a blood alcohol count ten times the legal limit.

"No! You need to listen! Forget Marjie! Jimmy should be fired instead! He's a creep! He's conning all of you!"

Yo Y o Yo.

VINCE

Tracey constantly scheduling him with the big fat bossy girl—Marjorie, or the mute girl—Huong, or weird one—Nadine, or the aloof goof—Emma, wasn't working for him. After Jo, and then Miss Lil, and of course Vita left the wheels came off the spindle as far as Vince was concerned. Every night got worse and worse, and dragged more and more, until he said enough.

So he left, but visited the bay often to fist bump Jimmy. That's where he was headed when Dominique, running backwards trying to blow Jimmy a kiss, collided into him.

"What you doin' in here?" she laughed. "I heard you quit."

He had. He found a hook up, working a gig that was commission based, but paid twice as much as what the Big B paid. He might've stayed though, had Tracy scheduled him with the cooler crew... like Dominique. She was hot. Like the sun hot. So hot he could barely look at her.

"Yo man," he grinned sheepishly at Dominique. "I'm just stopping by to say hello and ssshit—"

"—Come here child," Dominique laughed, playfully wrestling him into a headlock, twisting two knuckles into his skull. "Who do you keep calling yo man? What I tell you about that?"

Vince broke free, patting his hair. "Yo man, why you trying to mess up the curls." Really he wished it hadn't been so easy to escape that hug. That's the kind of environment he could go for. He might even forgo a few coins for that type fun.

"Don't you realize you're talking to a grown woman," Dominique laughed in her woodsy voice. "I'm not one of your boys," she said, mushing him in the head before strutting off.

Vince pulled out a comb and combed through his hair. "So, yo, yo man, what happened?"

"Aww man, nothing happened," Jimmy replied. "That girl was sick. They figured that out themselves."

"So, you didn't have nothing to do with that shit she was accusing you of?" Vince teased.

Jimmy looked over at Emma, thumbing through a fashion magazine. She wasn't kidding nobody. Clunky shoes, no name frames and unpainted nails, he bet she was a snitch. So he kept his voice low.

"Hey man, I wished you had stayed though. I wanted to get the Town Marshall for messing with Jo."

"So where's Jo now?"

"Why? You trying to hit that?"

"Aww man, no!" Vince said acting offended, doing little to hide his grin a PGA tournament could sit in.

"So, you hook up with Clarissa yet?"

"No. How about you?"

Jimmy looked back over at Emma before answering. Clarissa worked for Radio Shack. Half the guys working in the mall drooled over her, something like Dominique. Both were fast and easy.

"We're supposed to be hanging out after the mall closes—"

"—Aww DUDE," Vince howled, causing Emma to look over.

"Sssh! Sssh," Jimmy hissed. "It's a group of us," he whispered, not that it was a Corinthian secret. He just didn't want her in his business, especially after the Vita incident. Somebody was trying to set him up and it could have been her.

"Yeah…yeah…" Vince continued, his voice lowered, but not because Jimmy had hushed him. "But you do plan on hitting that, right?"

"Naa, I told you it's a group thing."

"Can I hang out with y'all then. I wanna do the group thing," he laughed.

"Would you cool it. Clarissa is cool."

"Yo man, I hear," he scoffed in a chuckle. "She be givin' Kareem rides home like every night."

Jimmy knew that. "That's because his broke ass don't have a car."

"But do you think he's hitting that?"

"I doubt it," Jimmy replied, his tone mixed with jealousy and fatigue. He cared, but didn't. Truth was, every dude cared about another man hitting something he wanted to hit. Human nature 101.

"I heard Lynne gave him a ride one night," Vince egged on. "A two-hour ride," he snickered.

"Where'd you hear that?"

"Lynne. Yo dude, she said they were lost in the woods for two WHOLE hours…" he laughed.

"She told you that?"

"Yo dude. She said that…" he said looking down, slowly raking his foot over the carpet. "Man one night I— I—"

Jimmy waited, looking at the glistening strands of hair streaking the top of Vince's head. "—What dude? You want Lynne?"

Vince looked up. "Aww no man. Yo dude, that girl ain't all there upstairs."

"How old is she anyways," Jimmy asked. This wasn't anything he cared about either. He was just trying to run out the clock.

"Yo man, she's about 40," Vince replied. "I heard she got about 4 or 5 baby daddies'."

"Lynne!?!" Jimmy belted, glancing over at Emma again. He lowered his voice. "...Wait...what?"

"Yo dude, I told you. The girl is messed up."

"Messed up," Jimmy wryly chuckled. "That girl is messed over!"

Vince laughed. "Yo man yo. I definitely wouldn't go near it."

"Well, did you ever speak to Tracy or —"

" — Aww naw dude," Vince cut in. "Tracy is the reason I left. She was trippin' about me supposedly burning the clock."

"Aww dude, but were you," Jimmy laughed. "Is that why you blew out of here?"

"Yeah, they said I was punching the clock a bunch of times, but guess what?"

"What?"

"I'm straight now, yo," he squealed laughing.

"You wild boy," Jimmy laughed too. That's why I wished you had stayed."

"Well, why don't you leave...and come hang out with me?"

"Aww man...the first of the year is right around the corner..." Jimmy sighed, running a finger over the keyboard before taking another peek at Emma. "Besides, I might get straight hours after the season."

"Yo dude, you can't be serious," Vince said, his voice elevated, reminding him to remember Emma as Jimmy took another peek that way. He held up a roll of scotch tape. "I should throw this down there at her..."

"Naw, don't do it. It's already enough going on back here."

"But come on man, why?"

The reason why was simple, and kosher, but nothing he cared to explain to Vince and his raging hormones. So he let the conversation go its natural course.

"Don't tell me you're messing with one of these airheads," Vince whispered. "You messin' with Nique?"

"Aww hell naw," Jimmy moaned. "You should've seen her the other day. She came in here in some asstight leopard pants. No panty lines man…"

"I know. I saw her yo," Vince dryly chuckled. "I saw her outside the theatre talking to some dude." But now he was really curious. Who was Jimmy dealing with that would keep his heels so dug in?

"Don't tell me it's…" and he snapped his fingers trying to recall the name of the girl with the afro.

"Hell no! Not Zoe," Jimmy blurted, looking back down at the other end of the counter. Emma was gone though, so he repeated with extra emphasis, "hell no! I like Zoe but she would have me not running, but bolting for the exit," he laughed stringing him along.

"Well, who?" Now this thing was killing Vince. He'd gone through the entire bay staff directory. Vita…Dominique…Lynne…Tracy… even Emma, and the most unlikely of all, Naomi. "Come on man, who? Who got your nuts in a sling!?!"

"Alright. Alright. Take one more guess," Jimmy teased. He'd never guess because he was on the wrong track to begin with.

Vince thought hard, one hand under his chin and facing the ceiling. And then Jimmy smirked, and threw up both hands and did a Cassius Clay dance.

"Awwwllllll dude no," he said shaking his head, and slowly backing away from the counter. "Nooooo," he dragged out again. "Nooooooooooooooooo," he howled.

Jimmy thought he'd never hear the end of Vince's howl. He heard that long yowl until he was out of the store.

Silent Night.

Lynne walked into the service bay bypassing Huong, head down, probably reading, looking as depressing as the night seemed to be headed. But Good. Last thing she needed was a chatterbox. Her silence would be golden.

"Hey, by chance did Tracy leave?" she decided to ask Huong.

"Huh?"

"Tracy…you know the girl with the white hair that puts your paycheck in mail slots…"

Huong just stared at her.

"Never mind," she scoffed. That girl was a lot like Vita. Unenlightened. Simple-minded. And majorly annoying. So she went into the office hoping the first person she didn't see was the exact person…still there, head down too, doing paperwork…. she did see!

When the door closed Tracy looked up and as soon as she parted her lips, up went Lynne's hand. "Not now…not in the mood," she said, following suit of her favorite vanguards…Zoey and Dominique.

How long did Naomi and Tracy think they could string along this charade of an investigation and no one not get tired of it. Besides Zoey, who didn't want to get caught up in mess, Dominique, who she became close with over the weeks since working together, specifically told her not to get involved.

"Well, I only need you to sign this form," Tracy said, not committed to her theatrics.

"What form?"

"Nae nominated you for seasonal employee of the week… and you won! You got the most kudos. It comes with a $100 bonus. It's a tax form," she explained with a weak smile.

New money was always good, but with the kind of day she had, made her skeptical. Her hair already a mess, she hardly needed Tracy digging deeper, getting past her roots, like beneath her scalp.

She scribbled a signature on the piece of paper and held out her hand. Tracy looked at her, and down at her wiggling fingers. "What," she asked, her lame smile doing a complete 360.

"My money. The cash…or check, give it to me," Lynne said with attitude.

"It'll be attached to your paycheck," Tracy said, swiveling in her chair and turning her back on her.

See. It was the same premonition she got when she woke up. She should have gone to her regular hairdresser, but noooo, the sistas' told her she needed to put her dollars back into the community. And what did she get for listening? A half day wasted driving to someplace in NE hell. Her sistas' said the place was all that, and the Internet backed them up. Chic, state of the art, licensed beauticians who worked on reputable people's heads. But Merry Christmas my sistas', it wasn't!

She got there to find no parking. Why hadn't they told her that when she called? Why hadn't they said she'd need a thumb, a leg, and a pair of comfortable pumps to get there?

Didn't mention none of that. She had to drive

through hell's hood to find the only parking available was on a lot Otis patrolled. At a dollar-fifty an hour, Otis would have every car on the lot towed.

But she didn't get towed, owing to the fact that she wasn't in the shop long enough. Locreesha and twenty-five crude handwritten signs posted behind 15 operators doing anything from press & perms, to weaves & haircuts, chased her the hell out of there.

Power to the people, but dag-dog-gonnit, did all they know was NO! Every sign in the shop had NO written in big fat Red chiseled markers before every rule. And every other word needed to be triple-underlined. Why not hang a sign on the door — Keep the F Out? Act like they were serving monkeys in a cage.

Wow! Like, even chickens were back there. Dead obviously; bones left discarded in a napkin on the manicurist's station. What they didn't know, and not No, was that she'd lay two bills on the table, plus pay for parking, and towing if necessary, if the service was right. And she was broke as a dog. She could've sat in her nana's kitchen for krokernall curls. That SHIT was FREE!

Now, after wasting a whole day down at the SAloon — and yes, that was saloon spelled with the double O's — she had to come into the Big B and get bamboozled by the promise of a forthcoming c-note!

"Are you okay?"

Tracy actually made the effort to turn around and ask that dumb ass question. Hell no she was NOT okay. And if she didn't want her to reach over her shoulder and rip up that piece of paper she just signed, she'd better get back to her scheming paperwork.

"Well, Emma just called out, so it's just you and Huong tonight."

Lynne stood there in a puddle of attitude. What were white girls doing with fat asses? They used to have flat asses. Somebody needed to be checking their roots, and not the ones trapped beneath the blonde straw.

"Well, what about you?" Lynne spat.

"Ugh, what do you mean?" Tracy spat back, clearly sharing the same moody puddle. "I've already worked 12 hours," she snipped. "But I'll call Faye if you two need help," she sighed...turning around to get back to her paperwork.

Her roots really needed to be checked, like the ones squeezed in those tight-ass pants. "Well do that," Lynne replied. She could talk like this because Tracy's back was up against the wall. She needed her, since it was only poor, sweet, no talking Huong out in the bay. And since that form was laying signed on her desk.

She left the office and headed for the exit, as in the Big b exit. She needed something to eat. F Tracy. She had put in 12 hours too, which didn't count the six hours she was about to put in, and practically alone, for a job that required at least four people.

Before skipping out of the bay Lynne leaned over the counter and called out to Huong sitting in a corner scribbling in a notebook. "Hey, you want something? I'm going to the Kitchen."

Huong looked up, slow-eyed and mouth hanging. "Ugh, no thank you."

'Ugh, no thank you, Lynne mimicked beneath her breath. People like Huong should come with buttons, so she could spin them around and start mashing and pushing, just to see which ones worked.

"If it gets too busy in here, call Faye. She's on page 32... I think," she tossed down to Huong.

"Okay."

'Okay,' Lynne mimicked again. Come to think of it, that girl could almost be Vita's clone. Save for the emotional mix, which Huong had none, both of them otherwise were one-word Sallys...though she wouldn't dare mess around with mashing any of Vita's buttons. She did laugh to herself however, thinking about a conversation with Vita.

"Hey Vita, we're short-staffed. Is anyone else coming in?"

Vita: 'okaaay.'

"Hey Vita, I'm taking a 40-hour break."

Vita: 'okaaay.'

"Hey Vita, Jimmy wants to fu — you…"

Vita: 'okaaay.'

Oh no wait, her mistake. That's where the burnt rubber and 500-foot skid marks would bring this jingle to a full on cold-blooded stop.

All Tracy needed to do was drop her car keys, or croak in the 4-inch heels she strutted around in, and she'd have walked right over and by her headed to the Kitchen. Tracy and Vita were a lot alike too. Hollow and nondescript. A big chunk of their soul was missing. So maybe Tracy's genes might check out after all.

The Kitchen was as empty as everywhere else. In less than five minutes she had her favorite pizza, the Hawaiian deal. Headed back to the bay she nibbled on a slice while window-shopping; the best part of her day… until she passed a window and caught a reflection of her profile — from the side view. UGH! Jeeennnnyyyy! Heellllppp Me!!!

To her relief, she passed a window filled with books. She threw the pizza slice in the box and hurried inside. Fifty books in the window, none she liked, but inside was a book lovers haven.

She picked up one book. Nope. Too long.

She touched another. Nope. Too thick.

She flipped through one. Nope. Too flimsy.

She looked over her shoulder and couldn't even pronounce the title of that book. Nope. Nope. Nope.

She looked at the wall. Nope. Covers too boring.

She squinted trying to read the back flap of one. Nope. Cost too much.

Hey! Wanda Sykes! That girl was fucking funny. 'That's Right, I Said It!' She was on her way to check out.

She returned to the bay to find Huong standing in front of a customer. Both stared at each other. That being Huong and the customer, eyeball-to-eyeball. Neither looked distressed—stupid maybe—but not distressed. She continued walking… to the office to store her purse, already laughing at some mess Wanda had written. It was only by coincidence when she happened to look up, something like fifteen minutes later.

"Is everything ok?" Like God help them all if the place caught fire and those two were the only anomalies left to help save people.

"She wants to make a credit card payment," the half mute child nonchalantly answered.

"Well go ahead and take the payment."

Lynne, like everyone else by then, knew it was outside the policy. But she wasn't arguing with no one at the beginning of the shift. No Thanks. She'd save her breath for the last customer… and that was a big iffy if.

Huong wasn't arguing either. Despite the credit card payment key no longer being an option, she somehow accepted the payment anyway.

After that, every transaction was approved. They never had to bother Faye. One minute she was up and the next Huong was up. Once she overheard a customer telling Huong that there was no price on an item, which she didn't know what Huong did, but that issue was quietly resolved as well. No hassles, no stresses.

By 10:30—it was the late season, ten days before Christmas when the store closed at eleven—she was sleepy as hell. Wanda had worn her the hell out. At some point she had to have dozed off because she woke up to find Huong sitting across from her just staring.

She swiped at her mouth. "What time is it?"

"10:55."

"Damn! You close that register and I'll get this one." What a complete fruitcake! How could she watch her sleep like that!?! The store closed at 11!

It took less than a minute for Huong to close the first register. Huong was quick. But for her it took forever. First she couldn't remember her employee number. She had to go get her purse to find it. When she returned, two customers — that being two absolute fools — were in the service bay grazing over a wall of gift-wrap at 11:15.

The dip and a twip.

The dip: "Babe, I don't know. That one looks kind of nice."

And the twip: "I don't know. I think I like that one better."

Dip: "Which one?"

Twip: "Number 4."

Dip: "Ah, I don't know. I think I like number 16."

Twip: "Yah, that one does look nice."

The twip looked at Huong, almost as if she realized for the first time Huong was standing there. "I think we'll take number sixteen," she smiled high-noon bubbly.

It was quiet for a second. Well, it was quiet save for the racket the register was putting up trying to close.

"Ugh, they want number sixteen," Huong said after a while, knowing the last register had closed and there was no way to complete the transaction.

Lynne didn't turn around. Her head was nestled in the crook of her arm waiting on Harold, the man she had put on hold, to waltz back into her life without having to go begging for him to come back.

She was in a dream…waiting…when she heard toenails clicking over linoleum. She fought with her feet, pushing layers of comforter onto a floor covered with straw, scrambling to get up, and get moving. "Oh, man!" She had to get the heck out of the store. Two Dobermans were coming after her.

Spitting out straws and feathers, Huong's voice, soft as it was, was all that saved her. For the second time Huong repeated, "uh, they want number 16."

Lynne, still trying to lift her head out of the crook of her arm, had to use two hands to open an envelope and stuff the transaction papers inside. So, there was no way she could focus on hearing Huong.

When she finally got the 'closing envelope' ready to be dropped in the night box, again...this time for the third time, Huong repeated herself. Lynne looked over and saw the customers, the dip and twip, staring at her ...as if she was the crazy one.

"Oh no they don't," she told Huong. "They want a box and a bow!"

'*Come sifting in here like they don't know the store closed thirty minutes ago,*' Lynne muttered. People had lost their minds!

A box and bow handed to the dip and twip, they, she and Huong, deposited the envelopes and headed to the office to retrieve their coats.

"Girl, you did a marvelous job tonight," Lynne praised little cute Huong. "Thank you so much!"

She didn't know what she would've done without that girl. She definitely wasn't the ditz she originally thought.

Chirpy and now wide awake, Lynne skipped on Huong's heels into the office to retrieve their coats.

"Oops... you dropped something," "Lynne said, bending down and retrieving a small yellow post-it-note that had fallen from something Huong was carrying.

Huong stopped short in front of her and turned around. "Huh?"

Who's the Boss?

BEATRICE

"I thought we already did Black Friday? Didn't Black Friday pass like two Friday's ago?"

"Oh, you didn't get the memo? Black Friday now falls on every day that ends in 'y'…"

"Umm…" Naomi stood in the center of the office scratching her head, holding another note for Jimmy. "Well all I know, is someone really loves our choir boy."

"Yeah, well he is a really sweet guy."

"That's what boils me over!"

"Jimmy being sweet boils you over?"

"No!" Naomi scoffed. "Hue and his stoking coals pandering to fear mongering!"

Beatrice let loose one of her gummy grins, a too broad of a grin she often tried to conceal by covering her mouth. It was a habit that followed her from childhood; getting teased for smiling like a horse. "Gotta admit, though," she said with a hand covering her mouth. "His comment box did turn up some good scoops."

Naomi rolled her eyes. "Yeah right! Like Lynne really deserved a hundred bucks," she scoffed. "Ask me I'd say we got robbed!"

Beatrice brought her bony fingers back up to her lips to mask her bucking giggle. "Agh yeah, but then it's better than tossing a whole carton of eggs because of one rotten egg."

Of course Bea had a point, why she held a major position on the executive team, and why she and Naomi were close. Still, Hue had a cockeyed messaging problem she felt necessary to dwell on. "Well, so long as you also believe in chickens coming home to roost!"

"Girl, it's only a week or so left. All of them will be out of here, and then the next batch will come in."

"You're wrong there," Naomi huffed relieved. "There'll be no next for me!" She shuttered, moving on to continue describing Hue's sub-zero memos.

Beatrice let loose another gummy laugh. "Girl, no one is paying them memos any attention."

"I am!" Naomi huffed.

"Everything he sends is so downright negative," she quipped. "No greeting whatsoever! He just dives straight into the muck and keeps digging! Wouldn't surprise me if that man had no pulse. You should see me! I have to put on a coat, hat and gloves just to read them!"

Beatrice quietly agreed. "You know Nae, I almost called headquarters on him," she sighed. "He had the nerve to think I'd be okay with him trying to secretly put cameras in the restrooms!"

"He tried to do what," Naomi gasped.

"Girl, yes..." Beatrice went on, eyes popped open and teeth candidly exposed. "All I could picture was his eyes watching my behind using the toilet!"

Naomi shook her head. What a perverted creep.

"Yeah, Helga had been complaining about thefts in lingerie...saying because her department was right next to the restrooms, was why her loss prevention reports were so high."

"And so, that was his solution," Naomi said in a fog trying to erase the visual of Beatrice's behind.

"Yeah, that WAS his solution," Beatrice said with extra emphasis on the word was. Not no more—"

—The office door swung open and in charged Nadine...shaking and carrying on about something a customer wanted to return that was outside store policy.

"Nadine, just give it to her," Naomi said, eager to get back to her conversation.

"No! This is fraud! I know fraud when I see it," Nadine argued, involuntarily rattling and quivering. She rarely gave in. For her, the rule was the rule, and policy the policy. No exceptions. She was unbendable. No sirree bob. Not this time, the last time or the next time. No one got over on her.

"Here, bring it here. Let me see," Naomi huffed. Geez, she loved Nadine like a sister, but sometimes the woman was a good-sized pain in the rear.

Hands quivering Nadine showed Naomi the well-worn bra. "Nae, look right here. Anybody can see these are deodorant stains. She didn't even have the decency to wash it!"

"What did she say was wrong with it?"

Either Nadine hadn't asked, or hadn't taken the time to listen. "It's a manufacture defect," she exclaimed. "I told her she needs to contact Bali! That's whose problem it is!"

"Nadine, just ask her what's wrong with the thing," Naomi sighed, unfolding the bra and holding it up. "Geez..." her eyes stretched out. "Bea... you wanna share a bra?"

Hand to mouth Beatrice shook her head.

"Dine, first tell the customer we will refund her money," Naomi said, taking her time to explain things. "Then give her the money," she added.

Nadine wasn't happy. Naomi was her Shero, but be damned if this shady customer should be allowed to get over. "...Ugh, these people are incredible," Nadine muttered, head quivering as she left the office.

Naomi looked over at Beatrice. "See. What I tell you? Hue did that to her. Got my girl so afraid she can't even think straight," she wryly chuckled. "It isn't even her money."

"Nae, I'm so sorry to have to tell you this, but I think your girl was born that way."

"Well at least she's not like that bozo downstairs… selling books out of housewares when we don't sell books anywhere in the store!"

"Yeah well, then we might want to be grateful she can't write because I'm sure she would try!"

"Oh my gosh Bea, sometimes Dine really mystifies me," she sighed. "The other day I specifically told her to go grab us some blank invoices. A simple request. I mean, my dog knows how to fetch what I want, and he is a really dumb dog," she chuckled. "But you know what she did?"

Beatrice shrugged, exposing the gums some. "Well, she didn't come see me so…"

"…So the next day I ask where are the invoices, and oh, you're gonna love this one. …She says, 'Office Depot was all out.'"

Beatrice let the gums go wild. She burst out laughing so loud she had to cover her mouth, this time to muffle her sound. "No! Stop lying on our girl!"

"No lie. I kid you not. I'm telling you. It's all Hue's fault. He's screwing with my girls. His fixation on security is doing this!"

"Yeah well, putting cameras in the bathrooms is where I draw my line! That has to be a major violation of some privacy law."

"Well my line is him scheduling these ridiculous mandatory meetings, harassing and riling up my girls, and then leaving the country to tour the globe!"

"…And bringing back junk," Beatrice sneered." Sophia in purchasing quit last week. She said we've been sending out top quality designs, and they send us back crepe paper. Those overseas manufacturers are robbing us blind! All over the globe, they hate our guts!"

"...Umm," Naomi hummed. "...And what does the genius do? Invest billions in new computers to ring that mess up to make sure no one's stealing," she wryly laughed. "What a joke," she sarcastically quipped. "I'm telling you. It's already backfiring. Our directors better jump on this and get them a new store exec!"

"Well, maybe it might excite you if you know how much Hue really likes Vita."

Naomi's mouth dropped. "Hue likes who!?!"

"Vita," Beatrice repeated. "He's really pissed about her resignation."

"...Umm, well this should get interesting because he also is heavily invested in Jimmy too."

"Follow the money," Beatrice sang.

"I am," Naomi quipped back. "But I'm wondering what's next?"

"Have you considered giving blood," Beatrice joked.

"I seriously doubt someone wants my blood," Naomi ruefully replied. "My pressure is way too high!"

Beatrice's bulky eyes flashed once, opening wide and getting stuck open. "You know what!? Why don't we have Marjorie handle orientations for a while...just until the Christmas rush is over?"

"That's a good idea," Naomi said perking up. "I'm sure I won't have to break her arm to convince her. She's been so eager to run a show."

"Great. I'm just trying to get you closer to your retirement date," she chuckled.

"Well...just remember, I don't need an alcoholic, a devil worshipper, or thieves by the droves!"

Beatrice laughed out loud. "Well, if we survived a 5% increase in profit margins against a 66.75% loss in actual revenue, resulting in Forbes taking us off the list, then you can deal with a pirate for a few months!"

"Wait," Naomi mused, leaning back in her chair. "Forbes really took us off the list!?!" She laughed. "I'm canceling my subscription!"

"Good luck with that," Beatrice laughed too. "Check Nas? Forbes is no longer on it!"

"God help us..." Naomi sighed.

No Returns.

Leaning over Nadine's shoulder Dominique howled, "damn Dine! How much more sugar do you need?" She might as well have drank a bottle of syrup, laughed the fizzing harlot in her quivering coworker's ear.

"…But my blood sugar is low," Nadine replied, her voice and hands shaking. "I'll get faint and pass out if I don't," she explained.

"Well damn, either way you're about to drop out on us," Dominique said, leaving the office to join Lynne, Jimmy and Kareem in the bay.

Now Nadine was a real shaking mess. Doctors had been telling her for the longest she was going to die if she didn't get her blood sugar levels in check, and now here Dominique confirmed her worst fear.

Oh Man! She meant to scoop up another spoonful of sugar, but instead knocked over the cup. If everyone would stop interrupting her and leave her the hell alone she could finish updating Naomi on all that went down that day. Out of everyone, to include Tracy and especially Naomi, she had taken the inquiries to the next level…serious as a heart attack.

She wiped up the spill, knocking over a cup of pencils and almost tripping in the process over the chair. Thirteen incoming calls later, spending five minutes per call easily, she finally sat down and pecked out more thoughts to add to her statement. Never mind the fact that the statements had been turned in. She liked the idea of keeping tabs on happenings in the bay.

But half her shift was over, and another call was coming in. She hopped up from the chair, slapped the desk hard and dashed off for the bay. "Dammit, you guys need to answer the phones. They're supposed to be answered by the third ring," she spewed, fluid from her mouth flying in various directions she was so angry.

For as off-balanced as she appeared, Nadine knew the customer service handbook back and forth. It was her job to answer the phone, ONLY IF, the call was not answered by the third ring. But when she ran into the bay, all four associates were sitting on wedding crates slacking off. The phones were still ringing and no one bothered to move.

But it was hard to read Nadine. She looked past the point of being concerned about ringing phones. So they stared, thinking about the possibility of running for their life.

"What are you looking at," she screamed. "The phone is ringing!" And she hurried over to the counter and picked up the receiver. "Hello, Hello," she yelled into the phone.

"We're open til' midnight," she yelled at the caller. "Next time press 2 and the automated voice will tell you the hours," she added. "Huh?" She covered one ear, struggling to hear the caller over the overhead speakers playing 'Carol of the Bells'.

"Huh," she grumbled. "Well...we don't provide directions. I suggest you get a map. You can find them in grocery stores or bookstores. They usually cost about—huh? —Hello! Hello!"

She slammed the receiver on the cradle and spun around to address the group still huddled together staring at her. "I'm sorry! I have to report this! Dominique you should—"

—BRRRNG! BRRRNG! Again no one moved... but Nadine. She snatched the receiver off the cradle and starting yelling in it again. Moving papers and materials aside Nadine started with 'goshes' and 'shucks' and 'oh shoots'. "Hold on please," she huffed, tossing the phone over her shoulder.

"Dominique, you need to take this call. The customer needs to know where to return a table she bought from housewares. No one downstairs is answering the phone!"

Dominique didn't speak. She walked over and took the call, remembering what happened the last time she and Tracy were gently teasing her about the way she counted nickels in twosies. It meant nothing. At least not to them. It was just a little comical she counted like few others her age did. Next thing they knew, Nadine was on the floor pitching a fit like a two-year old. Scared them to death. They thought she was having a seizure.

Nadine stormed back to the office, returning to the manuscript she was working on, not among her paid duties, but strictly on her own volition. She typed words and phrases like; not listening. Slacking. Missing calls. Drinks on counter. She was about to add another infraction but couldn't find the proper word.

Gosh... it was on the tip of her tongue too... rhymed with procrastinate.

The office door opened and in walked Zoey singing, "hello," ready to begin her shift. She moved around Nadine, about to hang her coat when Nadine sprang from her chair.

"I can't do this! I can't do this!" Nadine cried. During the springy lift off she hit her knee on an open drawer, so she was hopping and crying.

Zoey having worked with Nadine before, tried to ignore her. Everybody who had worked wih Nadine before avoided antagonizing her. But it was challenging. Anything was liable to set the woman off.

"Someone needs to get maintenance up here to do something about these drawers," she muttered, hopping on one foot and dabbing her bleeding knee. "That's exactly why companies are always getting sued," she claimed, tossing the soiled bloodied tissue in the trash.

Yuck. Disgusting. Zoey had her own unique set of issues. She was a clean freak. So she skirted around Nadine, grabbing a can of Lysol, careful not to touch anything on her way out.

That's when it happened; the clicking inside her head she described as white noise. "What are you doing in here," she shouted at Zoey. "You're not scheduled tonight! We don't need you!"

Zoey frowned, and doubled back to check the schedule. Nadine was a little fragmented, but quite a few times she'd been right. Actually, technically she was mostly right. But few followed rulebooks as closely as she did.

But nope. That time she was wrong. Right there in black and white, hanging on the wall for all to see, Tracy's heavy hand edit had inserted her name on the schedule. Nadine saw it too. So she picked up a red marker and promptly drew a long litigious thick line through her name.

"Naomi doesn't need any more seasonal help. I heard her say it," Nadine revealed. "She's tired of all the attitudes and problems in here."

Hesitant about what to do next Zoey stood by the white board for a sec, tapping the back of her neck. It became a truth or dare moment. Truth was, crazy people were scary. And dare; Somebody was paying for the half a tank of gas she just burned up getting to work, if the crazy woman got her sent home.

Saved by the bell Dominique walked in. It was about to get busy out there and she wanted to swing by Slades for a cigarette and a 'pick me up' drink.

"What's going on? What's taking you so long..." she started, halted by the look on Zoey's face.

Lynne appeared behind her. The trip required the three of them. But bouncing into the off-colored vibe in the office wiped the grin off her face too.

"First I got to figure out if I'm on the schedule today," Zoey spoke up.

"But didn't Tra—"

—Dominique didn't finish before Fritz literally leaped to her chair and started punching the keyboard. The three of them watched from behind a shock of frizzy red hair and flattened-torpedoed head wobbling on a pencil neck, rambling a series of hushed quips at the computer and into the phone interchangeably.

"—no, not that one. The other one. I don't—" she stood up and leaned over the desk, squinting to read the calendar where Tracy made her heavily edited notations in green marker.

Meanwhile Jimmy entered the office. He needed Dominique's stamp of approval for a customer he was helping, but got caught up in the standstill surrounding Nadine's urgent whispering into the phone.

"Huh? No, I thought—Huh? No but after— No! Absolutely not! That's not what I said. I said—Huh? I'm trying to, but—okay…okay…un huh…okay."

The call ended and Nadine coolly hung up the phone. It took her a while before she turned around. About 15 seconds or so; a long time to be staring at the back of someone's head.

Turned out, her Shero let her down...again. This kind of happened a lot. Naomi wasn't always able to go by the rulebook Nadine liked to follow. So she was mistaken. Tracy had scheduled Zoey. They might even need more help. It was supposed to be a busy night.

Nadine was done. Officially done. These people were slacking and not answering phones, and Tracy was wrong to mark over the schedule. Anyone could have made that edit. The proper procedure was to print a new schedule!

The constant unanswered ringing phones, her Shero not backing her up, at least twice in the past few days...and on major issues, plus she bumped her knee...twice too, and really badly, along with the knocking over cups and spillage she had to wipe up...it was all too much. She completely lost her train of thought. Holy smoke! She flipped out!

Nadine fell to the floor and commenced kicking and screaming, shaking her head from side to side like asylum patients seen in characters...like in The Exorcist.

Dominique called Faye. Beatrice wasn't in. "We got a code nuts down here. Might need an ambulance."

The code wasn't a joke. It had been used before. Those in the exec office knew the nuts code. Nadine was the only employee, out of over 10,000 people regularly employed at the Big B, permitted to use that code more than once.

Faye showed up and knelt over Nadine. "Come on, Dine...it's okay. Get up. You don't want to end up in the hospital."

Just like that Nadine got better. Slowly she sat up, and then stood up, and everyone but her and Faye filed out of the office.

"Damn," Kareem scoffed. "We could never get away with no bullshit like that!"

"Don't try it," Lynne muttered. "You'll never see your family again..."

"That shit is messed up," Kareem carried on. He knew Nadine had issues, everyone working in the bay did. Even those who didn't work in the bay detected this. But he had never seen this level of crazy. He couldn't understand why Jordana got the hate, but not this chick!

"Leave it alone," Zoey muttered to Kareem. "It's not worth it. You know the deal..."

A few minutes later after Zoey, Dominique and Lynne left out to pick up grub, a customer walked into the bay demanding to speak to a manager. Jimmy looked around, not because he was powerless to deal with whatever the situation, but because the office door opened. Nadine, draped around Faye's shoulder, limped out of the bay, prompting Kareem to speak up.

"Don't look over here chief," he wryly chuckled. "Look over there," he nodded in front of them. "That's your manager right there getting carried away."

Funny Boy.

SAMMY

~~

They needed a drink! They'd been half discussing it all night between customers. So when Sammy came through, redeeming a handful of kudos, and offered to buy them all a round of drinks, they accepted.

Lynne and Zoey left their vehicles in Big B's parking lot and all six of them hopped in Sammy's Tahoe and headed for Georgetown.

"My guy owns a bar out there...well, it's a bar and restaurant," Sammy said. "So—"

"—Good! 'Cause I'm hungry," Zoey groaned.

"Girl...when you not hungry?"

"Boy, you don't know me and my eating habits," Zoey snapped back.

"I don't have to," Sammy laughed. "Them hips telling on you!"

Those two, Sammy and Zoey, were always going at it, and both claimed not to be the other's type. Sammy was part Somoan, and Zoey all black.

Turned out the restaurant Sammy's guy owned was packed, and he couldn't be reached.

"His guy..." Zoey muttered to Dominique.

But Sammy did manage to get a table for six across the street, and Zoey stopped groaning. "Girl, you got to know people to get a table in here," he bragged. "You can't just walk up in restaurants out here and without reservations get a table for five people and one hooch," he laughed loud.

"Who you callin' a hooch," Zoey fussed. "I thought you knew somebody at the other spot. The only reason they probably let us in here is because everybody but you know not to eat here!"

"Alright now y'all, let's leave work on Tyson's Corner," Dominique piped in. "Let's try to enjoy this..."

"Yeah, cuz first of all I didn't say I was feedin' nobody! I said one drink!"

"Aww...y'all alright. I'll take care of it," Jimmy spoke up.

"Damn kid. Alright then...I already know what I want," Sammy chuckled.

"Thank you Jimmy," Zoey said rolling her eyes at Sammy. Contrary to the way they treated each other, she didn't have no hate for him though. They always tangled. Like two pups sniffing each other.

"Well, I'm getting the Battle Creek Oysters," Dominique said, squirming in her chair, licking and popping her lips. She was all bubbles and holiday happy. From the natural glitter in her hair, the result of too much coloring, to the jewels swinging around both wrists and four fingers, she was all sparkles.

"Woman, your mother must have been addicted to caffeine when she carried you," Sammy teased.

"Ha-ha. Funny! My mother actually tried to abort me. Didn't think she could feed another mouth," Dominique giggled, moving aside as their waitress poured water in her glass. "I was the tenth kid, yep, she carried around sacks of potatoes, hung curtains, drank like a fish and ran ten miles a day but nothing she did made me come out."

"DAYAM! Somebody probably glad she failed," Sammy teased.

"Yeah I bet," Jimmy slid in, in a mutter. Kareem, who'd been holding a side chat with Zoey over the menu cut an eye over to Jimmy. He didn't notice, and neither did Sammy. Actually, no one noticed the eye cut.

"I think we would have some cute kids… what do you think?" Sammy asked Dominique, oogling her over the rim of his eyeglasses.

Dominique fanned him away. She wasn't finished. "…I was born breeched you know. That's because I was in there hanging on!"

Laughter circled the table on that one, all except for Zoey. "You lucky she wasn't carrying you today," she murmured, staring at a menu. "That morning after pill would have taken care of your ass."

"Awww man, girl! Where's the love?" Sammy lightly tapped Zoey on the arm. "Don't hate, there's enough of me to go around." He leaned into her ear. "When I'm around you, the earth moves," he teased.

"Will you back up! Your big head is blockin' my light." And she popped him on the forehead with the menu. "I got your movin' earth…" she teased giving him another eyeroll.

Aside from ducking Zoey's swing, Sammy's smile grew wide. "I'ma big boy. You don't think I can handle your earthquake. But I used to live in Cali. I survived the Loma Prieta shake. Seven point one!" he drooled.

"Six point nine. Read your history."

"How would you know Ms. Eye-Witness? I was there."

"Umm um… measure that with your little shoe horn?" — Zoey again.

More laughter. The vibe around the table was good…jovial and genuine. Even Kareem, who came across a little stiff, cracked a smile.

"So who's looking up your skirt?" Sammy asked Lynne. He heard rumors about the woods incident and wanted to check her pulse in front of everyone.

Lynne, though, glanced at Kareem. "It is none of your business," she replied. "But if you must know, I don't wear skirts," she extended her hand and batted her eyes. "I now wear Vera."

Jimmy instantly started choking, water going down the wrong pipe. And Sammy started howling, "Oh, O, O, Ohhh," he laughed fist bumping his mouth. "So that's it!"

Lynne looked around the table confused. No one saw the tiny stone on her finger. Zoey had to clue her in. "Is that Vera as in Tiffany's, or Vera as in the rainbow?"

She still didn't get it. Dominique had to draw her a picture. "Is Vera a man or a woman?"

"Ugh! What!?! I don't—"

"—Let it go," Zoey said. "It's okay. We know."

Kareem didn't appear thrilled. He was showing a few teeth, but he wasn't smiling. All he wanted to know was what was the deal with the 'cray-cray' chick. "Y'all think they gonna cut her loose too?"

"Who? Nadine?"

"You answered your own question. She crazy. So, no," Zoey flatly answered.

"Look, we all have our bad days and good days. Sometimes—"

"—Aww naw," Kareem said vigorously shaking his head. "No black person could ever get away with the crap she pulls."

Lynne held her breath, and Zoey exhaled and smiled. "Yeah, that don't fly for us so-called angry black women. They're still looking for trees to hang us—"

"—Wait…whaaaddt," Sammy cut in. "Hang on. This ain't Woolworth's 63," and he tapped the arm of the waitress who reached him to take his order.

"…Ugh, I'm going to go ahead and order for my

friend in honor of freedom seekers in 1963," he said clearing his throat. "Now her people survived," he said gesturing towards Zoey, "but I think she'd be honored if one of your chefs could whip up a batch of collards and a couple of hog maws."

The waitress didn't even crack a smile. She stared down on the top of Sammy's head as if she wanted to take it off and hurl it out the door.

"By the way," he added, pinky extended, a hair away from touching the girl, wearing a gorgeous round cut serious baguette full of diamonds on the pinky. "How are you today? Are you seeking freedom too?"

Lynne squealed, loud. Kareem did not.

Zoey looked over at Lynne, long tongue sticking out and squealing. "What are you laughing at? It wasn't but two seconds ago we thought your face was gonna drag the table cloth on out the door."

"I'll have the Calamari—" Jimmy started before he was interrupted.

"—Say listen," Sammy butted in… tapping the waitress on the arm with that pinky. "Did you get those greens? I didn't see you writing."

Abruptly the waitress turned and walked away. She tucked her little pad in a hip pocket and scurried off.

Slowly Lynne closed her mouth. "Ooo…what happened? Where'd our waitress go?"

"See, that's what he gets for taking a joke too far," Zoey said.

"Aww, she didn't have to be like that," Jimmy said. "He was only kidding. I hate stuck up women like that."

Dominique looked over at Sammy and playfully slapped him. "Why'd you run off our waitress? Lean over. Let me smell your breath!"

"What he needs examined is his brain," Zoey muttered, not indebted to Sammy's antics.

"Wanna take me home and—"

"—Aww dude, it looks like she's bringing over a manager," Jimmy said holding a menu up to his face.

"But what? What I do?" Sammy asked holding a hand up to his chest, showing off the jewel, and a comically obtuse expression.

"Ut…roll back the tapes," Lynn muttered fingering a tress of hair. "Like how many trials have we've seen played out on CNN?"

The manager wasted no time explaining how Clyde's reserved the right to refuse service to whoever acted an ass. "Now, I'm sending another waiter over, but if there's still a problem at this table I'ma have to ask you all to leave," said the big bear, surveying each of their faces.

Sammy turned up the charm, apologizing and loading up on the sirs.

"Sir, I simply asked the young lady if we could get my friend a special order because she's on a diet," he said, his hand wavering towards Zoey's midsection. Of course her batting him away didn't help his cause.

"I didn't mean to offend the lady," he continued, bowing towards the waitress. "Miss, please accept my apology. I didn't mean to offend you."

The waitress, same withdrawn expression, said absolutely nothing. But the big bear followed up for her though. "We only serve what's on the menu. If you want something else, then you need to go someplace else."

…And POOF!—they were gone.

Sammy stayed quiet for a second, looking pie-faced until Lynne stood up. "F— this! You think I'ma eat here after that speech!"

Zoey looked up. "Girl, sit your bony ass down. You the main one who needs to eat!"

"Yeah, they aren't going to mess with your food," Dominique plowed. "If they mess with anyone's food, it'll be Sammy's!"

Not funny. No one laughed. Not even Sammy.

"Merry Christmas funny boy," Zoey teased in one of her dry voices. "They got some bread sticks on the menu. At least you'll know what's in it."

"Aww...people are so touchy nowadays," Jimmy said. "She's messing with her tip."

"Ah dude, it's cool. I got it," Sammy said less the joking tone. "Nobody's night gettin' messed up here."

Kareem shook his head...in the negative. "But brother, it's not always about money. It's about respect," he said talking like a wanna be scholar, but looking like Urkel's big brother.

Sammy, and especially Jimmy, stared hard. Both looked like they wanted to laugh...or smack him. Fact was, neither were his brother, in any interpretation; in either by race, class, culture, hobbies, DNA...nothing. They didn't even care for him. As evidenced. He was far too uptight.

"I fail to see where you're going," Jimmy replied.

"Where I'm going is to episodes like that one that happened in the office tonight," Kareem said. "Some of us get away with doing and saying whatever we want to others, while others are supposed to accept it and take it as all fun and games..."

"Whoa dude," Sammy interjected. "What's up?"

"Yeah, come on. Tiz the season," Dominique said, raising a glass of water to toast air, which was funky at the moment. "We're supposed to be having fun," she snickered, knowing just what was up with Kareem.

"Well, where do I fit in this WE—"

"—Alright! Look!" Zoey cut in, throwing up the hands. "I get it K—, but in a few days most of us sittin' around this table right now won't be there, so let that woman eat! This is God's show. Besides, this knuckle head over here," and she lightly tapped Sammy upside his head, "...don't even know what you're talking about...and really, neither do you," she added.

Kareem chuckled and tried to grin off his extra.

Only Zoey could handle her people. During the knicker and petticoat days, she would've been like Harriet, not crying in the fields talking about the mean master and how he won't set her free!

"Girl, you got your preacher's license?"

"Boy hush," she chuckled waving Sammy off. "I thought you knew people!"

"Apparently not like you. I only deal with earth people...you know...regular humans, not all them devils and demons and whatnot!"

Zoey waved Sammy off. The man came with an inbuilt battery. He didn't need wending up.

"Hey, hey," he continued teasing, tapping Zoey with the pinky finger. "Can I meet one of your demons..."

"...Boy, I swear! — Touch me again and I promise you'll draw back a nub!"

"Alright... chill y'all. Here comes waiter number two," Jimmy whispered.

"Okay, so who asked for the greens? I got my boy out back cutting up leaves," the waiter laughed. "...He can boil 'em, fry 'em, or charbroil 'em if you want..."

Lynne, sitting next to Kareem, used this moment to lightly stroke his hand. "It's alright. It's cool. I get it too. It should be fairness across the board!"

Kareem smiled. Faintly. She hardly got it, falling right back into Sammy's mouth!

"...Now, they cuttin' off them stems, right? Can't be no stems on them greens..."

And there was Lynne doubled over laughing, though when the waiter came to her and asked what she wanted, she got serious. "No thanks," she replied. "I just came for the drinks!"

Dominique leaned across Kareem to whisper at Lynne. "They can spike your drink too, you know."

Kareem hopped up. "Look, I'ma grab a cab. I'll catch y'all later. I gotta get home."

His exit was noticeable, though Sammy stayed

on his roll. "Now, this is my friend," he said to the waiter about to take Zoey's order. "...She's the one celebrating her ancestors who were in the 63 Freedom riots," he went on, ducking Zoey who tried to bop him in the face with the menu.

"Sir, I'll have the Shanghai Black Angus—"

"—Shank who?" Sammy yelped, adjusting his glasses to revisit the menu. "Woman, where do you see that on this menu," he asked pulling the menu close to his face. "...That ain't nowhere on this menu." He put down the menu. "Woman, we got to get you out the hood... talking about shankin' people and whatnot..."

"Let it go Sammy. It's not funny no more," Lynne said pouting, sad about Kareem's abrupt departure.

"Oh come ooonnnn," Dominique moaned. "This is the holiday! Everybody let it go! I mean let it go! Let's laugh a little."

"Agreed," Sammy said, not that he was having problems keeping the humor-mill rolling. "Hey sir," he said, calling back the waiter headed to the kitchen. "Now don't let us down. Make sure y'all cut them stems off the greens. 'Cause that's important. Can't no stems be on them greens."

"Sure thing hot shot," the waiter chuckled, given Sammy a little fist bump. "We gonna hook y'all up!"

"Your mother must've nursed you too long," Zoey said after the waiter moved on.

"Ugh no, that would be incorrect. My second grade teacher holds that record."

Dominique and Jimmy doubled over laughing. A third of Jimmy's drink was on the table.

"But now, you can try to break that record," he teased. "I don't mind a demon mommy."

"Boy, you should be a comedian," Jimmy laughed slapping the table.

"Naa, I'ma shoe salesman," he said. "Besides, I don't have no material to make black people laugh." He turned back to Zoey. "Do you know what would make y'all less angry and more …like laughable."

"Maybe slowly hanging yourself," Zoey replied, that time sending Lynne into hysterics.

"Take that—IN YOUR FACE," Dominique teased Sammy. "Lynne's laughing. Now what!?!"

"Well, Lynne ain't black!"

"WHADT—" shrieked Lynne.

"—All right, where you from," Sammy asked.

"I'm from Maryland, right here!"

"But we're NOT in Maryland darling," Sammy chuckled. "Do you need more time to think about this?"

"Oh shut up," Lynne said waving him off. "My father is black, so I'm black! And that's FACT!!!"

"No, no, no…" Sammy said wagging his finger. "That's not fact. Let's hear it. Give it up…" he added, wiggling his fingers.

"Give what up," Lynne scoffed.

"Well, let's take Zoe—"

"—Ut, wouldn't go there," Zoey warned. "Don't say it. I will jolly up your night and call your wife!"

"His wife," shrieked Lynne, Dominique and Jimmy simultaneously.

"Yes, his wife. Funny boy is married! Ain't that a hoot FUNNY BOY!?! "

No Ask, No Matcha.

~~

HUONG
~~

They never asked her. And she was in plain view. She could get away with murder, because everyone walked around her. They never ever asked her.

It was how she got away with lots when she first came to America. She wasn't raised a thief, but in the U.S. there were no fields to search for edible veggies, or trees to climb for fresh fruit, or rivers to gorge for fish, or baths, or anything.

But she was always so hungry, why she stole her classmate's lunch, and sometimes money from their backpacks and often lifted cash out of teacher's purses. A few times she took the whole purse. Like once she stole a laptop, right out of a public library. And she stole lots of books from libraries too. She even walked out of stores, like AT&T and Verizon, and Forever Young, and Blockbuster, and any store that looked easy to get away with phones and cute costume jewelry and movies. She probably could've robbed a bank and gotten away with that too, because no one ever suspected her. Nobody ever asked her a thing. They moved around her as if she was invisible.

Her parents would die of humiliation if they knew. They worked hard to take care of her and her siblings. But then it was their fault, sense they hoped and prayed she, or at least one of her sisters married a guy that was young...and handsome...and nice...and smart ...and doctor worthy and wealthy... someone like...aka Jimmy Chen.

Jimmy was so fine in Huong's eyes that it was her number two reason that she really missed working with the two fired black ladies. It was never a dull night when they were there. Ghetto one, she called her, liked to tease her. She called her 'stupid girl,' and mocked the way she talked. Her favorite slurs was, "Fact Book senh tay dey says they be da smartest people."

She knew they were talking about her. But she didn't mind. Not even when they talked about her, right in her face, acting like she didn't understand English... or just plain wasn't there.

"Move child! Move!" That was how they got her to step aside. Once she flat out told them, "I'm not from China, I'm from Vietnam!"

Of course they laughed and ignored her. "Umm hmm. Same ting. Asians senh tay no phase me," Ghetto one would say.

And yet, the real reason she really, really missed Ghetto one, aside from watching her be mad at Marjorie, was she made her nights in the bay go super fast watching Jimmy, watch her.

He didn't know it but she had major eyes for him, and on him, why when she walked in the bay and saw him in there, and no Jo-Jo, her knees buckled and she froze.

DUN, Dun, dun... the pressure multiplied when there was no Jo-Jo. She was more invisible then. She could hide behind Jo-Jo's antics...or her big butt.

"Umm, 'cuse me," Zoe fussed, pushing her aside wielding Lysol and a hand full of paper towels.

So she stepped aside and watched Zoey's dark wrinkled hands, with a ring on each finger, including the thumbs, and bangles jingling around her wrist, wipe down the counter like her mother washed windows.

"Move child! Back up!"

So she moved further aside, to the holding bay, where she planned to hide all night. It was going to be difficult to be in his midst with so many witnesses.

All hands on deck had been scheduled this night. The fat jolly fake Zeus Americans adored, in a few days would be flying over houses and twisting his big fat butt down chimneys. There were so many customers it looked like Black Sabbath was about to perform.

Unlike slower nights however, she wasn't sitting in the holding bay. She was back there catching boxes Zoey, Lynne, Dominique and others threw at her, Chung Kung Fu style. Nadine was back there too, as usual struggling to keep up. For every thirty gifts she did, Nadine barely finished one. But at least her vibrating kept her zen.

At one point, during a lull in wrapping gifts, due to her wrapping them so fast, and while Nadine was on break, Tracy poked her head in the back. "What's going on back here," she asked. "It's busy out there. We need all hands on deck!"

But there also was no room out there. It was all elbows in the bay. Plus Jimmy was out there! Good thing Lynne heard Tracy. "Don't worry about her," she said after Tracy returned to the office. "She can't fire nobody, even if she had the power."

An hour later the gift boxes started piling up, and there was no Nadine, not that she was much help. Back in her rhythm she got to fantasizing again…about her and Jimmy. She pictured them looking deeply into each other's eyes, and holding hands, and kissing, and… Zoey tossed a few more boxes at her. "Do these next…in number 22. The customer is waiting."

This meant the customer didn't want to do a little shopping and come back later. So she wrapped the gifts, in under 3 minutes, and took them to Zoey. Surprising, it was so busy Tracy called in for even more reinforcement. She called Marjorie. Not good.

She overheard Marjorie in a word brawl with two Slavic women. She only assumed they were Slavic when she caught sight of a Rolly-Polly doll hanging from one of the women's key ring. It was the same Rolly-Polly doll Mrs. Truchet, one of her teachers in Hanoi used to wear in her ears. Her mother hated the teacher. 'Slavic ÇÒ mÃt dåy'! her mother used to curse. In fluent Viet language she would add, "what does she have we don't have, but to teach our children immoral greedy ways." Her mother said other things too, what she always associated with the Rolly-Polly doll.

"Ma'am these went off sale last week and we're no longer accepting rainchecks," the Town Marshall said in one of her familiar bossy dress downs.

"No. No," the Slavic women cried together, like synchronized pillarists, albeit shedding no tears and using the word no ad nauseam. They didn't mean no, as in 'NO' STOP! Their no's meant no as in this is beautiful.

The major problem was the women talking at the same time in this heavy vroom, vroom modulation, not speaking English well and rambling on different channels throughout their over usage of no's.

Their velvety phonetic passion, so reminiscent of Vita who never listened, also reminded her of how close she came to having Jimmy all to herself...if just for a lousy moment. If only Jimmy had bothered to call the number. If only any of them had bothered to verify the number! What a terrible missed opportunity.

"We like, we like," both vroom, man daram miravam, vroom, vroom women insisted. And then came the "pah-va-vroosta, no, yah, vroom, vroom," which they repeated more than their echoing off key no's.

Town Marshall understood none of it though. She just kept sighing and shifting her weight from one leg to the other saying she couldn't do it.

The women started getting angry. What did she mean she wouldn't take their money? Their money was good. They were holding good American dollars. They stopped trying to speak English and began speaking fluent Russian. Bad, ugly words everyone was criss cross sure positive. The Town Marshall had to be careful. While she was at it, she might want to back away from the counter too. Women like Mrs. Truchet, who carried around Rolly-Polly dolls, liked to go over counters and teach people manners. Something like Jo-Jo.

The bad part was these women were a pair. Meaning they were two of Mrs. Truchet's, or more precisely, Jo-Jo's. There was no telling what they were saying, or what they might do. Maybe they were saying they were simply going to turn her in and report her. Or maybe they were going to take her to a trough and pull out her liver and eat it, AFTER turning her in. Then they were coming back and taking the whole Big B to the stakes, burning it down—all the way down to the ground. The gut wrenching threats was sounding like a Russian roulette. It didn't sound like the Big B stood a chance. The entire, and any and all of its sister stores, was about to become ONE Big Empty Parking Lot.

Beatrice had to be called, and Naomi came running in... all the way from Dumfries, about a 30 minute drive with no traffic, but a half day hellish nightmare wondering what had Marjorie done now? How bad would it be? Would it cost her an arm and a leg? Or her whole retirement?

Huong stayed in the back, which by the way, was not completely out of sight of what was going on in the bay. Anything she couldn't see, she definitely could hear. If anyone ever thought to ask her, "what did she see," she could tell them a lot.

But after Beatrice and Naomi swept and mopped up Marjorie's ego, and the vroom women left the bay, which was after getting what they wanted, she got back to fantasizing about her and Jimmy. She pictured being held, one hand behind the waist, the other holding her hand...as they danced to her all time favorite song, by her all time favorite artist, 'You Give Good Love'.

They twisted and turned, and turned and twisted...all the way to Halong Bay where they married. On the French Riviera they honeymooned, and in Naples, Florida… on the waterfront, they brought children, pets, maids, butlers, chefs, chauffeurs and the whole works into their world.

Flouncing around, twirling and twisting, she was in this make-believe discovery when she heard… or thought she heard, "hey Huong." She looked up and thought she saw him. Six-feet tall, piercing bronze eyes, slim but chisel carved, and the most gorgeous hands a man could have. Clean slender fingers and fighting knuckles...just like the hands in her dream. "…You look pretty (something garbled)... tonight?"

Instantly she straightened up, and opened her eyes and looked up. It was him! She recognized him; his hazelnut voice. She stared into his mouth, committing to memory his flashdance smile.

Her instincts told her to scream, "Yes! Yes!" and then wrap her arms around his neck, and kiss him until they became one…literally.

But the reality of him holding her artbook, asking about her drawings, pissed her off. Nobody touched her personal things!

His expression cast a shadow of doubt over her. She was fully out of this dream.

"Did you draw these?"

She only stared at him, her ire turning to fixation. He seemed awed by her artwork...but was about to turn the page.

"Hey Zoe," he called out to Zoey, in the bay cackling with Dominique and Lynne. "Come check this out!"

"You're good," he said to her, as Zoey made her way to the holding bay to hang over his shoulder.

"Who does this look like," he asked Zoey, before turning back to her. "Did you draw these? Are these drawings supposed to be us?"

She continued staring, not only due to Jimmy's commanding presence, but because her art suddenly had a live audience. Dominique and Lynne too were glued to the page Jimmy was on, laughing and pointing at the drawings, matching the cartoon caricatures to each of them hovered over the book.

A customer interrupted their amusement. Zoey and Dominique returned to the bay.

This left Lynne...and him...and her.

But Lynne wasn't as much interested in the art, as she was in him. "You need to let me trim your bangs," Lynne giggled in his face, using her hand to flip the hair he kept swinging left, out of his face.

During one of the swings, flipping hair out of his eyes, his face hardened and he looked down at her. "Who's number is this?"

Though her thoughts ran laps around him, circling him like a cat chasing its tail, she kept quiet and continued to stare as he muttered..."This looks like the note Vita found..."

"Haha," laughed Lynne. "What a damn shame! That girl been dropping them post-its everywhere!"

Lynne joined Dominique and Zoey in the bay and he looked back down at her again.

"Is this your number?"

She couldn't speak. "Huh? Ugh, I dunno."

Sorry. If he, too, couldn't read her, he'd never get it out of her.

Tiz' the Season...

TRACY
~~

"Trae, you won't believe who I just saw..."

"—Who?" Tracy was thinking Naomi Campbell or Sebastian Siegel, but somehow, "Tyson Beckford" came out.

"No! Hue!"

Tracy shook her head. "So, I guess we're about to be blamed for last night too!"

"I doubt it. At least I hope not," Naomi sighed. "That man is so oblivious. He looked through me, as if I was his mother who he probably hasn't seen since she paid off his student loan!"

Tracy laughed out loud. "Scary... but did you say something? To get a read on what to expect today?"

"Absolutely not," Naomi replied. "I'd rather open my mouth for a dentist first. Didn't even look back," she tossed over her shoulder, headed to her little closet. "But I have an idea," she said, her voice trailing behind her.

Tracy didn't get up to hear Naomi's idea. She stayed put, comparing and stapling mini spreadsheets generated from Excel. Despite the optics and how the seasonal workers saw her, acting like her work was the most important in the store, more important than the Big B's electricians that kept the store powered so that her mini spreadsheets would print, she really was holding it down for Naomi. The back end of customer service work was her bread and butter, and pride and joy. She absolutely loved the work...and wasn't shy about making sure others knew how critical she was to the flow of operations within the department.

So, of course anyone who'd ever spoken to her, at length, knew her feigned headaches included having to work on schedules, and pull reports, and nonwithstanding, create one more Excel worksheet...when she wasn't babysitting the seasonal workers and dealing with her problem childs; Marjorie and Nadine.

"Hey, you hear me," Naomi said, about an hour later, after gossiping with Beatrice about seeing Hue.

"No. What's up," Tracy said.

Naomi pulled a six-inch binder down from a shelf over Tracy's head. This binder was the holy grail of all the seasonal workers that had worked for the store since 1986. She opened the binder and thumbed through it as she talked. "I have a project for you," she went on, concerning Tracy greatly when she looked up and saw the size of the binder.

"Please don't tell me it's going to involve overtime," she kind of moaned. She loved her job, but not that much. She did have a life outside of the Big B.

"I'm thinking about pulling off a spectacular season," she went on.

Tracy's ears...and eyes were open. Wide open. It scared her when Naomi had an idea. Not a one of them ever panned out.

Flipping through the binder Naomi got distracted and started complaining. "You know, I've been here over two decades and it never ceases to amaze me... the worst CEO's are the shortest."

Tracy laughed. "...And least sexiest," she added. "Napoleon complexes..."

"You got that right," Naomi said, turning a page in the binder so hard it ripped. "I tried to tell that little Napoleon about the elevator. He ignored me. And what happened?"

"A customer got stuck in it," Tracy dryly recalled, finishing her sentence. She recalled that day with clarity. She was there. It happened a week after 9/11. She got the first call, and she fought with a half dozen big shots; departments and agencies to send help. But no one knew what to do. The predicament wasn't within their purview. Three hours later she witnessed the extraction, and was very privy to the fallouts.

"But what else happened," Naomi snarled. She stopped turning pages, pausing to let Tracy have a stab at answering the question. "We got blamed!"

Yeah.... Tracy remembered that. It was the one and only time she almost got fired.

"He blames us for everything! We try to tell him about the silly credit card policy, and what happens? Customers start complaining when Marjorie tries to do what he told her to do. There's no winning with him. NONE!"

"UGH!" She shut the binder and reached for another six-inch whopper. She had the wrong binder. "Now, we're supposedly stressing out Dine! Apparently we're not team playing correctly!"

"He said that? Did you speak to him?"

"No. Bea told me."

"Well, did she tell you what's the fix?"

"Kareem ever give you his statement," Naomi asked switching topics. So much was on her mind, to include the big idea she had.

"He said he gave it to Nique, 'bout a month ago."

"A month ago," Naomi shrieked. "What was she doing? ...Aah never mind," she sighed. "He and I had a really good talk the other day. But I can't remember what we talked about."

Tracy chuckled. "Boss, if you can't recall what y'all talked about, which was only the other day, then I'm not sure I want to hear this idea."

The remark didn't seem to register with Naomi. She was really distracted. "You know, maybe we can have Dine come in this Friday to collect feedback from each customer that visits us..."

Tracy threw an arm over her chair and gave her loving and caring, but spastic boss 'the look'. Naomi had lost her everlasting mind.

"...Well...it's better than letting her work on that long ass statement," Naomi chuckled.

"You mean that manuscript, don't you?"

"Whatever it is," Naomi huffed. "And to think he started all this." She reached for yet another six-inch binder. There was a row of them. Inside were the file of every employee that worked in customer service... since 86. Just one more thing Tracy was a superstar at. She'd done a fabulous job memorializing this history.

"Actually little Napolean reminds me a lot of my grandfather..."

Naomi stopped turning pages. "Seriously? You actually have a grandfather like that? Geez, I really feel so sorry for you."

"Oh, don't be. We all hated him. Even my father; and it's his own father." Tracy pulled a carrot from a ziploc bag and snapped down on it.

"I forgot to ask you... do you know how many steps it takes to close a sale?"

Tracy turned around, crunching on another carrot. "This isn't a Hue test is it? I always fail them."

"We're up to one forty-four!"

Tracy stopped chewing. "Did he just celebrate another birthday? How'd the count get that high?"

"No. He held us hostage in another meeting!"

"Okay, so let me hear it. I don't want to later get dragged over the carpet for missing a step!"

"Trae, I'd be lying if I tried repeating all the steps, but I almost burst out laughing in Reyola's face listening to her spelling out them steps as if she understood what she was talking about."

Tracy wasn't a big laugher, but she laughed at the thought of Reyola, who taught some of the new hire training classes, and who always looked like she was running downhill, talking more stupid than she looked.

Naomi pushed the remaining binder back in place, pooped. She couldn't find one past employee that she wanted Tracy to call to see if they would come back. Not one. And she really thought she might find dozens!

"You know…I think I'll take these binders home to see if I can find someone to help us this weekend."

"Oh, so your great idea is to have me transport all those binders to your car," Tracy laughed.

"No. I want you to see if my left arm wants to work Saturday…the morning shift."

"Marjie," Tracy asked stunned. Beatrice was going to have a conniption after the brawl she caused with the vroom vroom women. "…But I thought I was your left arm," she sulked.

"No. You are my left and right arm."

"…Which you never told me what my part is…"

"Oh yeah, that…" Naomi smiled. "I want you to send me your Christmas list."

"That's it!?! What if—"

"—You aren't about to bribe the boss, are you?"

"No ma'am," Tracy said tucking her head, before springing it back up. "But it seems that you're setting Marjie up to replace you when you retire—"

"—Now Trae, really think about it," Naomi said greatly humored. "Why on earth would I dare hand this job over to some one I really liked!?!"

Boss Lady.

Thank God her grant had come in. The SBA awarded her $50,000 to start a fashion boutique. Thank God thank God thank God. The haggling over punching time clocks and dealing with micromanagers was finally coming to an abrupt and beautiful end.

"Anyway, when did this start?" She was asking about the requirement to have six positive comment cards filled out by the end of her shift.

But Nadine couldn't tell her. She didn't know. She wasn't even sure if it was six, twenty-six, or none. Naomi wasn't specific, and she failed to clarify. And yet, she answered Emma anyway.

"All you have to do is politely ask the customer, once they finish their transaction, to fill this out," she rattled, flipping the cards between her wrinkled fingers.

It wasn't what she asked, but WTH... she had fifty grand sitting at the bottom of her purse. Tell her anything. She only had to play boo-boo the fool for two more days!

"Sometimes you have to be a little more persistent with some customers, more than others," Nadine insisted. "It's on you if you fail to meet the quota. They probably won't call you back next year."

'Oh really,' Emma chuckled. 'Because she wasn't planning on returning. EVER.

But then Nadine was a numbskull to start with. She was a real nut case, best displayed by the number of ambulances that had to swoop by and scoop her up off the floor. If the Big B could keep this nut ball on payroll, then she could burn all the bridges in London and still be qualified to return.

"So, what do you suggest I do, short of tackling people and forcing them to write nice things about me," she went on and humored herself. Might as well. Next year she was going to be her new boss.

Nadine hadn't heard her though, or she acted as if she hadn't heard her. She kept shaking her head — involuntarily it looked like — and kept talking.

"It's hard, and I know it gets frustrating at times, but it's what our boss wants, so we just have to do it." Nadine smiled an ugly smile. Stains and crud outlining each tooth were on full display to anyone who could stomach looking at her. "We want to please our boss you know," she tossed on.

Emma knew her upper lip was turned upwards because she felt it touching her nose. "Well since I'm only part-time seasonal, I'm not going to worry about it too much. If I get—"

"—oh no, this is for everyone," Nadine cut in. "It doesn't matter how junior you are. All of us are Big B employees. It doesn't matter how many, or few hours you work. Nao—"

"—fine. Every customer fills out a comment card! Got it!" Because if she heard boss, or Naomi's name one more GD time, she just might choke the living Naomi out of Nadine. Damn waiting til' the first of the year.

Of course all of this was besides the point. Rarely did the customers give her a hard time, unlike the frequent ambulance passenger. Besides, did she forget to mention? She had fifty grand sitting at the bottom of her purse. She'd even hand Snow White and the Seven Dwarfs a comment card, with a big goofy Gumby smile, knowing good and well she could care less what any of those characters thought.

Nadine shook her head in a never-mind fashion. "Don't worry," she promised. "I'll show you on the next customer."

The next customer walked into the bay no less than a minute later. The woman was well-dressed, as most that came in, soft-spoken, and seemed as if she would be one willing to play along. She didn't look harried or in a super delicious hurry. Christmas was right around the corner and this customer was cool as iceburg lettuce.

The customer laid a few gifts on the counter and calmly looked over the wrapping paper on the wall. Turned out she couldn't make up her mind on which one to select, so Emma, being into the fashions and all, decided to assist.

"Who are the gifts for?"

"Oh, one's for my dad and the others are for my husband."

Emma turned around looking over the selections on the wall. "Number 7 and 23 are masculine Christmas-sy patterns. We can always substitute the bow."

"Umm, you know, I think you're right." She lifted her chin out of the palm of her hand and stood back sort of tilting her head to be sure. "Yeah, I like them too… and I even like the bow that comes with it as well," she added.

Nadine didn't say a word. She helped Emma pull the selected wrapping paper off the roller and quietly, sparing Nadine's occasional 'oh shucks' and 'oh cripes' began wrapping gifts. About 10 or 15 minutes later, save for the bow Nadine still had left to get right, the gifts for the most part were complete.

"Ugh ma'am, would you like a gift card with these," Nadine asked over her shoulder.

"Don't they all come with gift cards?" asked the woman.

They sure did… just as the display showed on the wall… the wall that hadn't changed since the day Emma arrived… the same wall Nadine faced for the past ten or eleven years.

"We only include gift cards if the customer specifically asks," she added… over her shoulder.

"Well, ugh… yeah." The woman looked baffled, but smiled when Emma winked at her.

Whenever Emma's staff began to grow, the one prerequisite she was considering when hiring, and that was the ability to answer one simple question. "So how do you take your coffee? Black or with lots of sugar?"

There were no laws against asking that question. Just as there wasn't any law against hiring people based on answering correctly, "I don't drink coffee." Any other answer and the interview was over. Say-la-vee darling, sweetie-pie, or chap! Her premises were going to be totally coffee free.

Emma placed the gifts she had wrapped on the counter, and turned to see what Nadine was up to. 'Oh dear'. She didn't know which, but either it was the wrapping paper, the box, the tape, the bow or the scissors giving Nadine pure 'D' hell.

With tape on one thumb, scissors dangling around the finger next to the thumb, and between the 'oh Christs and cripes,' Nadine had turned a simple task into a monumental disaster. None of the corners were neat and crisp, and tape was everywhere… about fifty errant pieces. One gift she even had to re-wrap because she forgot to put the gift in the box!

But Nadine seemed oblivious, which was all the funnier. Emma imagined the humming going on inside her head as she fumbled rewrapping the last gift. When she was almost finished, near to the point of wrestling the gift, she turned around and asked the woman to fill out a comment card.

"Sure!" The woman brought out her own pen, clicked the top and started writing...as Nadine...after a deep exculpatory sigh, laid the gifts she had wrangled into submission on the counter — eye-level to the woman seriously writing.

Emma turned away. She didn't want to watch the woman's expression the moment one of those errant pieces of tape got her attention. The experience could scar the woman for life. Both boxes looked like a portrait of death.

Next came a soft gasp and an "oh my goodness!"

She knew at that moment the woman was staring the portrait of death directly in the eye. Emma turned around to see the woman rotating one of the boxes following the madness around each side.

"I think we might have to redo this one," the woman edged out slowly. She was shaking her head too.

"Excuse me..."

"Umm..." the woman laid the pen on the comment card to spend more time examining the gift-wrap. "Do you think you can redo these?" — obviously the two Nadine had wrapped. "They don't look too good." Obviously she was trying to describe these portraits of death as nicely as she could.

"Ma'am, once the gifts are wrapped you have to pay for them. We don't rewrap for free. Sorry, but that's our policy."

"Oh no, I can't pay for this." The woman stepped back, still calmly, as if she was afraid the gift-wrap was going to jump off the counter and snatch her inside the portrait. "This certainly isn't worth seventeen dollars."

Who knew what was going on in Nadine's head at the time. She certainly wasn't listening. "Our policy is once a customer requests a gift-wrap and you allow us to wrap it, you have to pay for it. We don't guarantee that what you see on the wall is what you'll get."

"…But this isn't even close…"

Emma's eyes ached. Her jaws ached. Her sides ached. Even between her toes ached. It was difficult laughing as hard without letting a sound escape. So badly she wanted to intervene, but she was determined not to step on Nadine's toes.

"Ma'am, I'm sorry," Nadine apologized for about the tenth time.

"I'm sorry too, but I'm not paying for that…" the woman said shaking her head, not sure what to do next. "Can you call someone, because I'm not paying for that?" There was no way the woman was turning a gift wrapped Nadine-style over to anyone. Father, husband, clergy, or her worst enemy.

Nadine snatched the gifts from the counter electing to call neither Faye, nor Beatrice. She was going to reinvent the madness, however she could.

Dropping the boxes on the counter Nadine got to huffing and shucksing and oh cripes'sing all over again. The woman looked over at Emma helplessly, desperately pleading for assistance. Like Stop the Abuse! Nadine needed a time out.

Cautiously Emma eased over to Nadine who was snatching and jerking on the boxes, turning the yes ma'am's and I'm sorrys into a scrooge gift-grinder from B-Witch's Hell.

"Here," Emma smiled, "let me try. This paper can get a little tricky."

"I told Naomi not to get this kind of paper. I don't know how she expects us to work with it!" Nadine threw up her hands and stepped back.

"I know… it's the weirdest paper I've ever seen," Emma agreed… blaming the defenseless wrapping paper as old as the display on the wall, times ten.

Still muttering, Nadine's credibility shot to smithereens, she looked over at the customer and apologized again. "Ma'am, she's going to try and redo the wrap. The paper is a little difficult to manage, but we'll do the best we can…"

And she offered this apology, scooting aside the gifts Emma had wrapped—the ones wrapped in the same paper that needed no redoing. Emma guessed the woman was wincing because she didn't answer. But oh man! Did it not feel like a poltergeist wind blowing through the service bay. It was chillllll-ly in there!

"We really work hard back here and we really try," Nadine went on, "but some things, as I am sure you are aware, are outside our control."

Nadine went on playing before an evacuated stadium. Shucks, she didn't need spectators. All she needed was a stage. "But if you wouldn't mind taking the time to fill out one of our guest comment cards, we can address any and all concerns you may have."

Still nothing. The woman said absolutely nothing. Surprisingly, when Emma turned around, the woman was still writing… filling out the comment card! She only paused long enough to privately inspect the gifts Emma had quietly placed beside the others. She wrote a few more words before heavily dotting the period that was to conclude her comment.

She looked up at Emma, and Emma looked at her. 'Please lady, please take your gifts and don't look back,' she conveyed through a straight face. With Nadine going on like a scratched record it would be a fluke if she didn't chase after the woman and ask her to fill out another comment, and then shoved one in her purse if she told her she already filled one out.

Too bad she wasn't going into comedy. Nadine'd be her first act. She'd make her first mil before the lights came on.

Not My Circus.

~~

TERESA
~~

She didn't care what the wanna be white girl said. A
Devil Wears Prada was too a good movie, and Naomi
did remind her of Miranda, and for that matter, Naomi
reminded her of Meryl Streep, too!

It was the craziest reason to get pissed at her.
Not only was the movie not about race, Teresa's comment wasn't even about race. So why did race come up
at all!?! And by a supposed black woman at that!!!

Like so what she'd rather shuck corn, pull hairs
out the crack of her butt, watch paint dry, and jump off
a bridge than watch a Meryl Streep movie. Like who the
fuck was she? And who the fuck cared? Teresa didn't
personally know either Meryl Streep, or the Miranda
character Streep played, but would bet her whole next
paycheck, from the Big b and the check she got from her
full-time job at Oracle, that the producers of that film,
plus Streep herself, could give a fleck less if she jumped
from a bridge. Like the beat that goes on, no one would
care. Her death wouldn't generate one solid headline. So
there! Take that! It'd be all the weaponry she'd need to
play the movie on repeat until she did jump.

Almost the entire night she listened to Lynne talking about us this, and white that, as if screaming at white men was going to fix her situation. Puleeze! The white man's system was going to screw with her head, and the rest of their heads, for the next 300 years, and the 300 after that, just to watch them point fingers at ghosts slapping them in the face.

Wake the fuck up Lynne! Which didn't mean she hadn't seen movies, or been stereotyped herself by white racists. Ignorance was everywhere, none more prevalent than in this ridiculous argument.

"Well, that's good you got a VCR and all. I got one too," Lynne smack-talked. "But we still gonna need you to work Saturday night!"

Like the hell she would. First of all, who was Lynne, but seasonal help like her! Secondly, the whole matter started with Lynne asking if she wouldn't mind switching shifts. And she told the snot, she'd first have to call her mother to see if she could watch her son, which had her mother agreed, she would've gladly switched with her. But now here she was facing this nasty cunt telling her what she was going to do, with her trick friend, the other troublemaker, Dominique Oliver.

She should have never let them bluff her into that ridiculous idiotic scuttle, as if they wanted to be her friend. She got sucked into that one. Walked face first right into their little stink bomb. The definition of two bitches. Two full grown adult cunts that threw up their fists to solve issues.

The whole lot of them, a detriment to society; Lynne and Dominique as described a given, but Jimmy with his instigating, Nadine with the craziness, and the golden girls Marjorie and Tracy with their entitlements, and Naomi who enabled it all. For a company that put these sores ahead of customers and employees, deserved to go down with this stinking sinking ship! She wished them all a future of tears in hell. Dress accordingly.

Quietly she moved to the opposite end of the bay and proceeded to help customers far away from the agitators. But even at a 15 foot distance, this wasn't far enough to block their words. They hurled CVS filled plastic bags, loaded with hate meant to knock her out.

Laughter filled the holding bay.

"Bet her people sat in first-class on Columbus's paddle boat."

'Hahahaha!'

"No wait, no wait…" Dominique catching her breath, "Mo tea sah."

"But massa, we has no tea."

"No tea! Off with your head!"

'Hahahaha.'

Teresa heard this, and it was hardly funny. Not even a little. Reminded her of her high-school days, sitting around with friends trying to be cool, rolling over themselves laughing at dust balls like they got it. Eye roll. Those girls looked dumb then, and these old skanks weren't funny now.

"What gets me is her coming in here wearing them tired uptight suits like she's better than everybody, like nobody don't know we all in here makin' $13.50," Lynne lamented, dressed herself like she owed every bank in the nation, along with nations overseas, enough currency to be destitute for hundreds of reincarnations.

That's why she chuckled. The stupid bitch didn't know an 870 credit rating in her case was NOTHING to brag about. A Gold American Express cardholder driving a Lexus and wearing Prada shoes and carrying Coach bags was a fucking joke. If she didn't know, she should go ask her momma taking care of her kids!

Of course Lynne got offended by the cynicism in her chuckle. The truth fucking hurt. Which was precisely how the night got more painful.

The hate continued. They pitched a tent, started a fire, and decided to roast every marshmallow until she was toast. They laughed about her clothes and big nose and made wild guesses about her dating habits, and why she was so pale.

"Girl need to get up under some sun, or stick her head in an oven," Lynne laughed, joined by her groupies who didn't mind being cruel.

Teresa's nostrils flared and her lips quivered she was so angry…and hurt. If Lynne was drowning, she'd throw her a sandbag. And then beat her over the head with another sandbag if she wasn't drowning quick enough. People wondered why co-workers walked into their jobs without warning and shot up the place. This was why! Groupies latching on to troublemakers without a care or conscience, all because they don't want to be the odd man out. Group-think. Herd followers. Sheep. And this behavior wasn't only in the bay, or in the Big b. She dealt with it at her real job too. And in her case, the ringleader was always supposedly black!

She couldn't stand it no more. What hurt most was the fact that they were sisters, women, as in black female sistas, whereas everyone Lynne showed out for, belonged to a group that reportedly disdained them; the framed portrait of an absolute sellout.

So Teresa took off…initially thinking she needed a break, but ultimately deciding she was done.

SHE QUIT!

She couldn't be around that much hypocrisy and hate any longer. Her mother used to tell her to get away from those type people. "They will do nothing but camp out in your spirit and eat you up from the inside."

"Hey, hey! Umm, excuse me," Dominique called after her as she hoofed it out of the bay, coat draped over her arm. "Where are you going? We have customers in here!" Not too unbelievable, Dominique found the event amusing. She actually laughed.

Teresa kept walking. Fuck you. December 1865 the 13th Amendment said she could work for whoever she wanted to work for. She didn't have to take this shit. Especially not from some black Sambo Aunt Tom, and no disrespect to the true Uncle Tom, Josiah Henson.

Truth was, had she turned around they would've seen her tears and known they'd gotten to her. That's all they wanted. To bend someone bendable.

But had she turned around holding an Uzi, it would've been another story. She would've given anything to hear them apologizing, begging for their life. It's why she understood those that went boom boom ballistic on coworkers.

She continued to the escalator, looking up and calling on God. "Lord, please forgive me. I am so sorry." Though she meant every word.

Jimmy caught up to her. "Hey, hey," he started, gently grabbing her arm. "Come on. Don't do this. It's not worth it."

Her face was really wet by this point, as if she had put her face beneath a running spigot. "I don't need that job," she said between clinched teeth. "It's not worth it!"

"All right…that was messed up how she jumped on you like that," he said, riding the escalator down to the lower level with her. "But she just found out she lost one of her children's fathers."

"And I lost one of my toenails," Teresa shot back.

"Well, do you mind if I apologize for her," he asked once they reached the parking level.

She looked into his eyes. In that moment she saw her mother, and heard a quote her mother attributed to MLK. "Only love can conquer hate."

"Jimmy thanks," she said, though she was pissed at him too. Had she been armed, he'd been gone too.

"I accept your apology," she said wiping her *large nose*. "You should run for office. Seriously. I'd vote for you. But don't worry about me, or the Big b. It's them who need saving," she said, nodding at the escalator… in the opposite direction where she headed.

SHAKEDOWN!

~~

DOMINIQUE
~~

Naomi was on the phone asking Dominique about what happened. "I just got a call from Teresa telling me she was assaulted."

"Oh my god," Dominique chuckled. "That's not what happened at all. That girl is exaggerating. Her and Lynne exchanged a few words but..."

"Nique, we need to talk first thing in the morning," Naomi said in a voice in need of resuscitation. She had come so close and gotten so far to end up back at square one.

Over and over along the course of her good size life she'd been told she was foolish to think she could solve the problem of inhumanity when, like four legged animals and every other living thing, the basic function of life was to copulate, multiply and repeat. And news flash, no matter how many tried to interfere with this order, only God got the final say.

"But I'm off tomorrow," Dominique said.

"Nique, I need to see you in the office, first thing tomorrow!" She didn't care who was in charge of human order. She was in charge of the Big b's customer service department, and so far that hadn't changed!

Dominique hung up and turned around to face Tracy standing by the office door with her hair tied up in a bright yellow scarf.

"I don't see what all the excitement is…I mean, since when have you ever had to come in here over some seasonal employee having a personal crisis?"

"Maybe because Naomi trusted you to manage the bay, not arm it," Tracy spat, hurling a huge hobo bag hoisted over her shoulder in a chair and kicking off her snow boots.

"Oh, so all this is my fault," Dominique hurled like Tracy had hurled her bag. "And what? Am I about to be fired!?!"

"I have no idea what Nae is planning to do," Tracy huffed, pulling off sweats too, changing into her normal tight-assed slacks. Her snappy jerky movements made her look honestly angrier. "All I know is I'm back in here and pissed too," she grumbled.

"Oh, so she told you to get up out of bed and come in here and you didn't ask why!?!"

"Actually, yes," Tracy replied, her lips pursed and eyes speared, shooting daggers at Dominique. She stuffed the clothes she pulled off into the hobo bag and threw the bag in the coat closet, slamming the door shut.

"Oh, so I guess she didn't know I was in here," Dominique huffed.

"Well, I don't ask questions when my boss tells me I need to get back to the store after I've been here for 10 hours already," she hissed. "I trusted she needed me, and she trusted I'd be here."

Dominique stood in the center of the office, no longer looking like the citified deal-broker princess that made things jump in the bay. She looked pathetic staring at the back of Tracy busily getting ready to deal with work she had been entrusted to do. And still, she went on and lied anyway.

"Well, I have a doctor's appointment tomorrow so I might not be able to make it in, in the morning."

Tracy held up both hands; tiny translucent pretty hands. "—Ugh Nique, you don't have to explain what's going on with you to me," she said reaching for the door. "It's on you what you decide to do tomorrow."

The truth. Long before Dominique's shady dealings with Kareem, she was hardly a poster picture for ethics. She was caught twice accidentally forgetting to ring up sales and pocketing the money. Rumors also swirled around her entanglements involving married male employees. And upper management, to inlcude Naomi knew about her less than honorable release from the military. The only benefit to keeping her around was her personality. She was easygoing, outwardly bubbly, and she came to work and did the work. Generally she related well with staff and had zero complaints from customers, so other than her propensity to be involved in less than ideal personal situations, the good side of her was unfailingly trusted.

Dominique remained in the office while Tracy helped close the registers in the bay. She was nervous, knowing what happened between Lynne and Teresa was unnecessary.

Even Lynne knew she was wrong, why she faked a seizure hoping to generate sympathy. Unfortunately, the act was so good, thanks to Nadine anxious not to be an anomoly, she got an unnecessary trip to the hospital... via paramedics.

"Hey, you all right—" Dominique whispered.

"Girl, I'll be okay," Lynne replied, trying to sound sick, but sounding more like someone looking around for eavesdroppers.

"Looks like they might let me go," Dominique said. "They called Trae in...so, I doubt if Nae is going to keep me..."

"Damn, girl," Lynne sighed. "I should've called

in. I knew my levels was off when I left the house," she coughed using her sick voice. "I'm so sorry."

"Don't worry about it," Dominique replied. "I'm not sweating it. I've got some savings saved up to get me through a couple of months."

"Yeah, but…" Now Lynne really was sick. Over the past couple months the two had become close. They started hanging out more frequently and calling each other after work to gossip about work. If they didn't have the Big b in common, what was left to keep them connected?

"Well…at least you have your real job. Maybe you can hook me up with David," Dominique laughed. "I know how to make broke people pay their bills!"

Making Peace.

She had witnessed lots during the course of her career. Only 38 years old, and she had double the years of HR experience. The culture in department stores had gone from candidates interviewing in suits, neckties, skirts and pearls, to a woman showing up dressed in a t-shirt with BITCH emblazoned across the front. And then there was the woman, Mary-Jean Roberts, who worked beside her for 8 months, right there in HR, who turned out to be an ex-felon.

Sweet soft-spoken Mary-Jean with the bob hair-do and modest decorum blatantly lied about her past, claiming to have a degree from Old Dominion, when she had no degree at all. She hadn't even graduated from high-school. She also wasn't married as she claimed, not that it meant much considering she shook the department learning she escaped from a mental institution.

Seeing these scenarios was enough to double her age, and why retaining employees like Dominique was easy. Unless she murdered someone, the chances of her retiring from the Big b was very likely.

But when Naomi called asking to call back past employees like Jordana and a few others that left under messy circumstances, she got concerned. "Why on earth would you want those people back!?"

"Oh, it'll just be for one day," Naomi said. "Trae and I have a 'little bet' going."

Faye tilted her head. Naomi...and Tracy as well, were among the most loyal and level-headed leaders in the store. "A bet," she asked incredulous. This sounded not only irresponsible coming from Naomi, but entirely preposterous.

"Well, in a matter of months five people just quit on me," Naomi explained. "That has never happened before," she said.

"But Nae, you've lost twice that many last year! Remember—"

"—Those I fired," Naomi contended. "Well, most of them," she admitted. "If I remember correctly, only one left, well technically anyway," she chuckled. "I'm not sure if unexpectedly dying can be counted as quitting. That one is an iffy call. Won't you agree?"

Faye sighed. She had a lot on her plate. Housewares had a manager suspected of drinking on the job. She just finished listening to someone trying to describe what his breath smelled like. And then there was her real nightmare. The manager in Jewelry who took it upon himself to threaten employees with termination if they didn't take proper steps to prevent a domestic abuser from attacking his ex. He couldn't do this. Not only were his demands outside of store policy and dangerous, he was creating impossible legal quagmires for the store. Not even police wanted to deal with domestic cases, citing them as their worst calls. But this wasn't the worst part. Her nightmare was trying to undo written communication he sent to these employees, that Hue co-signed!

It was awful, because she genuinely cared about women dealing with abusive spouses or partners. But she couldn't see the entire store put at risk, similar to the lesser problem childs just as touchy; like the hairy sexual harassment rumors stacking up on Sammy, almost reaching his pile of kudos, along with the normal trove of suspected thieves, like the nuisances coming out of the customer service department, to include the foible Naomi was presenting, sure as bright sunlight apt to unmask other legal quandaries.

And yet, the unforgivable part was her husband taking a turn for the worse. He was his sickest since the diagnosis, and she had three innocent children looking for a visit from Santa.

"Look Nae, I don't need Hue on my back—"

"—Oh, I'm going to be here," Naomi cut in. "Me and Trae...since we're both trying to win this bet!"

"Tell you what," Faye said. "Send Eli their names so he can activate their employee numbers...but," she continued in her warning tone. "Hue will be in. He's hosting some kind of dinner party for the board."

"On Christmas Eve," Naomi near shrieked. It wasn't that she even remotely expected anything to go wrong, but when she called Hue a fool, it was a kind of tongue and cheek thing. What sober person wanted to be sitting around a card table, on Christmas Eve, talking about forecasts and projections with other sober people?

"Okay...okay..." Faye said a little humored. This ask really wasn't too big of a deal, even if there had been a revolving door of birdbrained incidents going on in the customer service department. For this reason Faye made a trip to the bay before heading home.

She entered the office and found Dominique and Lynne talking forehead to forehead by the closet, and Nadine hovered over a copier slamming doors and lids.

Even though she had two eyes and 20/20 vision she asked anyway. "Hello ladies, how are things going?"

No one greeted her back, unless Nadine fussing how she couldn't make the darn copier work, counted.

"Here, let me take a look," Faye offered, noticing a note, apparently scribbled in haste by Nadine, taped to one of the copy machine's doors:

'BROKEN!!! DOMINIQUE SAID SHE WILL FIX!!!'

The note looked written earlier, going by dried shoe prints criss-crossing the paper when it lived on the floor while others either used, or attempted to use the machine. Now Nadine reaching the end of her rope was making another desperate attempt to fix the darn thing!

Faye opened and slammed drawers and doors too, before calling the HR department. "Katie, do me a favor and send a tech to customer service. The copier isn't working."

"The tray she's trying to use is probably out of paper," Lynne offered immediately after the call. It was a high point when Faye realized Dominique and Lynne were a canolli away from a fork and a knife.

She turned her attention back to Nadine. "How many copies do you need?"

"Two thousand," Nadine replied. This was the manifesto she'd been diligently working on.

Faye's eyes googled, spinning two full circles. Usually jobs that large were farmed out. But "no problem" later and Nadine was on her way to HR, with the manifesto draped over one arm to finally make her 2000 copies, while Faye made her way over to the forehead huddle.

These two, like most, were not bothered by her presence. Faye was an acutely fair-minded person. Most didn't turn colors until they saw...or heard from the likes of Hues... or Katies.

"Ladies, I need you to go to HR and help Dine make those copies. It's a couple thousand, so be quick. Katie might need to use the copier."

Dominique's full head of Flash Dance hair came up out of her purse. Katie was the Big B's legal assassin.

Follow the Leadership.

NAOMI

Due to the shorter store hours she kept the schedule light. Just she, Tracy and her best and brightest helpers were called to work in the bay this day.

Faye decided to pop in, just to check on things before she returned home and turned off her phone.

She giggled soon as she saw Naomi. "Oh my Goodness Nae, Hue is going to kill you in cold blood," she laughed out loud.

"Let him," Naomi said. "He's following green. I'm following red, the spirit of the season," she laughed, twirling around so Faye could check her out from behind too. And this much was for sure. She was a sight to see. Especially the back view. The version she presented of Mrs. Claus few ever got to see, and that was of either of her... or Mrs. Claus!

"Nae, I say you're going to kill someone, dead in the water," Faye giggled, staring in awe with a hand up to her cheek. From the Peter Pan hat Naomi wore, to the too tight pilgrim corset and short knit skirt, had every employee arriving to the store that morning jerking around to do double takes. Covered in red, from the striped candy cane colored leotards and bloomers, to the red patent leather buckled shoes and significant coats of ruby red lipstick and rouge covering her face, and whole ample behind hanging from beneath the hip hugging skirt, she looked risky hilarious!

"Alright, let's get that coffee brewing," Naomi cheered once she and Tracy made it beyond the gawkers to the customer service office. "We have nine more hours to go!"

It was a little after 6am. The store opened at 7, the only time of the year when the Big b opened this early. Employees would soon be arriving.

"Oh, I'm ready," Tracy said. "I brought Jesus in with me today." This was something her grandmother used to do when her family got together, mostly Thanksgiving and Christmas. There were a few drinkers in the family, whose tongues got loose when they drank. All that spared the family from making trips between the hospital and jail was granny holding that door open.

Jimmy arrived first. He usually did. He walked in the office to see Tracy opening the registers, and Naomi on her tip-toes reaching for Lysol stored on a top shelf.

Instantly he froze. At first he didn't know who's rear he was looking at. Actually, he wasn't sure what he was seeing. All he saw was a lot of red meat!

"Hey Trae, where's the grab—ber—"

—Jimmy standing there surprised her, as did her turning around nearly sacked him. He stumbled backwards, mouth agape.

"Hey Jimmy! Merry Christmas," Naomi smiled, turning a six-inch spread into 10 or 11 inches.

"Oh, hey Naomi," Jimmy muttered, about to turn around and leave, thinking he stumbled on her getting dressed for work.

"Where are you going," Naomi called after him, as if all was copacetic in Ms. Kringle's world. "After you hang your coat, I need your help reaching this Lysol.

You know when Zoey gets here, it's going to be the first thing she'll be looking for."

He quickly hung his coat and grabbed the Lysol, and swiftly headed for the door refusing to turn around. He hoped he never had to go to the office for anything. He might even brave the elements and go home coatless.

Like a zombie he moved to the register furthest from the office, praying Naomi didn't have to leave the office for anything either. The sight of her was not only painful. It was torture. At that moment he didn't care to ever see another thigh again.

Five minutes later he forgot all about the deluxe thighs when Zoey...and Miss Lil walked in!

"Mizz Lil," he howled, leaving the counter to give her a warm hug. "What are you doing here!?!"

"I'm only in here because Nae said y'all short... and to collect me a lil extra shopping money," Lillian laughed.

"Aww...don't lie Mizz Lil," Jimmy teased. "You know you came back here to see me."

"That's true Jimmy," Lillian laughed, about to head for the office when he suddenly remembered.

He reached for her arm, largely because she was closest... Zoey was already at the door. "Watch out—"

—But too late. Zoey had already opened the door and Naomi was on her way out to the bay.

Lillian shrieked. Actually she yelled, as if someone was snatching her purse. "Mizz Naomi!" she shouted shocked. "What are you doing in here half-naked!!!"

"Oh, Lillian, we miss you," Naomi said hugging the famed Miss B, who leaned back, out of this embrace as if she smelled something foul.

"Hang your coat," Naomi said, appearing to not notice Lillian's reaction to her costume.

"Come on, Chop! Chop!" she happily yapped, clapping her hands. "The store opens in fifteen minutes! Let's be ready," she rejoiced, using her recent holiday manicure to peck at keys, one at a time, checking to see if her employee number still worked.

Maybe on the other side of the counter this all might go over well, but from where Zoey, Lillian and Jimmy stood staring, it looked like they were headed for one long hilarious day. They gave each other a final look before the morning started rolling.

Right off, most titilating was Naomi and Tracy pushing up their proverbial sleeves. They moved away from the registers to the gift-wrap counter... to do the 'picking cotton' work. Acting like they were working at a take-out deli, they took requests asking 'who's next,' and following those orders as best they could.

At one point when a customer asked for a different ribbon than the one shown on display, Naomi turned to Jimmy and asked, "do we mix bows and wraps?"

He struggled to answer, because he couldn't get his eyes off the sight scrolling in his mind. "Ugh, it's fine he ended up, robotically, telling her.

From then on, Naomi and Tracy kept the gift wrap flow moving, of course with Lillian's assistance. "Oh Mizz Naomi, we don't use staples or glue on the wraps. The seams are supposed to be invisible."

And Zoey and Jimmy instructed Tracy on 'how to track packages...from the bay registers.' It was an entirely different operation from the back office.

Service was moving, flowing, jelling, going well... despite Jimmy's difficulties trying to keep Naomi's rear out of his peripheral...permanent sight. At first break he had to call Vince.

"Dude, you got to get over here and see these glukes," he laughed from inside a bathroom stall.

"Aww...Yo man, she called asking me to work for a few hours, but I told her I'd think about it. We're swamped over here..."

Clearly Vince wasn't comprehending his pressing need to share his pain. "Aww man, if you get a break, you gotta come over here and check her out. Man, she in here half naked!"

Suddenly Vince got unswamped. He nearly cartwheeled from behind a counter where he was helping a customer install a new sim card in a phone, to direct a co-worker (also with a customer) to hold the fort down. "Yo Pete, get him next," he said to the co-worker, racing out the exit.

The Big b was at the opposite end of the mall, about a half mile jog. But Vince was young. He reached his destination within a few minutes, weaving and bobbing around strollers, wheelchairs, holiday shoppers and whatnot.

Like O.J. in the airport commercial he hurdled a furbaby kiosk, landing on the heels of two holiday browsers who happened to be Lynne and Dominique.

"Where you going, running around here like that," Dominique teased. "Isn't Clarissa the other way?"

Never in that much of a hurry to diss the diva Dominique, he paused long enough to quickly ask if they'd seen Naomi.

"No! Why!?!" Lynne sneered. "Who the fuck wants to see her!?!"

"*They* say she's up in the bay butt naked!"

Whaddttt!!! All three flew up the escalator.

Vince was so excited, laughing and dancing and twirling around that he also didn't see Nadine, at the moment he spun into the bay. BAM! He collided with her, causing her to drop an arm full of boxes she was about to have wrapped.

"Damn! You need to look where you're going," Nadine huffed...summoning Naomi from behind the counter, hurrying with her wide load to make sure her basket case was okay.

Nothing in the boxes were breakable, and though down on the floor, Nadine was not hurt. The only injuries arising from the collision, appeared to be dozens of eyeballs staring at a big bounty of bunny booty squeezed in candy stripped bloomers. There wasn't an unscathed eyeball among the hordes in the bay watching Naomi helping Nadine up.

From that point 'til closing the bay rocked and rolled. Employees from all over the store dropped in to check out the *half naked* Naomi. Sammy made several trips, telling his customers they needed to check out the nativity nutcracker freakshow in customer service.

But Naomi? She paid none of the jabs or taunts an iota of attention. Instead, she posed for pictures with hundreds of customers; some only interested in adding an x-rated photo to their holiday album, along with little ones who really thought she was Mrs. Claus.

Hue, who initially did not recognize Naomi, or rather did not know she was one of his store directors, even stood begrudginly beside the big juicy thighed woman and allowed this moment to be memorialized. He obviously didn't have much of a choice. His board meeting members thought he knew about 'The Nativity Nutcracker' merriment, and perhaps would question a confession in front of so many amused customers.

Later, as Bing Crosby continued crooning above, Lillian asked why she did it.

"You know... sometimes you gotta take one for the team," she replied. "Wished more leaders realized the value in us playing the piñata...since we sign the paychecks," she chuckled. "More gets done. And everybody goes home happy!"

By-the-way, Tracy won the bet.
But she won the war!

Other Books by the Author

Memoirs

Black Table
God Be the Glory
Babies Raising Babies

Novels (Series)

Leiatra's Rhapsody (I)
Something Xtra Wild (II)
This One I Got Right (III)
Rye n the Rump (IV)
My Love (V)

Other Fiction

Pretty Inside Out
A Piece of Peace
Tehuelche
Pleasure
Double Dare
Lock Box
Big Bully
Copy Cats
Mindless
Painted Cats
* * *NEW Front Page News
* * *NEW Anthill

Short Stories

My Blackberry
Storytella

Poetry

Atlóta
GEM
A Blast From the Past
Civil Talk

About the Author

RYCJ is a book reviewer, blogger, publisher, and storyteller. Since 2009 she has written dozens of books in a mosaic of genres, and has read and reviewed hundreds of books. She is the ultimate book lover, passionate about reading and writing stories that educates, entertains and inspires.

www.ingramcontent.com/pod-product-compliance
Lightning Source LLC
Chambersburg PA
CBHW020753190726
48285CB00006B/2007